**EASY PREY** *The Shark* was badly wounded and no match for the Soviet *Q-21*. She'd be an easy kill.

"Target," the SO reported, "Bearing one eight nine degrees . . . Range eleven thousand yards . . . Speed two zero knots . . . Depth one five zero feet."

"Roger that," Boxer said; then turning to Cowly, he said, "*The Sea Savage* is closing in on us."

Cowly nodded. "Damn lucky he's not on the surface. Even in this blizzard the wreckage off our stern must be visible for miles."

"You can bet on it," Boxer said.

Boxer took the wheel himself and slowly eased it up. *The Shark* responded, turning slightly to its portside. He estimated that the wreck was less than a hundred yards away.

The Sonar Officer gave Boxer another target position. *The Q-21* was now ten miles out.

"I think Borodine has a fix on us," Boxer said softly.

"Then we're in trouble," Cowly whispered.

Boxer didn't reply . . .

# DEPTH FORCE #4

## BATTLE STATIONS

### BY IRVING A. GREENFIELD

**ZEBRA BOOKS**
**KENSINGTON PUBLISHING CORP.**

ZEBRA BOOKS

are published by

Kensington Publishing Corp.
475 Park Avenue South
New York, NY 10016

First printing: July 1985

Printed in the United States of America

# 1

The wind slammed into Boxer. He grabbed hold of the support bar. Under the woolen face mask he wore, his beard was covered with ice. He glanced at Cowly, his EXO. Ice covered the lower part of his face mask too. And the goggles he wore made him look like some kind of monster.

Boxer fought the need to drop below the rim of the outside bridge. A force nine storm was blowing. The combination of wind, snow and sub-freezing temperatures made life on *The Shark*'s bridge a living hell.

Boxer wiped the snow from his own goggles and looked down at the console of the COMCOMP. The bridge unit had malfunctioned. And because of the various electrical and electro-magnetic disturbances, the master unit on the main bridge was erratic.

Boxer keyed the communications officer. "Are you still in contact with our protecting angle?" he asked.

"Say again, Skipper."

Boxer repeated his question.

"Roger that," the COMMO answered. "He's close by . . . Can't make it back to his base . . . He's going to ditch close to us."

"Roger that," Boxer answered. He moved closer to Cowly and said, "That plane is coming down . . . We're going to have to put a rescue team out."

Cowly nodded; then he said, "If we don't get those flyboys out of the water within three minutes, they'll die."

Boxer nodded and keyed Lieutenant Vargas. "Need four volunteers to go into the drink . . . Our protecting angle can't make it back to their base."

"I'll go—"

"Negative," Boxer said. "You're in command now . . . Can't lose you too, Spic . . . Send the four men to the bridge ready to go over the side."

"Aye, aye, skipper," Vargas responded.

Boxer switched off the radio.

"I think I hear the plane," Cowly said, pointing toward the port side.

Boxer strained to hear it too. But the grinding noise of the constantly shifting pack ice and the shrieking of the wind made it impossible for him to hear anything, except Cowly and the radio. He shook his head.

"Target," the Radar Officer announced, "bearing two four four degrees . . . Altitude three thousand feet . . . Range one zero miles . . . Speed two zero zero knots . . . Closing fast."

"That must be our lost angle," Boxer said.

Cowly nodded.

Suddenly the hatch opened and four men came up to the bridge. Each wore a wet suit and face mask specially insulated for use in the Arctic.

"You men hit the water the moment the plane goes in," Boxer said. "Hopefully they'll come down real close to us . . . It'll be up to you to get the flyboys aboard."

The four men nodded.

Boxer keyed engineering. "Stop all engines," he said.

"All engines stopped," the EO answered.

"Target . . . two four four degrees . . . Range . . . zero two miles . . . Altitude one thousand feet . . . Speed one five zero knots . . . Closing fast."

"Roger that," Boxer said. "Better get down on the deck," he told the rescue team.

"Aye, aye Skipper," the man in charge answered.

Boxer waited until all of them were below; then turning to Cowly, he said, "Here goes." An instant later *The Shark* was completely illuminated by high intensity floodlights.

"Skipper," the COMMO said, "The pilot says he sees us."

"Tell him to come down as close to us as possible . . . And to come in quickly . . . If he sees us, the Ruskies might be able to, too."

"Roger that," the COMMO answered.

The roar of the plane was loud enough to be heard over the shrieking of the wind and the noise of the ice.

"Should see it any moment," Boxer commented.

"I'd like it better if we could talk him down," Cowly answered.

"Makes it more interesting this way," Boxer said.

"There she is!" Cowly exclaimed pointing off the star'b'd side.

Boxer peered down on the deck. The rescue team was standing by.

The roar of the jets was deafening.

Cowly made a gesture to indicate the plane was big.

Suddenly it was down! A huge curtain of water shot into the air; then the thunk of the ice as it smashed against the metal. The portside wing snapped off. The fuselage fell back into the water and quickly began to settle.

Boxer switched on the bridge searchlights and trained them on the wreckage. The plane was sinking fast. But it was close enough to *The Shark* for the rescue team to reach it in minutes.

Even with the searchlights on it was hard for Boxer to see anything clearly through the blowing snow.

"Target," the Sonar Officer said, "Bearing one eight nine d e g r e e s . . . Range twelve thousand yards . . . Speed two zero knots . . . Depth one five zero feet."

"Roger that," Boxer answered. He was positive that his Russian counter-part was still searching for him. He would, if he were in his shoes. After all, *The Shark* was badly wounded and was no match for the *Q-Twenty One*. She'd be an easy kill!

Cowly tapped him on the shoulder. "Someone just clambered onto the fuselage."

"Set those damn flotation bags!" Boxer exclaimed aloud.

"Target," the SO reported, "Bearing one eight nine degrees

. . . Range eleven thousand yards . . . Speed two zero knots . . . Depth one five zero feet."

"Roger that," Boxer said; then turning to Cowly, he said, "Borodine is one one miles off our port side."

Cowly nodded. "Damn lucky he's not on the surface . . . Even in this fucking blizzard the light around us must be visible for miles."

"You can bet on it," Boxer said.

Suddenly two yellow flotation bags bloomed under the fuselage of the downed plane.

Boxer keyed the EO. "Give us two thousand rpms," he said, knowing that it translated into approximately two knots.

"Aye, aye Skipper," the EO said.

Boxer keyed the helmsman. "Going to bridge, helm," he said.

"Aye, aye Skipper; the bridge has the helm," the helmsman said.

Boxer took the wheel himself and slowly eased it up. *The Shark* responded, turning slightly to its port side. He estimated that the wreck was less than a hundred yards away.

The Sonar Officer gave Boxer another target position. The *Q-21* was now ten miles out.

"Borodine is still coming toward us," Boxer told Cowly.

"Too bad our SUBROCS are iced up, or we'd be able to surprise the shit out of him," Cowly answered.

Boxer agreed and brought *The Shark* directly behind the downed aircraft. He keyed the EO. "Stop all engines."

"Aye, aye Skipper," the EO responded.

*The Shark* lost headway, slowed down and within minutes began to drift toward the wreckage.

Boxer keyed the OD. "Send a four man detail topside to take aboard personnel."

"Aye, aye Skipper," the OD replied.

Within minutes the men of the rescue team were back in the water with the survivors of the crash.

Boxer switched on the MC system. "Deck detail stand by to take men aboard."

The first member of the team reached *The Shark*.

"Go get them!" Boxer exclaimed.

The survivors were taken aboard and quickly moved below; then the rescue team clambered onto the deck. As soon as the deck was cleared, Boxer keyed the EO. "Give me everything you can."

"One zero knots, Skipper, is the best I can deliver," the EO said.

"Do it," Boxer answered, switching off all the lights.

"Aye, aye, Skipper," the EO answered.

A moment later *The Shark* shuddered and got under way again.

Boxer keyed the bridge helmsman again. "Transferring helm to main bridge," he said.

"Aye, aye, Skipper," Mahony answered.

"Helm transferred," Boxer said. "Come to course three one degrees."

"Coming to course three one degrees," Mahony answered.

Boxer looked back to the wreckage. It was already hidden by the blowing snow.

Suddenly the hatch opened. Still wearing his wet suit and mask, one of the men lifted himself onto the bridge. "Came to make a report," the man said.

Despite the face mask, Boxer recognized the voice. It belonged to Vargas.

"Survivors are bedded down in sick bay," Vargas said. "The three of them are shook up . . . But the doc says they'll be okay in a day or two."

Boxer nodded and said, "Good work . . . But I ordered you not to go."

"Goddamn," Vargas exclaimed, "and I thought you said to go. I was really pissed at you . . . I apologize . . . I mean who the fuck wants to go into the drink up here?"

"Spic you're a lousy liar," Boxer said.

"Hey, Skipper, but I got other talents," Vargas answered.

Suddenly the roar of an explosion rolled across *The Shark* from the direction of the wrecked plane.

"Torpedo?" Boxer asked, looking at his EXO.

Before Cowly could answer, another roar rolled over them.

Under his face mask Boxer grinned; then he started to laugh . . . Borodine's sonar officer had mistaken the wreckage of the plane for *The Shark*. And obviously didn't try to ID it, or couldn't because of the weather . . .

Cowly began to laugh too.

Vargas looked at Boxer; then at Cowly. "I always knew you Anglos were nuts," he said.

"Not nuts," Boxer answered. "Just fucking lucky . . . We were just sunk."

"What?"

"Comrade Captain Borodine just used two torpedoes to sink us," Boxer laughed. "The Ruskies think we've been deep sixed."

"Holy shit," Vargas exclaimed. "That's mother-fucking luck!"

Boxer keyed the EO. "Stop all engines."

"All engines stopped," the EO reported.

Boxer picked up the MC mike. "Now hear this," he said. "Now hear this . . . This is the captain speaking . . . I want absolute silence aboard . . . That means no movement and no talking." He switched off the MC and whispered to Cowly, "Let's hope Borodine doesn't realize his mistake until it's too late for him to do something about it."

Cowly nodded.

Boxer leaned against the side of the sail. He was almost too weary to stand. He closed his eyes . . . With a bit more luck, he'd be able to leave the bridge in a few hours. That, and having some hot food, was the extent of the luxury that he allowed himself to think about . . .

"Comrade Captain," the Sonar Officer said, "the wreckage is being quickly dispersed . . . Two large sections of the target have already sunk."

"Roger that," Borodine answered; then turning to Viktor Korzenko, his EXO, he said, "I never imagined it would be this easy to destroy *The Shark*."

"If I were you, I wouldn't complain about that," Viktor answered with a grin. "Better an easy time of it than a hard one."

Borodine didn't answer. He keyed the communications officer. "Send the following message to Admiral Goshkov: Sank the American submarine *Shark* . . . There were no survivors . . . Returning to base . . . Send it code ten."

"Aye, aye Comrade Captain," the COMMO answered.

Borodine leaned back into his chair. He rubbed his eyes.

"Excuse me, Comrade Captain," the political officer, Karenski said.

Borodine lowered his hands and looked at the man. He was tall and thin and had a hawk-like face.

"Permit me to congratulate you on the destruction of *The Shark*," Karenski said, offering his hand.

Borodine nodded and shook the political officer's hand. "Thank you," he said. "But it was more luck than skill."

Karenski smiled. "I was sure you'd say something like that."

Borodine let go of Karenski's hand and stood up. "If you'll excuse me, I'm very tired and need a few hours sleep."

"Yes, of course."

Borodine turned to the COMCOMP and dialed in a new course that would take the *Sea Savage* into the Bering Sea. "Viktor, turn the CON over to Lieutenant Popov and get a few hours sleep."

"What about you?" Viktor asked.

"I'm going to my quarters. Leave word to wake me in two hours," Borodine said, as he left the bridge. He went directly to his room and dropped down on the bunk. The destruction of *The Shark* gave him no joy. If he felt anything, it was a certain sadness at having killed Boxer . . . at not having the opportunity to know the man better. He closed his eyes. These thoughts were not the kind of things he could communicate to anyone. He found himself wondering if Galena would understand them? He didn't really know. Boxer was his enemy. He had no doubt that given the chance, Boxer wouldn't have hesitated to destroy him.

11

COMMO keyed him. "Comrade Captain, there's a message from Comrade Admiral Goshkov."

"Read it."

"Congratulations. Report to me as soon as possible."

"Thanks," Borodine said.

"Out," COMMO answered.

Borodine stared into the darkness. "It shouldn't have been that easy," he said aloud. . . .

# 2

Most of the snow now was wind-blown, but that didn't make it any easier for Boxer to see. An hour had passed since sonar had lost the *Q-21*. But Boxer knew that sound traveled long distances underwater and longer in very cold water.

Suddenly something crashed against the port side, aft of the sail. The next instant tons of ice came down on the deck, tilting the entire boat to the port.

Boxer hit the button for the emergency klaxon. He switched on the searchlights and swung them aft. Large chunks of ice lay on the deck and a huge pressure ridge hung menacingly over it. He keyed the EO. "Give me one zero knots," he said.

"One zero knots," the EO answered.

Boxer keyed the Damage Control Officer. "Emergency detail on deck to clear ice," he said. "Check for structural integrity."

"Aye, aye, Skipper," the DCO answered.

The EO keyed Boxer. "Skipper st'a'b'd propeller only partially grabbing . . . Getting max zero seven knots."

"Roger that," Boxer answered, looking down at the deck, where the detail was already chopping at the ice. He played the lights on the pressure ridge. There was open water between it and *The Shark*.

As the ice on the deck was chopped away and thrown overboard, *The Shark* began to right itself.

"No structural damage," the DCO reported.

"Roger that," Boxer answered.

"Skipper," Cowly said, "I can't take much more of this topside."

"I don't think I can either," Boxer responded. He keyed the Duty Officer. "Send two deck officers topside to relieve Cowly and me."

"Aye, aye, Skipper," the Duty Officer answered.

Within minutes the two officers were topside.

"Keep her on this course," Boxer said. "Look out for pressure ridges," he warned. "If either of you feel the least bit uncertain about anything you see, key me immediately. I'll have our surface radar scan for pressure ridges too. Any questions?"

"None, Skipper," one of the men answered.

Boxer nodded. "I'll arrange to have you relieved in two hours," he told them, as he lowered himself into the hatchway. To suddenly be out of the wind and the numbing cold was a pleasure so intense that Boxer uttered a deep sigh of satisfaction.

"I don't know what I want to do more . . . Have something hot or sleep," Cowly said.

The deeper they went into *The Shark*, the more they steamed until they looked as if they were actually smoldering.

"I have to take a quick look at our flyboys and our prisoners," Boxer said.

Cowly nodded. "Mind if I don't go with you?"

Boxer shook his head. "Get some sleep," he said, removing his Arctic storm gear. He took a few moments to wipe the moisture from his beard and hair; then he went directly into the sick bay. The three flyboys were sleeping.

"Gave them a shot to knock them out," the doctor said, walking alongside of Boxer.

"What about our wounded Russian?" Boxer asked.

"He'll need extensive surgery to rebuild his knees."

Boxer had decided to deal with the two Russian officers the following day, or when time permitted. Now his main task was to make sure *The Shark* was out of Russian waters and close to an American, or Canadian base. "Where are the other Russians and our men?"

"In the mess area now," the doctor said. "But the men will sleep here and the two women — well, we have not found quarters for them as yet."

Boxer had forgotten that two of three people coming out were women.

"One of them will have your quarters," Boxer said.

The doctor nodded.

"I'll find a place for the other," Boxer said. He left the sick bay and went to the mess area. For a few moments he stood in the doorway and said nothing.

Sanchez was speaking to a man who was one of the men taken aboard *The Shark*. Meagan, the reporter assigned by Kinkade, the Company's chief, to do a story about *The Shark*, was speaking to the two women who were also taken aboard.

Suddenly one of the men saw Boxer and started to stand.

"No need to get up," Boxer said, entering the mess area. "I'm Captain Boxer."

Sanchez introduced Boris Donoski.

Boxer shook his hand.

"I was the one who identified this submarine for the Russians," Boris said with a laugh.

Boxer frowned.

"I had to do something to earn my keep," Donoski said.

"He was one of mine," Sanchez said. "I recruited him several years ago when he was visiting Paris."

Boxer looked at the other two men.

"Paul Hardy," one of them said.

Boxer shook his hand. He knew Hardy was the leader of the group. "Glad you made it out," he said.

"Dean Foster," the other man said, offering his hand.

"Welcome aboard *The Shark*," Boxer said, shaking the man's hand.

"May I present Doctor Natalia Jannovich and Nicole Pushkin," Sanchez said.

Boxer looked at the women. Both were attractive, but the doctor was beautiful. He shook each of their hands and welcomed them aboard *The Shark*. Then he said, "Doctor

Jannovich, you will take the doc's quarters . . . Miss Pushkin, I will find a place for you."

"She may share my quarters," Meagan said.

Boxer shook his head. "I think it better if all the women had their own accommodations. Now if you'll excuse me," he said, "I must get some sleep. But first I want something hot to drink." He went over to the soup dispenser and filled a plastic cup with hot beef broth. "I'll drink this back in my quarters," he said with a smile as he turned to leave the mess area.

"Captain," Sanchez called.

Boxer stopped and turned toward him.

"You have two other guests aboard *The Shark*. The Russian in the sick bay is Colonel Andra Stepanovich, KGB commander of the Vladivostok district and the other who's under armed guard in my quarters is General Valentin Yedotev, head of the KGB."

Before he could fully understand it, Boxer played back in his brain what he had just heard.

"We're coming out with more than we could have hoped for," Sanchez said.

Boxer managed a smile. "Not so much more," he said, "that it would make the Russians doubt that they sank us."

"Sank us?" Hardy asked.

"The two explosions you heard a few hours ago were from Russian torpedoes. They were fired at the remains of a crashed bomber that their sonar picked up."

"Then they're not following—"

"No," Boxer said. "More than an hour ago they disappeared from our screen."

"But that's wonderful!" Sanchez exclaimed.

"Lucky," Boxer responded. "With the people we now have on board, let's hope our luck holds."

"And why shouldn't it hold?" Meagan asked.

"We're badly damaged. We're in the worst ocean at the worst time of the year . . . and the Russians just might fly over us and wonder what the hell we're doing on the surface, when we were supposed to have been sunk."

"Aren't you being pessimistic, Captain?" Doctor Jannovich asked.

Boxer nodded. "But I have survived because I am a pessimist," he said; then he turned and walked out of the mess area. Having the head of the KGB and one of its area commanders on board wouldn't alter the weather conditions one iota. And for the present, the weather was *The Shark*'s worst enemy. He entered his quarters, gulped the soup down and without undressing, he stretched out on his bunk. He was grateful that sleep came quickly.

Boxer awakened before he was keyed by the OD. With his hands behind his head, he remained in his bunk. Until now he hadn't had time to think about, or react to Tom Redfern's death. Tom was a good friend and a fine officer. Together they had been a wonderful team.

Boxer pursed his lips. It was going to be difficult to face Sue-Ann, Tom's wife. "Damn difficult," he said aloud. He wondered just how much she knew about Tom's activities. Probably very little . . . Tom was a tight lipped man. He—

"Skipper," the OD said, keying him, "you asked to be awakened after two hours."

"Roger that," Boxer answered. "Any status change?"

"MET says the storm is moderating," the OD answered.

"I'll be on the bridge in one five minutes," Boxer said.

"Ten four," the OD said.

Boxer left his bunk, stripped and wrapping a towel around his torso, he crossed the hallway to the shower. Minutes later he returned to his quarters and dressed in clean clothes. He was beginning to feel somewhat more human. The feeling would be complete after he had something to eat. He tried to remember the last time he sat down and ate something. He couldn't.

Just before he left his quarters, Boxer tried the MINI-COMCOMP. An error signal came up on the screen, indicating that the master computer system was down. With a shrug, he switched it off and then left his quarters.

"I'm going to the mess area," Boxer told the officer who had the CON.

"Aye, aye Skipper," the young officer answered.

"If Mister Cowly comes to the bridge send him to the mess area."

"Aye, aye, Skipper," the officer said.

Boxer nodded and continued on to the mess area, where he found some of the crew eating. They greeted him warmly. All of them had been with him aboard the *Sting Ray*, his previous command.

"Skipper," a yeoman said, "com'on and join us here."

"Be with you as soon as I get something to eat," he answered, inserting his food card into the nutritional computer. An instant later his allowable caloric intake came up on a small video screen, followed by the choices available to him. Using an electronic pencil, he indicated what he wanted. His choice was approved and he went to the food station where the doors to the automatic dispensing units were already open.

Boxer came to the table with a tray of food that included roast beef already cut into uniform pieces, a baked potato and creamed spinach, apple pie topped with coffee ice cream and a cup of black coffee.

The men made room for him.

"What's the info on the Ruskies?" one of the chiefs asked.

Boxer removed his plastic chopsticks from their wrapper. "I don't know where they are and I hope they don't know where we are."

"Are we heading back to base or to the *Tecumseh*?" another rate asked.

Boxer swallowed a piece of roast beef before he said, "One or the other I hope. The sooner we get out of this ocean, the happier I'm going to be."

"Yeah," the rate answered, "the Eskimos can have it."

"Skipper?" Cowly called, poking his head inside the mess area, "there's a priority message coming in for your eyes only."

"Coming," he said, picking up the container of coffee with one hand and the tray of unfinished food in the other. "See you men," he said. On the way out, he dropped the tray into the disposal unit but kept the coffee.

Within minutes, he was seated in a closed-off section of

18

the Communications Center where the electronic decoders were located. He ID'd himself to the machine and a green light came on, indicating he could proceed with the decoding operation. The code itself used very large numbers of which only one digit became a letter in the alphabet, or a phonetic grouping of sounds. As each word was decoded, it came up on a screen. The message read:

FROM COMPANY CHIEF
TO CAPTAIN
RUSSIANS REPORT SHARK SUNK . . . BREAK
RADIO SILENCE AND ADVISE . . . MONI-
TORED YOUR TRANSMISSIONS TO FLYBOYS
. . . REPEAT . . . BREAK RADIO SILENCE AND
ADVISE.

Boxer hit the delete key and the message disappeared from the screen. He secured the decoding device and left the enclosed area. Ordinarily the COMCOMP would do the decoding, but he wasn't certain that it would be able to in its present state.

"Kinkade is worried," Boxer told Cowly, as they went to the bridge together.

"That's understandable," Cowly answered.

"He wants me to break radio silence and advise him about our situation. I want to think about it for awhile," Boxer said. "If we transmit, the Ruskies are going to know it's us."

Cowly nodded.

Boxer returned to the bridge and took the CON. He sat at the COMCOMP and thought about Kinkade's request. He had just about decided to ignore it when the DCO keyed him.

"Go ahead," Boxer said.

"Skipper, one of the pumps on the st'a'b'd side is becoming clogged with ice . . . We're going to lose it soon."

"Will the other one be able to do the job?"

"Negative . . . It will not keep all of the water out. We'll probably lose zero two to zero three knots."

"Roger that," Boxer said. He ran his hand over his beard.

The decision had been made for him. He couldn't afford to wait any longer to contact Kinkade. If he didn't, he'd risk losing *The Shark*. Unit after unit would malfunction until she'd be reduced to a floating hulk and it was questionable whether she'd continue to float. The other side of the coin was the Ruskies. They might come after *The Shark* and he couldn't do a fucking thing to defend the boat. He uttered a deep sigh. Neither risk was acceptable. But if he contacted Kinkade, he might be able to get aircover whenever the weather permitted.

Boxer keyed COMMO. "Signal our home base care of Kinkade . . . Use the same code and priority level as his message. Give our position and tell him we're extensively damaged. That we can't submerge and we need air cover on a twenty-four hour basis. Tell him we have retrieved all personnel and that we have taken the head of the KGB and one of the area commanders prisoner. Tell him that Major Redfern was killed in action and that we did not take the body out."

"Roger that, Skipper," the COMMO answered.

"Please repeat the message," Boxer said.

The COMMO read the message back.

"Ten four," Boxer answered; then motioning to Cowly to join him at the COMCOMP, he said, "I just put the ball in Kinkade's court. It'll be interesting to see how he plays it."

"What about the Ruskies?" Cowly asked.

Boxer shrugged. "I couldn't even begin to guess what they might do. In a few hours at most we'll be in U.S. territorial waters. But I just don't know whether that will give us any security. I just don't know."

"Skipper," COMMO said, keying Boxer, "message sent."

"Roger that," Boxer answered; then to Cowly, he said, "I don't figure Kinkade will waste any time getting back to us."

Cowly looked at his watch. "I'd say two hours at the very most."

"Two hours, eh. I have twenty bucks that says less. Are you willing to match it?"

"Sure . . . Why not!"

"Skipper," the senior officer on the bridge keyed Boxer,

"the wind has freshened from the sou'-sou'-west and the ice is beginning to build across our bow."

"How bad?"

"We're going to start bumping into big floes soon."

"Roger that," Boxer answered. He keyed the EO. "We might have ice problems soon. Will we have enough power to move through an ice field?"

"Negative."

"Roger that," Boxer answered and pursing his lips, he said to Cowly, "I think the worst is yet to come."

"Maybe we'll get lucky. Considering what might have happened to us, we've been lucky so far."

Boxer smiled. "I never realized that you're the kind of guy who drinks half of what's in a glass and says it's half full."

Cowly nodded. "And you're the kind who doesn't give a damn whether it's half full or half empty, as long as you can drink."

"Right," Boxer answered. "I leave the philosophical speculations to others. I'm only interested in whether or not I can do what I must or want to."

"That's why every man on the boat trusts you," Cowly said. "And a few even love you."

"Now that's pushing it," Boxer laughed. "That's really pushing it."

"Skipper," the bridge officer said, "there are heavy floes dead ahead."

"Roger that," Boxer answered; then he keyed the EO. "Reduce speed to three knots."

"Aye, aye, Skipper," the EO answered.

"I'm going topside," Boxer told Cowly. "Stand by here."

Cowly nodded.

Suddenly a loud grinding noise moved from the bow to the stern.

"That sounds like it could rip us apart," Cowly said.

"Enough of them banging at us could," Boxer answered. He left the COMCOMP, grabbed his Arctic gear and headed topside.

Kinkade paced back and forth in front of Admiral Stark's desk. This time he came directly to the Chief of Naval Operations. "He's got my people aboard and he got the head of the KGB and a lesser light also and — "

"You told me all this," Stark said.

"He's your man," Kinkade answered. "You tell me how to get him and that boat out of there."

"If I knew I would have told you," Stark answered. He was a tall dignified-looking man, with a full head of very white hair.

"I need a fucking miracle," Kinkade roared, "and I don't even have a magic trick up my sleeve."

"If there's a way to bring *The Shark* out, Boxer will find it."

"He's going to have to," Kinkade answered. "I can't send anything in. The only guys who go up there are Met teams — wait a minute . . . Wait a minute . . . I think I've got it . . . Stark, I'm a damn fucking genius. We have two Met teams up there on ice islands. Why didn't I think of it before. Once *The Shark* gets to either one of those bases, we can fly in some metal shielding, laser weld it over the damaged sections of the hull and she can get out."

"Those aren't navy teams," Stark said.

"Air force . . . Air force . . . They'd be more than willing to help once they know he fished three of their people out of the drink."

Stark agreed.

"Okay . . . What we need to know — "

"Where those islands are in relation to *The Shark*," Stark said.

"That's right," Kinkade answered, dropping into the chair alongside Stark's desk. "The head of the KGB! Good Christ, it's the intelligence coup of the century!"

Stark picked up the phone and dialed Gen. George Powder's number. Powder was on the Joint Chiefs of Staff with Stark. As soon as Powder came on the line Stark nodded to Kinkade and said to Powder, "George, one of our ships is in difficulty in the Arctic and I want to know the exact location of your floating Met bases."

"Don't bull me, Stark," Powder answered. "One of your

spook subs is trouble. Got the word from a fighter bomber."

"That same plane went down and my spook sub, as you put it, fished your flyboys out of the drink . . . Now give the fuckin' positions of those bases."

"I know that too, I mean about our plane going down."

"The positions, George."

"My guys aren't going to fly any drops up there," Powder said.

Stark put his hand over the phone's mouthpiece and repeated what Powder had just said; then added, "This kind of attitude really burns the shit out of me."

Kinkade nodded.

Stark removed his hand from the mouthpiece. "I don't want to go to the president over this one. But I fuckin' will. Your men will fly the missions and make the drops. I have a sub and its crew out there and I'm going to fucking well see that they come back. Are you reading me, general?"

"Loud and clear."

"Have two C-90s standing by . . . As soon as I receive word that my sub has reached one of your bases I want those planes in the air."

"What about having them loaded?" Powder asked.

"Don't be a wise-ass . . . They'll be loaded and ready to go . . . Now the positions."

"Able base is at latitude seven four degrees, fourteen minutes, twenty-two seconds north; longitude one hundred and sixty-five degrees, ten minutes, eight seconds west."

Stark jotted down the position. "Now the second base."

"That's off the coast of northern Greenland," Powder said.

"Let's have it," Stark said, guessing that Powder probably knew the sub was too far west to make an attempt to reach it. But he wasn't going to let the prick get off without giving him what he had originally asked for.

"Latitude eighty-four degrees, twenty-eight minutes, forty seconds; longitude seventy degrees, forty minutes, ten seconds west."

"Thank you George," Stark said politely. "Have those planes standing by."

"Anything else, Admiral?"

"Nothing . . . Goodbye," Stark said and put the phone down.

"He must be doing a slow burn," Kinkade said.

"Right now I don't give a fuck if he incinerates himself," Stark said, opening the lower right hand drawer to activate the electronic projection equipment. In an instant, the far wall was covered with a map of the Arctic. "*The Shark* will head for Met base Able. We'll drop the necessary supplies to enable Boxer to make repairs to get the hell out of there and meet the *Tecumseh* just south of Greenland."

"Will I be able to get my people out?" Kinkade asked.

Stark shook his head. "No one comes out before anyone else."

Kinkade knew better than to argue with Stark, when it came to *The Shark* and its crew. They were special to him, especially Boxer.

# 3

Boxer was back on the bridge. *The Shark* was caught in a mass of ice and because of her shape; the ice was sliding over the bow. Boxer keyed the EO. "How much live steam can you give me?"

"All you want, Skipper."

"I want as much as you can deliver through pipes run to the bow."

"Hosing would be better," the EO answered. "I'll get it going with the DCO."

"Now," Boxer said, "or that fucking ice will push our bow down."

"Roger that," the EO answered.

Boxer keyed Vargas. "Spic, I need a demo man to blow away some of the ice . . . open a path for us."

"Roger that," Vargas said. "I'll send someone to the bridge . . . tell him what you want blown and he'll do it."

"Ten four," Boxer answered. He watched the ice slide over the bow. It was like a living thing . . . Something that wanted to devour *The Shark*. Even the noise sounded threatening. Sometimes grinding. Sometimes growling, the way a wolf or an angry dog would, low in its throat. And sometimes squealing, like a person gone mad with pain.

The COMMO keyed Boxer. "Message from HQ . . . Same code as before, Skipper."

"Acknowledge receipt," Boxer said. "I'll take care of it when I come off the bridge."

"Immediate reply—"

"Fuck that, just acknowledge," Boxer snapped and was immediately sorry.

"Roger that," the COMMO answered.

Boxer pursed his lips. He hated it when anything got in the way of his running *The Shark*, especially when it came from headquarters. . . .

Boxer suddenly became aware of the men on deck. They were attaching hosing to valves ordinarily used for washing down the deck. Within moments the hoses were smoking with live steam and two teams began cutting away at the ice. Jets of steam made *The Shark* look like a fire-breathing monster. But the steam blown back toward the men quickly turned to ice, making it impossible for anyone to man the hoses for more than a few minutes at a time.

Two men came up through the hatchway. "Miller and Hendricks, reporting as ordered, sir," one of them said.

Boxer knew their names and nodded. "I need to have a path blown open for us. We've got to get out of this ice jam and into open water."

The men looked toward the bow.

"As soon as the deck is cleared, you can work off the bow," Boxer said.

"Can't see much ahead," Miller said. "But I bet some of that shit out there is big."

"Probably," Boxer answered.

"Will start with one pound charges and throw them like grenades," Miller explained.

"How much RDX do we have aboard?" Hendricks asked.

"At least a hundred pounds," Boxer said.

"Let's hope we don't need any more," Miller said.

Boxer was keyed by the chief in charge of the deck detail. "Skipper, the ice on the bow has been cut away."

"Roger that," Boxer responded; then to Miller and Hendricks, he said, "Get us the hell out of here."

"Will do, Skipper," Miller answered.

"We'll sure as hell try," Hendricks said.

The two men opened the hatchway and disappeared through it. One of the men on watch closed it.

Boxer scanned the ice. It was awesome to look at and in a dozen different ways frightening to think about.

"Skipper, there's something on the ice directly off our midship," one of the officers on watch said.

Boxer made a quarter turn and scanned the ice.

"There it is!" the officer exclaimed.

"It's a polar bear," Boxer said, "and it's coming this way."

"It sure as hell doesn't seem to be afraid," the officer said.

"If you were that big, I guess you wouldn't be afraid either."

"Skipper," another officer of the watch said, "Miller and Hendricks are on deck and moving toward the bow."

Boxer turned his attention to the men; then back to the bear. "Better give that animal something to think about," he said and reaching below the top of the COMCOMP, he withdrew a flare gun, opened the chamber and loaded it with a flare-cartridge. A moment later he aimed the gun at a point over the bear and fired.

The sound of the explosion was very loud and white light very bright, made brighter by reflecting off the snow.

The bear stopped.

The Miller and Hendricks stopped and waved; then moved forward to the bow.

Even as the flare began to die, Boxer replaced the spent cartridge with a fresh one. Then suddenly he realized that by blowing the ice, he'd be giving the Ruskies a fix on him. The sound of underwater explosions would travel a great distance, especially in the frigid water of the Arctic and if there were several in rapid succession. He pursed his lips and looked down at Miller and Hendricks. He had to take the risk. If he didn't, the ice would creep over *The Shark* and sink her. He uttered a deep sigh and looked toward the bear. It hadn't moved.

"Skipper," Miller reported, "we're ready down here."

"Roger that," Boxer answered.

The first explosion sent the bear running in the opposite direction.

Boxer keyed the EO. "Five knots," Boxer said.

"Five knots," the EO answered.

Another explosion followed; then a third. All told, there were fifteen of them before *The Shark* gained an open passage way.

"Increase speed to ten knots," Boxer said, keying the EO. Then he keyed Miller. "Good work. Now go below. We'll probably need you to do that a few more times before we're out of this place."

"No sweat, Skipper," Miller answered.

"Ten four," Boxer said.

*The Shark* was moving well. The ice it did encounter, it easily pushed aside.

"I'm going below," Boxer said. "If you see anything unusual, call me."

"Skipper," the officer of the watch answered, "everything out there is unusual."

"You can say that again," Boxer said, opening the hatch. Moments later he was inside the sail and secretly glad to be out of the wind and the numbing cold.

Boxer went straight to the COMMCOMP.

"All systems are go," Cowly reported.

Boxer removed his cold weather outer gear and hung it within easy reach. "A short time topside and you feel as if you've been on watch for a couple of days."

Cowly nodded sympathetically. "I know the feeling."

Boxer said, "I have a reply from HQ."

"Did I win our bet?

"You won," Boxer answered with a grin. He keyed the COMMO. "I'll have that message now . . . Put it on the screen."

"Sure, Skipper."

Boxer switched on the video-message-interface device. The message came up on a screen to his left. As soon as he saw the coordinates, he checked *The Shark*'s position. The rhumb line position between the two was five hundred and fifty five miles. But there was little or no chance that *The Shark* would be able to travel in a straight line. He was certain that it would encounter other ice fields and storms that would force it off course. Given the speed of ten knots, it would take a minimum of fifty-five hours to reach its destination.

Cowly, who was standing close by, asked, "What the hell could be out there?"

"A ship maybe?"

"You'd think Kinkade would tell us."

"Why? He's telling us only what we need to know to get to where he wants us to be."

Boxer keyed COMMO. "Send the following message to Kinkade: proceeding."

"Just—"

"Just that one word," Boxer said.

"Aye, aye, Skipper."

Boxer turned to Cowly. "We'll keep the helm on manual and if we run into any more pressure ridges we'll use the same procedure to get through them."

Cowly nodded.

"I'm going to start interviewing our Russian guests," Boxer said.

"Which group: the willing, or the unwilling?"

"The willing first. Kinkade will want a report on Tom's death. I might as well get that down on tape now."

"He'll also want to know about how the general got shot up," Cowly said.

Boxer frowned. He hadn't really had time to think about that, but he was sure Cowly was right. It would be just the kind of thing that Kinkade would use against him in any way he could.

"Maybe he won't push it," Cowly offered.

"He'll want the report," Boxer said.

Cowly nodded.

"Take the CON," Boxer told him. "I'll be in my quarters. I'll do the interviewing there. I'll speak to our people first; followed by the three defectors; then the colonel. Have them come one at a time. When it comes time to bring the colonel, blindfold him."

"Aye, aye, Skipper."

"What will happen to us, Captain?" Col. Andra Stepanovich asked.

29

"That's not for me to say," Boxer answered.

Stepanovich rubbed his unshaven jaw. "General Yedotev needs medical attention."

"He is getting whatever he needs," Boxer said.

"Will the general lose his legs?"

"His knees will have to be rebuilt, or replaced with artificial joints. It's a routine operation either way."

Stepanovich's eyebrows went up.

Boxer wasn't sure he understood and was about to explain, when Stepanovich said, "It is not routine for one man to shoot an unarmed man —"

"Colonel, if you have any sort of complaint to make against any of my men, you will have the opportunity to make it when I turn you over to our people."

"You too will be named in the complaint, Captain."

Boxer nodded. He didn't know whether he should become angry or laugh. He did neither: he kept a straight face and nodded. "That will be your right," he said.

"Skipper," Cowly said, keying him, "the bridge reports heavy snow."

"Wind?" Boxer asked.

"Steady at zero five knots, out of the west-sou'west."

"Roger that," Boxer answered.

"You don't have a very good chance of reaching —"

"Colonel, I'm paid to worry about things like that," Boxer said. "But let me assure you that if, for any reason, we don't make it out of the Arctic, neither will you or General Yedotev." Then forcing himself to smile, he added, "Either all of us make it back, or none of us will. Now, I have other duties to perform." He stood up, walked to the door, opened it and summoned the two guards, who had brought Stepanovich to his quarters. "Blindfold the colonel and take him back to the mess area."

"Aye, aye, Skipper," one of the guards answered.

As soon as the colonel and his escort left, Boxer removed the cassette and placed it in his safe. He was sure it would take days, if not weeks of intensive work to debrief the colonel and the general. He sat down, filled a pipe and lit it. He was tired and needed a few minutes relaxation before going up to the bridge again. He tried to make his mind go blank, but he couldn't. He kept thinking about everything from the weather to Louise Collins and her beautiful black body.

"Skipper," it was the bridge officer who was keying him now, "visibility down to one five feet. Can't see anything beyond the bow."

"Roger that," Boxer said. "I'll be topside in a few minutes."

"Ten four," the officer answered.

Boxer emptied the pipe bowl into an ash tray and put the still warm pipe into his jacket pocket. He wasn't looking forward to going to the bridge again. But if *The Shark* was going to survive, every member of her crew would have to push themselves to the limit of their endurance and because he was captain, he'd have to push himself even more.

"Skipper," Cowly said, when Boxer stopped at the COMMCOMP on his way topside, "I ran those coordinates through the NAVCOMP and asked for a readout of all ships on station in the Arctic."

Boxer squinted at him. He should have thought of doing that. "What did you come up with?"

"Not a ship," Cowly answered.

Boxer cocked his head to one side. "It has to be a ship."

"It's a weather station," Cowly said.

"A what?"

"There's more."

"What the hell are we going to do at a weather station?"

"The station is located on one of the floating islands of ice."

"You're joking!" Boxer exclaimed.

Cowly shook his head. "I made a printout of the data."

"Why the hell are we being sent there?" Then he answered his own question. "Kinkade is going to use that fucking floe to fly his people out and keep us there to repair *The Shark*, or try to."

"Something like that, I would guess," Cowly answered.

"I don't fucking believe that man!" Boxer exclaimed. "I really don't fucking believe him." He went to the COMM-COMP and checked their present position. "I don't need an ice floe," Boxer growled. "I need the *Tecumseh*. Our last

31

rendezvous point was—" He stopped. "*The Shark* won't make it and even if it could, we couldn't risk a dive to get inside of her."

"Kinkade has all the cards," Skipper," Cowly said.

"This time. But no one will fly out. Everyone on board stays on board."

"Kinkade isn't going to buy that."

"He's not going to have a damn choice," Boxer answered.

# 4

At the COMMCOMP, Borodine studied the computer analysis of the sounds that had come from a point northeast of the *Sea Savage*'s position. The sounds had been, according to the sharp spike pattern, a series of fifteen explosions.

"I'd say there was at least a two to three minute interval between them," Borodine said, looking at Viktor.

"They could have come from volcanic activity," Viktor suggested.

"We'll know that soon enough," Borodine answered. "I radioed our seismological center in Moscow to see if their undersea instruments have picked up any disturbances."

Viktor nodded. "Do you think it could be a ship?"

"Could be. It's possible for a tanker, or even an American Coast Guard cutter to get caught in the ice and blast their way to open water."

Viktor agreed with that.

"It could also have been *The Shark*," Borodine said. "Our communications picked up sudden bursts of radio transmission. But the amount of electrical interference made it impossible to locate the origin."

"*The Shark* was sunk—"

"We assumed it was *The Shark*," Borodine answered. "Given the circumstances it was a natural assumption. But now, I'm not so sure."

"Are you trying to tell me that those explosions came from *The Shark*?"

"It's possible."

"Then she must have had something go wrong and—"

"That's a possibility," Borodine answered. "But there is also another possibility. *The Shark* can't submerge. She must travel on the surface."

"Yes."

"She gets caught in a pressure field and must blast her way out. Think about it!"

"The time interval between the explosions is just enough—"

"For two good men to throw explosive charges from the bow onto the ice," Borodine said, completing Viktor's sentence for him.

"You think those explosions came from *The Shark*?"

"I'm almost sure of it," Borodine answered.

"Then why don't we go after her again?"

Borodine waved the question aside. "I also think the radio transmission we couldn't ID came from *The Shark*. She's heading to a particular destination and my guess is that she has air cover, just as she had when we tried to attack her on the surface. If we attempt an underwater approach, her sonar will locate us and vector in the aircraft. We can't risk that kind of an attack."

"But where is she going?"

Boxer shrugged. "It doesn't matter. Wherever it is, we can't follow her. We'll have to wait until the next time we meet to destroy her."

"I thought we had done it," Viktor said. "I believed we had done it."

"So did I," Borodine sighed. "So did I. But I should have known better. I should have known that Comrade Captain Boxer would not let *The Shark* be so easy a kill."


Able base was a few minutes west of the rendezvous point. Boxer was below when the bridge officer keyed him and announced that the floating island of ice was two miles off their star'b'd bow.

"Roger that," Boxer said and grabbing hold of his gear, he

called out to Cowly, "Let's go see our safe harbor."

In a matter of seconds, the two of them were on the bridge.

Boxer keyed the EO. "Reduce speed to three knots."

"Reducing speed to three knots," the EO answered.

Boxer trained his glasses on the icefloe. There were three modified Nissen huts and a radio shack with what he estimated was a hundred foot tower. Suddenly he saw several figures leave one of the huts and run in their direction.

"We must be the big event of the season," Cowly said.

Boxer laughed and said, "Right now they're the biggest event in my life." He keyed the EO again. "Give me just enough to keep steerage."

"Twelve zero zero rpms, Skipper."

"Roger that," Boxer answered. He switched on the MC. "Mahony topside, on the double."

"Skipper," COMMO said, keying Boxer, "message coming in from HQ."

"Read it," Boxer answered.

"Received word of your arrival at Able Base. Supplies and equipment to make the necessary repairs are already airborne. Ready passengers for flight to States. Sending two anti-sub 'copters to you. Simmons will fly one. Another pilot is on the way. Signed Kinkade."

"Send the following answer: Supplies and help welcome. Passengers will return with *The Shark*. Signed Captain Jack Boxer."

"Roger that," COMMO answered.

Mahony came through the hatchway.

"Take the helm," Boxer said.

"Aye, aye, Skipper," Mahony answered, stepping up to the wheel as the other helmsman moved away.

The men on the icefloe were ten yards from *The Shark* when they stopped. One of them lifted a bull horn and said, "Welcome to Able base."

"Glad to be here," Boxer answered over the MC.

"Bring your boat close to our hotel," the man said.

"Is it safe to tie her up alongside your island?" Boxer asked.

"Not my island," the man answered. "I only have a six month lease. But it's safe."

Boxer put his hand over the speaker. "The man has a sense of humor."

"He'd have to have one to stay here for six months," Cowly answered.

Boxer nodded; then to Mahony he said, "Take her to the huts over there and ease her against the floe. You only have enough power to give you steerageway."

Mahony nodded.

It took the better part of ten minutes for Mahony to bring *The Shark* around the floe and to where the huts were.

"Deck detail topside," Boxer said over the MC. "Stand by fore and aft with lines."

Several of the men from the weather station were on the floe ready to catch the lines.

Boxer keyed the EO. "Stop all engines," he said.

"All engines stopped," the EO answered.

After a few minutes *The Shark* lay dead in the water.

"Let go bow lines," Boxer ordered.

Several men on the floe grabbed hold of the line and looped it over a stanchion made of ice.

"Will that hold?" Boxer asked over the MC.

"As good as anything else," a man answered. "In a couple of hours your boat and the ice floe will be frozen together. After the first blizzard you won't be able to tell them apart."

"Let go stern lines," Boxer told his men; then to the men on the floe, he said, "Come aboard, gentlemen." Minutes later he and Cowly shook hands with the commander of the Met base, Maj. Tore Hansen, a compactly built, broadboned man with blond hair and light blue eyes.

Tore introduced the two men with him: Captain Gray and Lieutenant Rinaldi.

"There are supply aircraft due here sometime within the next two hours," Hansen said. "The two big ones will drop their load on the floe but the smaller one will land."

"We need additional food—"

"Not to worry," Hansen said. "My cook has been cooking up a storm, ever since I told him we were having company.

Like all artists, he complains he's not appreciated."

Boxer smiled.

"I'd ask you and your EXO to visit our humble home," Hansen said. "But you'll see it when you come for dinner at eighteen hundred. Captain, you and every man on *The Shark* is welcome."

"Would your chef mind if the men ate in shifts?"

"He's sensitive about the food being served at the right moment," Hansen said. "But I think I can make him understand the logic behind your request."

Boxer nodded.

"Four more Nissens are being flown in," Hansen said, "and several specialists. We're even getting four very sophisticated anti-submarine 'copters. Another thirty people, I understand."

Boxer glanced at Cowly. "Weather permitting, I want one of those whirly birds in the air at all times."

"Aye, aye Skipper," Cowly answered.

"Put Simmons in the charge of them," Boxer said.

"Will do," Cowly said.

Boxer summoned all the officers to the bridge and introduced them to Hansen and his men.

"Tonight," Boxer told his men over the MC, "we have been invited to dine at Able base. We'll split the crew into shifts, Section chiefs will be responsible for the division. Now for the next few hours all members of the crew, with the exception of the sonar section, are on liberty. Anyone who wants to leave *The Shark* and walk around on the ice floe is welcome to."

"Well Captain," Hansen said, "I'll go back to my chateau and see how dinner is going."

Boxer shook Hansen's hand. "See you eighteen hundred," he said.

"Seems jolly enough," Cowly commented after Hansen and his men had left.

"Certainly does," Boxer answered. He was about to say that he was going to his quarters, when COMMO keyed him. "Skipper, the ETA for the supply aircraft has been changed to fifteen-thirty, or a half-hour from now."

"Roger that," Boxer answered.

"Two aircraft will land. The other two will make their drop from five zero zero feet."

"Tell them we'll be waiting," Boxer said.

"Aye, aye Skipper," COMMO answered.

"Better start the division officers on developing work details," Boxer said. "Have the DCO and EO coordinate their work."

Cowly nodded.

"The sooner we make the repairs, the sooner we'll get out of here."

"I don't think anyone aboard has any doubts about that," Cowly answered.

"I'm going to my quarters," Boxer said. "Give the bridge over to the OD. All the other officers can stand down until the air drop. Have the OD organize the pickup."

"What about our guests?"

"Kinkade's people are free to accompany us. The colonel remains under armed guard."

"Do the men work with us?"

Boxer nodded. "We're going to need lots of hands. Have them assigned to a work detail."

"Mister Sanchez?"

"The same," Boxer said.

"That leaves the women?"

Boxer ran his hand over his beard. "Maybe they can help out with some of the paperwork? The main thing is to keep them busy. We don't want any trouble and in this kind of situation, idle people can make trouble."

Cowly agreed.

"Skipper," COMMO said, keying Boxer, "four aircraft are twenty minutes out."

"Roger that," Boxer answered; then to Cowly he said, "I'm going to my quarters."

"You should have been there ten minutes ago," Cowly said with a smile.

Boxer left the bridge, went straight to his cabin and stretched out on the bunk. He closed his eyes and almost immediately drifted into a light sleep. Louise was in his arms. He ran his fingertips over her black breasts. "Louise I love—"

He was being rocked. Someone was pushing his shoulder. He bolted up! Cowly was keying him.

"Boxer here," he answered.

"Skipper, Met station advises a rapidly developing storm. The wind has veered to the southwest. Hansen says it's going to be a blizzard."

"When?" Boxer asked.

"Any moment."

Boxer looked at his watch. He had only been asleep for ten minutes. "Have our radar—"

"They have the planes on the scope, Skipper. Last report they're one two five miles out and coming in for their drop run."

"I'm going topside," Boxer said. "Have COMMO patch me into radio contact with the planes."

"Roger that," Cowly answered. "But contact is poor. A great deal of static."

"Ten four," Boxer answered. He ran from his cabin to the bridge and grabbing his Arctic gear, he scrambled topside. As soon as he left the hatchway, the knife edge of the wind slashed through his face mask.

Boxer peered down at the open water. It was already beating against the port side of *The Shark*. The floe was moving and *The Shark* was being taken with it.

"Skipper," the Radar Officer said, "four targets bearing nine four degrees . . . Altitude one thousand five zero zero feet . . . Speed one two five knots . . . Closing fast."

Boxer could hear the sound of their engines. He looked up. The sky was filled with rushing clouds.

"Skipper," the COMMO said, "I can't keep radio contact."

"Tell Hansen to put on his high intensity lights," Boxer said, switching on *The Shark*'s lights.

Suddenly the snow began to fall: a huge curtain of it dropped between him and the rest of the ice floe. He reached for the flare gun and fired both barrels. Moments later two brilliant balls of light exploded in the falling snow.

The roar of the planes was deafening.

"Skipper," COMMO said, "I can hear the pilots talk to one another. They can't see anything. Not even one another."

Suddenly Boxer heard the sound of crunching metal. An instant later a thunderous explosion rolled over the ice floe and a ball of orange flames came crashing down on the floe.

Boxer hit the MC switch. "All hands . . . All hands topside . . . All hands topside for emergency rescue . . . Cowly, Vargas report to the bridge."

"This is Otta One," a voice said, coming in over the radio. "This is Otta One . . . Do you read me."

"Skipper," COMMO said, "did you get that?"

"Roger that," Boxer said, looking at the fire that was raging, where the Met Station had been. "Otta One . . . One or two of your aircraft have crashed."

"Cannot hear you . . . Repeat, cannot hear you."

Cowly and Vargas scrambled through the hatchway.

Boxer pointed toward the fire. "Looks like all of the Met station got hit. Vargas get your men over there and see if anyone is alive."

"Will do," Vargas said.

"This is Otto One . . . Coming down . . . Coming down . . . Not enough fuel to make base . . . Coming down!"

"Holy Christ," Boxer exclaimed, "he's going to fucking crash!"

The plane roared over the bridge and slammed down on the ice. One of the wings came off and left a trail of flames.

"Cowly, get some men over to that plane," Boxer said, looking at the two fires that were now burning.

Another plane roared low overhead but did not attempt to land.

Boxer keyed the RO. "How many targets have you on the scope?"

"One, Skipper . . . Bearing nine five degrees . . . Altitude four thousand feet and climbing . . . Speed two zero zero knots."

"Roger that," Boxer said.

Within minutes, Vargas reported that there were no survivors. "The Met station has been completely destroyed. All hands were killed."

"Roger that," Boxer said. "Return to *The Shark*."

Cowly's report came a short time later. It was just as grim as Vargas's.

Boxer ordered Cowly back to *The Shark*; then he left the bridge and went straight to the Communications Center, where he sent a message to Kinkade, advising him of the two crashes.

When Cowly and Vargas were back on board, Boxer switched on the MC. "Now hear this," he said, "now hear this . . . This is the captain speaking . . . By now all of you have heard of the two crashes that have occurred . . . There were no survivors and everyone in the Met Station was killed, when it was struck by the planes that collided in the air. This means we're going to have to get out of the Arctic just the way we are. Nothing can be repaired. We have a long hard voyage ahead of us. There's nothing else I can tell you. If we're lucky, we'll make it." He switched off the MC and looking at Cowly, he said, "Prepare to get underway."

"Aye, aye Skipper," Cowly answered.

Boxer sat down in front of the COMMCOMP and placed his hands along its edge. If he could have prayed for divine intervention, he would have. But prayer would not bring *The Shark* safely home. Only he could. He and the men with him could do it, if they were lucky.

He turned to Cowly. "I'll take the first watch topside."

"I'll go—"

Boxer waved the suggestion aside. Now it was more important than it ever had been, that he push himself harder than he would push the men.

"Make sure that every officer and man has his turn on the bridge," Boxer said.

"Aye, aye Skipper," Cowly answered.

Boxer slipped back into the Arctic gear and climbed up to the bridge. He wasn't looking forward to the next few hours.

Kinkade prowled the width of his office. Admiral Stark and Thomas Williams was seated in front of Kinkade's desk.

"Three planes lost, more than thirty people killed and an Air Force Met Station completely wiped out," he said in a low voice. "I can't believe that it happened."

Stark stood up. "Where is *The Shark*?" he asked.

Kinkade stopped. "I don't fucking know!" he shouted. "Your Captain Boxer didn't see fit to include his position in this message." He waved the paper in front of him.

"Stop shouting," Stark said sharply.

Kinkade looked at him.

"The rescue mission was your idea, not Boxer's. You can't blame him for what happened. If he can bring *The Shark* out, you know fucking well that he will. And if he can't, then no one can."

Kinkade walked back to his desk and bracing his hands on the back of the chair, he said, "Williams, where is the *Tecumseh*?"

"Off southern Greenland," Williams answered.

"Can she go into the Arctic?"

"It wouldn't make any difference if she could," Stark said, "*The Shark* can't dive to get under her. Boxer is going to have to bring *The Shark* down to where she can be picked up by ocean-going tugs and towed back. But if I know Boxer, he's not going to let any damn tug bring *The Shark* in."

"Williams?"

"Stark knows him better than we do," Williams answered.

Kinkade dropped into his chair. "Just suppose the Ruskies try to get back their people, what the hell do you think will happen?"

"Boxer will fight," Williams said.

"Will he fight or will he go by his own rules?" Kinkade asked, looking straight at Stark, who was still standing.

"He'll fight, if he stands a chance of winning," Stark answered. "But he won't throw away his entire crew to bring back two KBG—"

Kinkade was on his feet again. "Not just two KGB officers, Stark, but the head of the whole damn KGB and one of his lesser lights. By Christ, those two don't fall into your lap every day."

"They're not exactly in your lap," Stark answered.

"That's the fucking trouble," Kinkade snarled. "That's really the fucking thing that has me worried."

"Boxer will do whatever he must do to bring *The Shark* back,"

42

Stark said, "and if that includes—"

"I'm telling you this, Stark, if he makes any sort of deal with the Ruskies, I'm going to have him up on charges of treason."

"Easy, Kinkade," Stark cautioned. "I don't take kindly to being threatened, or having any of my men threatened."

Kinkade's eyes narrowed. "It's a promise, not a threat."

"I think this has gone far enough," Williams said. "Kinkade, why don't you calm down. Boxer wasn't responsible for what happened. And whether you'll admit it or not, he's probably the only man we have who can bring *The Shark* out. He's hard-headed and most likely to do the unexpected, but that's what makes him the kind of man and officer we need. He'll probably try to sail *The Shark* back to Norfolk and to help him I suggest we send two, maybe three destroyers to guard him when he comes out of the Arctic."

"Good idea," Kinkade said.

Kinkade nodded. "But where the hell is he coming out: to the east or west of Greenland?"

"He doesn't have to tell us," Williams said. "We'll pick him up on our fly overs. We'll see him long before he comes out. I don't think he'll object to the protection of two or three destroyers."

"I wouldn't bet on it," Kinkade growled.

"Then the matter is settled," Williams said, ignoring Kinkade's remark.

"The destroyers will be there," Stark responded.

"I'll go with it," Kinkade said.

Williams nodded and smiled. "Now," he said, "I could use a drink. What about it, gentlemen?"

"That's a good idea," Stark said.

"Kinkade?" Williams asked.

"I have work—"

"Come on, Kinkade," Stark said. "C'mon and have one on me."

After a few moments, Kinkade nodded. "All right, all right. There's a place down the road from here."

# 5

Borodine sat on the right side of Admiral of the Fleet Goshkov. Immediately across from him was Comrade Chernenkov, the Prime Minister, and next to him sat Comrade Vice Admiral Vorshilov. The rest of the chairs at the table were empty. The room, like the table, was very large and when anyone of them spoke their voices almost had an echo.

Chernenkov smoked American cigarettes and said very little, though now and then he jotted something down on the yellow pad in front of him.

Gorshkov and Vorshilov asked the questions. Their tone was friendly but business-like.

Borodine glanced at his watch. The meeting had already lasted more than two hours. During that time he had essentially told them what they had already learned from the listening to the tapes from the *Sea Savage*.

"You realize, Comrade Captain," Chernenkov said, breaking a long period of silence, "that America now has revealed to you a new weapon."

"Yes, Comrade Prime Minister," Borodine answered. "That 'copter would have forced us to crash dive, even if the bomber wasn't there,"

"How long did it take you to ID the aircraft?" Vorshilov asked.

"Too long," Borodine answered. "Both aircraft were almost on us before we ID'd them."

"And why was that?"

"The radar equipment had been affected by the atmospheric conditions," Borodine answered.

"Was the same true for the sonar?"

"No," Borodine answered. "I made the mistake. I was sure the debris was from *The Shark*."

"But now we know for certain that *The Shark* was not sunk and is presently making its way toward Greenland."

Borodine nodded. He had not known that until the meeting opened and Chernenkov informed him of it.

"Having thought you sank *The Shark*," Chernenkov said, "you started back to your base."

"Yes, Comrade Prime Minister."

"But you did hear the explosions, which even you guessed could have come from a ship attempting to blast its way through the ice. Isn't that so?"

"Yes, Comrade Prime Minister."

"The question is why didn't you attempt to investigate the source of those explosions?"

"Even if I did investigate them," Borodine answered calmly, "I would have found nothing. There were perhaps fifteen explosions in all. After that there was silence. That meant the vessel had gained open water and by the time I would have reached the origin of the explosions, *The Shark*, and now we can assume it was *The Shark*, would have been gone."

"Is there any way we can stop her?" Chernenkov asked.

"Short of going to war," Goshkov said, "I don't see how. Three American destroyers are already in position to guard her when she comes out of the Arctic and they are giving her a twenty-four hour anti-submarine screen from the air. She is out of our reach."

"In that case," Chernenkov said, "we are confronted with a major intelligence problem."

Gorshkov and Vorshilov agreed.

"Comrade Captain Borodine," Chernenkov said, "your presence here is no longer required. You may leave."

Borodine stood up, nodded to Goshkov and Vorshilov.

"You did well, Comrade Captain," Chernenkov said.

Borodine thanked him, turned and quickly left the room. He was outside and the cold air had cleared his head when he realized that he had had a hearing; that if Chernenkov had, for any reason faulted him, he could have been placed under arrest. Despite the cold, that thought, was sufficient to make him break out in a cold sweat. He pursed his lips and quickened his pace. The idea that his life hung, so to speak, on the thread of one man's decision made him furious. "It could have just as easily gone the other way," he silently told himself.

He went to the first telephone kiosk he saw and phoned Irena. It took several minutes for her to come on the line. While he waited he lit a cigarette. Had he been arrested, he wondered what would have happened to the other officers who served with him? He shook his head. There were things the government sometimes did that were, in his opinion, stupid beyond measure. Stupid was the wrong word. "Wrong," he said aloud. "Absolutely wrong."

"What's 'absolutely wrong?' " Irena asked.

The sound of her voice startled Borodine.

"Igor?"

"Yes," he answered.

"Is everything all right?" she asked.

"Everything is fine."

"Are you with anyone?"

"No."

"I thought you said something was 'absolutely wrong,' " she said.

"I was talking to myself."

"You sounded very angry at yourself."

"Do you want me to meet you, or will you come straight home?" he asked. Whenever he was in Moscow, Borodine stayed in her apartment.

"What would you like to do?" she asked.

"Have you come home, make love to you and then go out for dinner," he answered.

She laughed softly. "I think I'd like that too."

"Good; then that's what we'll do. See you at eighteen hundred."

"Yes, my darling," she answered. "I'll see you soon."

Borodine hung up, stepped out of the kiosk and started to walk. The smell of snow was in the air. He looked up just as the first flakes came tumbling out of a leaden sky.

Boxer was on the outside bridge. *The Shark* had made it through the Arctic and was now sailing south through the Davis Strait. Except for having to blast its way out of ice jams twice and weather the usual Arctic storms, *The Shark* took twenty-five days to claw its way across the top of the world and now the Met officer reported a rapidly falling barometer.

"Roger that," Boxer said, aware that wind had veered around to the northeast, which meant it was blowing off the Greenland ice-cap.

The waves were already slamming into *The Shark*.

Boxer switched on the MC. "Now hear this," he said. "Now hear this . . . This is the captain speaking . . . Secure everything . . . Secure everything."

"Skipper," the helmsman shouted above the roar of the wind, "the wind is taking her off course."

Before Boxer could answer, the Met officer keyed him. "Skipper, that wind is blowing at sixty knots and gusting at a hundred."

"Roger that," Boxer shouted. *The Shark* didn't have enough power to hold steerage way and the sail was making it all the more impossible to hold any kind of a course. Boxer keyed Cowly. "Take the CON. Have Mahony at the helm."

"Roger that," Cowly answered.

"Clear the bridge," Boxer ordered. "All hands clear the bridge." He left the bridge last and dogged shut the hatchway. By the time he reached the COMMCOMP, *The Shark* was no longer able to hold any sort of course. "Lower sail," Boxer ordered.

Cowly actuated the sail controls. "Sail being lowered," he said.

The DCO keyed Boxer. "Skipper, the stress device on the damaged hull section reading red. If it goes, the hull could break."

Boxer ran his hand over his beard. He hadn't escaped from Borodine and beaten the Arctic to be beaten by it now. "We don't have a chance on the surface," he said. "This storm will break us up."

Cowly raised his eyebrow. "We don't have much of a chance if we dive either."

"We need just enough water between us and the surface to be able to hold a course," Boxer said.

"And if we can't surface, or if we dive and can't control the dive?"

Boxer didn't answer. He switched on the MC. "All hands," he said, "listen up . . . All hands, this is the captain again . . . We can't hold a course on the surface . . . We stand a good chance of breaking up if we stay on the surface . . . But if we dive to where we can hold a course, then we may not be able to surface again . . . And if we dive, we may not be able to control the dive . . . No matter what we do, we stand to come out on the short end of the stick . . . But I'm going to dive . . . I think it's the best chance we have . . . Standby all stations . . . We're on manual control . . . Standby . . . DO Ffood all tanks . . . Make five zero feet."

"Tanks flooding," the DO answered.

"Diving planes down zero five degrees," Boxer said.

"Diving planes not responding," the DO answered.

Boxer watched the depth gauge. They were through the twenty foot mark and already *The Shark* was much more stable. "Helmsman," Boxer said, "come to nine three degrees."

"Coming to nine three degrees," Mahony answered.

"Skipper, coming to five zero feet," the DO said.

Boxer watched the depth gauge above the COMMCOMP. The needle passed through fifty — hovered at fifty-five and slowly moved back to fifty.

"Depth five zero feet," the DO announced.

"Roger that," Boxer answered.

"Skipper," the DCO said, "we're taking on water on the portside."

"Can the pumps control it?"

"Not if we go deeper," the DCO answered.

"We'll maintain this depth," Boxer said.

"Roger that," the DCO said.

Boxer leaned back and activated the damage control net. "Everything is working," Boxer said.

"How long are we going to stay down?" Cowly asked.

"I don't see any sense in surfacing until we're off our coast and not then, if the weather is bad."

Cowly shook his head. "I don't know which is worse: running on the surface or being down here. Either one is hell on my nerves."

"Mine too," Boxer answered.

"But you don't show it."

"Sure I do," Boxer said. "Only you don't see it. I just hide it better," Boxer answered. "But I'm just as nervous as anyone else aboard. I have no way of knowing whether we'll be able to surface until we try."

Cowly nodded. "I know that and so do all of the men," he said, "but all of us know that if it can be done, you will do it."

Boxer flushed "We do it together," he said. "*The Shark* isn't just me . . . It's every man in the crew."

Cowly didn't answer.

"Take the CON," Boxer said, I'm going into the mess area."

"Aye, aye, Skipper," Cowly responded.

Boxer nodded. He was gambling. If the gamble didn't pay off, they'd all die. . . .


"Not a word from *The Shark* for twenty hours," Kinkade said, looking straight at Stark. "Boxer's messages, no matter how terse, were still messages."

Stark leaned back into his high-back leather chair. "There's a major storm in the Davis Strait. All our aircraft have been grounded. The *Tecumseh* and the two destroyers waiting for *The Shark* were forced to leave their station."

Kinkade frowned.

"The weather—" Stark began.

"I need to know that those KGB people are safe," Kinkade

growled.

Stark's anger ignited. But he kept it under control. "We're just going to have to wait. Once the weather clears we'll be able to find out more."

"What the hell would you do if you were out there?" Kinkade asked.

"I was a fighter pilot," Stark answered. "I have no idea what I'd do."

"I'd tried getting hold of Bush. But he's off skiing somewhere."

"You know," Stark said, in a controlled voice, "you're a fucking fool. You're going to ask a pear how an apple thinks. For the love of Christ, Bush would go by the book. Look at the fucking book and you'll know what Bush will do."

Kinkade was about to answer when the phone on Stark's desk rang.

Stark picked up the phone and said, "Stark here."

"Sir, Captain Gilhooly of the destroyer *Oak* is on the radio phone."

"Put him through," Stark said.

"Aye, aye sir."

"One of the destroyer captains," Stark told Kinkade.

"Admiral," Gilhooly said, "the weather has cleared and we haven't found *The Shark*. The *Emerson* and the *Oak* went up into the strait for a distance of forty nautical miles and found nothing."

"Continue to search," Stark said.

"The Met officer advises me that another storm is on its way," Gilhooly said.

"Then abandon search until the weather moderates again," Stark said.

"Abandon the search!" Kinkade exclaimed, starting out of the chair.

"Aye, aye sir," Gilhooly answered.

Kinkade put the phone down. "I'm not going to risk two ships and their crews—"

"But *The Shark*—Boxer is your fair-haired boy."

Stark was too angry to answer.

Kinkade sat down again. "I'm sorry I said that. But this

whole damn thing has gotten to me. I hold the most important man in the Russian intelligence system and I don't hold him. Boxer holds him and I won't have him until Boxer gives him up."

Stark nodded, opening the humidor and removing a cigar, he clipped its end and lit it. Nothing he or anyone else would say could help or hurt *The Shark*. He blew a column of gray smoke toward the ceiling and was almost sorry that he wasn't a praying man. . . .

Boxer checked *The Shark*'s position on the NAVCOMP. "Five five degrees north . . . five zero degrees, one five minutes west," he said aloud. "In another day or so, if not sooner, we're going to be crossing the main shipping routes, not to mention the anti-sub patrols. If I can't be deep, I'd rather be on the surface."

"Are we going to try now?" Cowly asked.

"Now," Boxer answered. "We'll make it as routine as possible." He hit the klaxon once; then switching on the MC, he said, "Standby to surface. Surfacing under manual control."

"All controls on manual," the DO responded.

Boxer glanced at Cowly. Beads of sweat stood out on the man's forehead. He was sure his was marked the same way.

"Target bearing four three degrees . . . Range six thousand yards . . . Speed eighteen knots."

"Course?" Boxer asked.

"One ten degrees."

"ID."

*"Sakari Maru."*

"Stand by," Boxer said over the MC. "We'll wait until the *Sakari* passes." He keyed the EO. "Go to five knots."

"Five knots," the EO answered.

Boxer keyed the SO. "Give me the target's position now."

"Bearing four three degrees . . . Range two thousand yards . . . Speed eighteen knots."

"Roger that," Boxer answered. He could feel the sweat on his back and in his crotch.

The sound of the *Sakari*'s four giant propellers began to fill *The Shark*.

Boxer keyed the SO. "What's her draft?"

"Four eight feet, Skipper."

"Helmsman go to five eight degrees," Boxer said.

"Five eight degrees," the helmsman responded.

Boxer switched on the COMMCOMP'S sonor display. The *Sikari* was less than a thousand yards off *The Shark*'s starboard side. The noise from her screw propellers was deafening. Suddenly *The Shark* began to roll slightly.

Boxer keyed the EO. "Give me everything you can."

"Roger that," the EO answered.

The rolling was becoming more violent.

"That fucking turbulence!" Boxer exclaimed.

"Skipper," Cowly shouted above the noise of the *Sakari*'s propellers, "We're rolling almost one five degrees."

"Standby to surface!" Boxer ordered. "Standby . . . Blow all ballast."

"All ballast blown," the DO said.

*The Shark* began to rise.

Boxer checked the sonar display. The *Sakari* was three degrees past *The Shark*. He looked at the depth gauge. The needle was steady at twenty-five feet. Boxer ran his hand over his beard. The last time they surfaced they had difficulty getting past twenty-five feet.

"Skipper," the DCO said, "we're taking on more water in the aft section than the pumps can handle."

"Roger that," Boxer said. He keyed the EO. "How much more power can you give me?"

"If I give you anything more," the EO said, "I'm going to burn out most of my bearings. Nothing is right down here."

"Burn them out," Boxer said, "or we'll never make the surface."

"Going to full power," the EO answered.

A shudder passed through *The Shark*.

Boxer watched the needle on the depth gauge move. They smashed through the twenty-five foot level. "Making one five feet," Boxer announced. He switched on the UWIS. The bow pierced the surface; then fell back. A few moments later the rest of *The Shark* came to the surface. "Raise sail," Boxer ordered.

"Sail up," Cowly answered.

"Bridge detail," Boxer said. "Topside."

"Skipper," the EO said, "number one and three drive shafts are out."

"Roger that," Boxer answered, taking deep breaths of the fresh, cold air that rushed into *The Shark* the moment the bridge hatch was cracked.

"I can't give you more than five or six knots," the EO said.

"That will have to get us home," Boxer said.

"Ten four," the EO answered.

Boxer keyed the COMMCOMP. "Radio headquarters and tell them we'll be coming into base under our own power. ETA five days. Will radio exact time before entering harbor."

"Aye, aye, Skipper," the COMMO answered.

Boxer rested against the back of the chair. "Cowly," he said, "I'm tired . . . very tired."

"Skipper, all of us are tired."

Boxer nodded. There was no need for him to say anything else. Of all the men aboard *The Shark,* Cowly was the closest to him. In many respects, Cowly was his other self and yet, he knew very little about him. He never spoke about himself, or about any member of his family. He—

"Skipper," one of the junior officers said, "Mister Sanchez requests permission to come to the bridge?"

"Permission granted," Boxer answered.

Within minutes Sanchez was on the bridge. He came forward with his hand extended. "Stunning," he said, pumping Boxer's hand. "Just stunning. On behalf of the civilians on board, I want to congratulate you."

Boxer separated his hand from Sanchez'. "Thank them for me," he said. "But the real praise should be given to the crew and the boat. I just managed to coordinate both."

Sanchez glanced at Cowly. "Is he always like this?"

"Most of the time," Cowly answered with a smile.

"I'll skip all the back slapping. When we make port, you and your entire crew are invited to my house for the best and biggest weekend party ever given in Washington. Does that meet with your approval?"

"I'm sure the men will appreciate it," Boxer answered.

"Tell them they can bring someone, or come alone."

"I'll make the announcement before we tie up," Boxer said.

"I wouldn't have missed this for a million dollars!" Sanchez exclaimed.

"I would," Boxer said. "What about you Cowly?"

"For a million, I would have," Cowly said.

"But—"

"Listen, Sanchez, you don't know how fucking close you came to never making another deal . . . never seeing the light of day again. We were lucky, very lucky, isn't that so, Mister Cowly?"

"Very lucky," Cowly repeated. "Very, very lucky."

Stark and Kinkade stood on the dock where *The Shark* would tie up before she was moved by tugs to the drydock. The day was gray and biting wind came off the bay. Their breaths steamed in the cold air.

"I offered to have him and the Ruskies airlifted off," Kinkade said, "but he refused."

"You should have known he would," Stark answered. "In all this time you should have known enough about Boxer to know that it would be a matter of pride for him to bring *The Shark* in." Even as he was speaking *The Shark* was slowly easing her way into the docking area.

"There's something I want to talk to you about before Boxer comes ashore," Kinkade said.

"You're not going to start with that crap about bringing him up on charges again?" Stark asked.

"Nothing like that," Kinkade said.

Stark was listening, but he was more interested in *The Shark*. "Good God, will you look at that. Half her starboard side is gone—midships and toward the stern."

Kinkade said, "It's about his latest woman."

"What?" Stark turned to look at him. "What about her?"

"It can't be," Kinkade said.

"What the fuck are you talking about?"

"Louise Collins—"

"Kinkade—"

"She's black."

"I know she's black. I met her. You saw her the night of the party at the Redferns."

"I had her investigated," Kinkade said.

"You did what?" Stark shouted.

"She's a very active lady in all the wrong directions."

"Christ, Kinkade why don't you mind your own fucking business and let Boxer live his own life."

"Because," Kinkade answered, looking straight at Stark, "he doesn't have a life of his own. His life belongs to the Company. He gave up his right to have a life of his own when he joined the Company."

Stark took several steps away from Kinkade. "Tell me what you did," he said.

"I had two of my best men visit her and explain the situation," Kinkade said.

"And—"

"She saw things our way," Kinkade said. "She is now living and working in a different city."

"Naturally you arranged for the new job?"

Kinkade nodded.

"What are you going to do when he tries to locate her?"

"That's been taken care of," Kinkade said. "She wrote him a letter, which ends the relationship."

Stark moved back to where Kinkade was standing. "You know, Kinkade, you're a first class shit . . . I mean really a first class shit."

"The woman is black. She was active in all kinds of liberal organizations. What the hell was I supposed to do? Boxer belongs to the Company."

"Just pray that he never finds out," Stark said. "Because if he does, I don't think your life would be worth much."

"He'll never find out," Kinkade said. "The men I sent won't talk."

"You shouldn't have told me," Stark said.

"I wouldn't have," Kinkade admitted. "But I wanted you to

55

know just in case Boxer has a bad reaction—"

"Bad reaction, you fuck. You're not talking about a reaction to a flu shot. You're talking about a man's emotional life."

Kinkade didn't answer.

Stark turned away from him. *The Shark* was alongside the pier. Boxer was on the bridge.

"Standby on the bow and stern lines," Boxer said over the MC. "Let go lines."

The docking detail on the pier wrapped the lines around the stanchions, while the details aboard *The Shark* fixed them to the cleats.

"All hands," Boxer said over the MC. "Now hear this . . . Now hear this . . . This is the captain speaking . . . Liberty commences at fourteen hundred . . . Remember the party at Mister Sanchez's house this weekend . . . Pick up printed directions from the OD." Then waving to Stark and Kinkade, he said, "Hello there admiral and Mister Kinkade."

Stark saluted him.

Boxer returned the salute.

# 6

Before he went to his room, Boxer picked up Louise's letter from the hotel clerk. The first time he read it he stood at the side of the bed; then he moved to the dresser and read it again. Finally he sat down in the chair next to the window and read it for a third time. When he finished it, he ran his hand over his beard and squinched his eyes shut to stem the tears, but they came and wet his beard.

After a while, Boxer stood up and tore the letter into small pieces; then he went into the bathroom and flushed them down the toilet. He washed his face and looking into the mirror, he said aloud, "You never were much good when it came to choosing the right woman to fall in love with." Uttering a deep sigh, he dried his face and returned to the bedroom.

Before he had read the letter, he had thought about going to sleep for a few hours. But now he was no longer sleepy. He put through a call to his mother.

"You don't sound right," she said. "Is something wrong?"

"Everything is fine," Boxer answered. "I'm very tired."

"Will you be coming home soon?" she asked.

"Sometime next week," he answered. "I have a few things to do in Washington for the next several days."

"You don't have to phone before you come," his mother said. "You come anytime."

"Sure, Mom," he answered. "I love you . . . See you soon."

"I love you too," she answered.

Boxer put the phone down, filled a pipe and lit it. He looked over the rest of the mail, which mainly consisted of back issues of magazines and advertisements. He neatly stacked the magazines on the night table near the bed and threw the junk mail in the waste paper basket.

Suddenly the phone rang.

He picked it up. "Boxer here," he said.

"Sam Ross," the voice on the other end announced.

Boxer sucked in his breath and slowly let it out. Senator Sam Ross was Tom Redfern's father-in-law.

"Sue-Ann and myself would like you to come out to the house and spend a day or two with us. I've already cleared it with the admiral and Kinkade. They said you're free as far as they're concerned. Do you have anything else going?"

"Nothing," Boxer answered.

"I'll pick you up at your hotel in about an hour," Senator Ross said.

"I'll be outside," Boxer told him.

"See you," the senator answered.

Boxer put the phone down. He was planning to go out to see Sue-Ann sometime during the next few days. It wasn't something he was looking forward to doing.

Boxer showered, packed an over-night bag and went down to the hotel barber to have his beard and hair trimmed. Then he stepped into the bar and ordered a Stoli on the rocks.

He tried hard to put Louise's letter out of his mind, but he couldn't. He didn't understand why she had decided to end their relationship. He loved her and was sure that she loved him. That she was black and he was white didn't matter when they—Suddenly Boxer realized that the barkeep was staring at him. . . .

"Anything wrong?" Boxer answered.

"Weren't you the guy in here New Year's Eve—"

"It was me," Boxer said. "I decked some creep who was bothering my—" He remembered saying that Louise was his wife.

"That guy came back here a couple of times with a few of his friends."

58

"If you see him," Boxer said matter-of-factly, "tell him next time I'll break every bone in his body." He lifted the glass of Stoli and with it gestured toward the barkeep. At that moment he would have enjoyed a fight. It would allow him to vent his anger and frustration. "Tell him I don't like creeps."

"Listen, mister, I don't want any trouble here."

"Won't be any if your friend behaves himself," Boxer answered, putting a five dollar bill on the dark wood bar.

"Are you having more than one?" the barkeep asked.

Boxer shook his head.

"That's two-fifty," the barkeep said.

"Keep the change," Boxer told him.

The barkeep effusively thanked him.

"Just don't forget to tell that creep what I said," Boxer said, knowing the tip he gave would help the man remember. He finished his drink, left the bar and walked outside to wait for the senator.


The senator's silver limo pulled up. The chauffeur got out, went around to the other side and opened the door for Boxer.

"Glad to have you back," the senator said, offering his hand as soon as Boxer was settled in the seat next to him.

"Glad to be back," Boxer said, shaking the senator's hand.

"Hard mission, wasn't it?" the senator asked, flicking a switch that raised a dark glass partition between the front and rear sections of the car.

"Hard," Boxer answered. "The Ruskies almost had us and then what the Ruskies didn't do, the weather almost did."

"The admiral said it was a miracle that you brought *The Shark* back," the senator said.

"Just luck," Boxer answered. "Nothing more than luck." He looked out of the window. The landscape was gray. Spring still hadn't come. "Looks like snow," he commented.

"Rain and sleet," the senator said. "But in the mountains the forecasters are predicting four to five inches of snow. A typical late winter or early spring storm."

For the next few minutes neither of them spoke; then the

two of them started to speak at exactly the same time.

"You first, senator," Boxer said.

"No . . . You."

Boxer nodded. "I wasn't with Tom when he was killed. Vargas was there and two of the other men."

"What happened?" the senator asked.

"Tom opened the door to a hut where our people were. He didn't know the Ruskies were also there. General Yedotev opened fire. Tom was killed."

"Instantly?"

"No . . . It took a few minutes for him to die."

"Tell Sue-Ann that he was killed instantly," the senator said.

Boxer nodded.

"Then what happened?"

"Vargas entered the hunt, demanded to know who fired at Tom and as soon as he was told, he shot Yedotev in the knees. His knees will have to be rebuilt."

"Too bad he didn't blow his fucking head off," the senator said, looking out of window next to him. "Tom was like a son to me. He was—" There was a catch in his voice. Several moments passed before he was able to speak again. "I have been trying to get his body back but the Ruskies won't even admit they have it or that we have several of their people."

"I guess they wouldn't. If the situation was reversed, we wouldn't admit it either."

"Probably not," the senator said.

"Mind if I smoke?" Boxer asked.

"No. Go ahead."

Boxer filled and lit his pipe. When it was drawing to his satisfaction, he asked, "How's Sue-Ann taking it?"

"Putting up a good front."

"Seeing me isn't going to help her much," Boxer said.

"She wanted to see you. She asked me to call you."

Boxer puffed on his pipe. Whether the senator knew it or not, he and Sue-Ann were not on the friendliest of terms. She resented his affair with Kathy Tyson.

"She wants the body back to give it a proper burial," the senator said.

"Do you want it back?" Boxer asked.

"If it will make her feel better, yes."

"I can't promise anything," Boxer said, "but I know someone who might be able to help." He was thinking of writing to Borodine.

"Who?"

"I'm sorry, senator, I can't tell you," Boxer said.

"I should have known better than to ask," the senator responded; then he said, "Have you any plans while you're ashore?"

"None."

"In about a month I'm going to go to Paris for a special meeting with several high ranking Russians. You might consider going along with me."

"What use would I be?" Boxer asked.

"None, really. I just thought you'd like to get away for a while," the senator said.

"I'll think about it," Boxer answered.

Neither of them spoke again until the car turned into the long driveway and the senator said, "Sue-Ann asked several other people to dinner. It's her way of keeping up a good front."

Boxer nodded.

The car stopped in front of the house and a servant was already there to open the door for them.

Sue-Ann came into the foyer to greet them. She kissed her father first and then kissed Boxer. "I'm so glad you could come," she said.

"It was good of you to ask me," he said.

She took his overnight bag and handed it to a servant. "Put Captain Boxer's things in the east wing guest room."

"Please," Boxer said, "no rank tonight."

"No rank," she said, taking hold of his hand and leading him into the living room, where a dozen couples were assembled.

Sue-Ann was a dark-haired woman, with an athletic body. Not much ass or breasts. But what she had was sculptured by the dark green off the shoulder gown she wore. She spoke with a decided western drawl.

"People," she said, stopping in the middle of the room, "I want you to meet Jack Boxer, a good friend of ours."

Boxer managed a smile and looked around. He recognized a few of the faces, probably having seem them the other times he dined with the Redferns.

"You just enjoy yourself," Sue-Ann said, "while I see how things are going in the kitchen."

"I'll be fine," Boxer answered. "Don't you worry about me."

"We'll talk later," she said in a whisper and left him.

Boxer nodded and headed for the bar on the far side of the room, where he asked the bartender for a vodka on the rocks. That he was now in such safe surroundings was almost unreal, when he thought about where he recently had been. . . .

He finished his drink and turned to the bartender for another.

"Dinner will be served in about ten minutes," Sue-Ann said.

He made half a turn to the right.

"I've seated you between my father and Mrs. McElroy. She's the wife of Congressman McElroy and the granddaughter of Mr. Kinkade."

"I didn't know Kinkade had a family," Boxer said.

"A son and a daughter. The son was killed in Nam and the daughter married one of the Lutzes. Trish is the result of that union."

Boxer didn't know who the Lutzes were and cared less. But he was interested in McElroy, who was beginning to make a name for himself. "Isn't McElroy—"

"Another Joe McCarthy?"

"Something like that," Boxer answered.

"Father says that Bill McElroy has his eyes on the White House," Sue-Ann said.

"Is the congressman here?"

"That's him with Trish speaking to Dad," Sue-Ann said, moving her head to the right.

Boxer looked at McElroy and his wife. He was a tall, thin man with an undercut chin and thinning dark brown hair. His wife was blond, with a womanly shape and pleasant smile.

"Trish is as ambitious as her husband, maybe even more," Sue-Ann said.

Boxer shrugged. "Politics isn't my department," he said. "But I'll tell you this, if she's got any of Kinkade's genes—and she's bound to—she's got to be a barracuda."

Sue-Ann laughed. "She may be, but you'll discover, she's also very charming."

The tinkling sound of the dinner bell interrupted their conversation.

Boxer offered his arm.

"Thank you," Sue-Ann said. "It's a pleasure to be escorted by you."

"The pleasure is entirely mine," Boxer answered, wondering what kind of game they were playing, or if Sue-Ann was so tightly wound up over Tom's death, that she couldn't accept it.

They went into the dining room.

Boxer helped Sue-Ann with her chair and then went to his own place at the table, where the senator introduced him to the McElroys.

"You look as if you've recently spent a great deal of time out of doors, Mister Boxer," Mrs. McElroy said.

"Much more than I had wanted to," Boxer answered with a smile.

"Boxer . . . Boxer," Congressman McElroy said. "That name is very familiar." He looked at the senator. "Captain Boxer . . . Miss Kimble's article . . . You're the captain of *The Shark*, aren't you?" His voice became loud enough to draw everyone's attention to him. "Well aren't you?" McElroy pressed.

"I'm afraid I am," Boxer admitted, casting his eyes down at his plate, on which a servant was just placing a chicken crepe, covered with a white mushroom sauce.

"My God, man," McElroy exclaimed, getting to his feet, "this man is a national hero, a leader in our fight against communism." He picked up his wine glass. "Ladies and gentlemen, a toast to this brave man and his crew."

Boxer flushed. He didn't know whether to laugh, call the

63

man a fucking fool, or pull him back down into his chair. He glanced at Sue-Ann.

She looked amused.

"Please, say something," Mrs. McElroy whispered.

"I have nothing to say," Boxer answered.

"My husband is waiting."

"It's his speech," Boxer said.

She glared at him.

Boxer smiled back at her. He was right: she was a barracuda.

"I'm proud to be at the same table with you, Captain," McElroy said and sat down.

Boxer picked up a knife and fork, cut his crepe and began to eat, though without much appetite. He was sorry now that he had agreed to come to dinner.

"I'd really like to have the opportunity to speak to you," McElroy said. "We fight the same good fight. You in your way, I in mine."

Boxer stopped eating, crossed his fork and knife at the top of his plate and said, "Congressman—"

"Please call me Bill."

"Bill then," Boxer said, "I don't fight the good fight, as you put it. I do a job . . . simply that and no more."

"Nonsense," McElroy exclaimed. "A man on an assembly line does a job. A clerk in an office does a job. But you and I, we're—"

"Bill have you ever killed a man?" Boxer asked. "Have you ever killed many men?"

"What?"

"Have you ever seen your friends die?"

"No. But—"

"With all due respect to you Bill, you're a horse's ass. Now if you'll excuse me, I'll leave the table. I need a stiff drink." He stood up, nodded to the other guests and as he left he heard Sue-Ann say, "He was with Tom when Tom was killed. They were very close. . . ." What other lie she told them was drowned out by the sudden upsurge of conversation at the table.

Boxer went into the living room. The barkeep was still

behind the bar. "Give me a double scotch neat," Boxer said. He drank it quickly and asked for another.

"On the rocks?" the barkeep asked.

Boxer shook his head. "I'm on a roll," he said. "You don't want to spoil it, do you?"

Without answering, the man poured the drink.

Boxer picked up the glass and walked to the window. Outside, the pane was covered with rivulets of rain. He finished the scotch, returned the empty glass to the bar and went up to his room.

Boxer removed his jacket and tie; opened his collar and slipped off his shoes. He lay down on the bed and switched off the night table lamp. Then placing his hands behind his head, he stared at the dark ceiling. Politicos like McElroy always pissed him off. . . .

"The good fight, shit!" Boxer said aloud. "It's never a good fight."

"Sometimes it has to be a good fight," Sue-Ann said.

Boxer turned his head to the doorway. She was silhouetted against the light coming from the hallway.

"Sometimes it has to be a good fight," she repeated.

Boxer pulled himself up on his elbows. "I'm sorry I sounded off."

"No, you're not," she said. "You just reminded McElroy that he was in the wrong pulpit at the wrong place and the wrong time."

Boxer leaned against the bed's backboard. "You know I wasn't with Tom when it happened."

She stepped deeper into the room and closed the door behind her. "I was wondering whether you heard me say that."

The room was completely dark now.

Boxer reached over to the lamp.

"Please, don't turn it on," Sue-Ann said. She came to the side of the bed and sat down alongside of Boxer. "I told Dad I had a very bad headache. I'm sure when he explains the reason for my absence from the table, everyone will be sympathetic." She reached out and took hold of his hands.

"You're cold," Boxer said.

She didn't answer, but he could hear her breathing. Then in a whisper she said, "I was never unfaithful to Tom."

"I'm sure he knew that," Boxer said, not knowing what else to say.

She circled his hands with hers and bending close to Boxer placed his hands over her breasts.

He started to draw away.

"Don't Jack. Don't. I want your hands there. I want you to—I was going to say, make love to me. But that's not what I want. I want to be fucked. That's what I want. I want to be fucked." She ended with a catch in her voice.

"Sue-Ann—"

"Please, don't say anything, or try to tell me it's not what I want, because, it *is* what I want. It will be something we've done together. It will be our secret and it will never happen again."

Boxer put his arms around her and drew her to him. Maybe when he first met her, he wondered what she'd be like in bed. But once he had gotten to know Tom, he never thought about her in a sexual way again. His tastes ran to more voluptuous women. Sue-Ann was the gamine type, at least in body, if not in practice.

"Sooner or later there will be other men," she said softly. "I know that and so do you. You're the closest to Tom I have." She drew away from him, stood up and reaching around to her back, she unzipped her dress. "That's better," she said, as she stepped out of the garment and left it on the floor. "You undress," she said.

Boxer stood up and stripped.

Sue-Ann slipped off the camisole she was wearing. "You want to take off my briefs?"

"Sue-Ann, are you sure you want this?" Boxer asked. This was a completely new experience for him. He wasn't sexually excited by her and he was certain she wasn't turned on by him.

"I'll take them off," she said, hitching her thumbs into the elastic waist band and pulling the skimpy panty down. She climbed into bed and settled next to him. "I didn't realize how cold it was," she said.

Boxer put his arms around her.

She was trembling.

He kissed her forehead.

"I never realized how muscular you are," she said. Then she took one of his hands and brought it to her crotch. "Finger me," she said. "I'm very sensitive there."

Boxer began to play with her cunt, moving his finger in and out of it.

"Yes . . . That feels good," she said, taking hold of his penis and rubbing it against her snatch. "I know what will stiffen it," she said. "You just lie back and let me get it hard." She swung around and straddling him, she began to lick his cock.

Boxer responded. She was good, alternately sucking and using her tongue. He was excited now and reaching under her, he caressed her small breasts.

She sat up and looked back at him. "I'd like it if you did me," she said.

"Bend over."

"This okay?" she asked, positioning her slit over his mouth.

"Yes," he said and began to tongue her vagina.

"Go to the clit," she said, "Ah, that's it!" And she pressed her cunt down on his mouth. "Suck it . . . Suck it hard!"

She was a great deal more sexy than Boxer would have thought.

"Play with my nipples," she said. "Wait, I'll do something for you." She changed her position, lying on her side, she buried her face between his legs.

Boxer felt her tongue against his ass; then she slowly moved it to his balls and back again. He placed his hands over her breasts and teased the nipple on each small mound.

"I'm ready," she said and crawling over him, she took hold of his penis and guided it into her. "Good," she whispered, "feels very good." She leaned back and ran her fingers over his scrotum.

"You're throbbing," Boxer said.

She reached down to his ass hole and teased it. "I'll do anything you want, Jack . . . Anything!"

Boxer put his hands under her armpits and slowly drew her forward; then he began to move.

She bent low over him and offered him one breast and then the other.

He sucked her nipples and placed his hands on the cheeks of her ass. He could feel her body begin to tense and quickened his pace.

She grabbed hold of his shoulders.

He heard her say something but couldn't make out what it was.

"Tom," she gasped.

Boxer stopped moving.

"No . . . No don't . . . Oh please don't stop!"

"I'm not Tom," Boxer said.

She continued to move. "I know you're not Tom . . . I know . . . But—But he would have wanted me to do this. He would have wanted you to fuck me!" Her body tensed and she flung herself down on him. "Move . . . Oh please move!"

Boxer thrust into her.

Her body shuddered and spasm after spasm shook it.

Boxer's passion surged out of him. . . .

Sue-Ann stretched out on top of Boxer and softly wept.

He put his arms around her. He didn't know what to say and even if he did, it wouldn't end her pain. Only time could do that. He caressed her head.

"I'm sorry," she said. "It's unfair of me to cry now."

"Sue-Ann, we may not be lovers, but we're certainly friends. You go ahead and cry if that's what you want to do."

She raised her head. "I never realized you were such a gentle caring man."

Boxer patted her rump. "Just like anyone else, I have many sides."

She didn't answer and lowered her head. "I'm glad I did it with you and what I said about Tom, I meant. He thought you were the—"

"Don't say anything else," Boxer said. He didn't want to hear about Tom, or any of the other men who had been killed.

"Would you mind if I slept with you tonight?" she asked.

"No," Boxer answered. "I'd like company."

"Is that what I am?"

"No," he said. "I already told you that you're a good friend."

She lifted her head kissed him gently on the lips; then settled down again. "You can put your hands anywhere you like," she said.

Boxer wrapped one arm around her shoulders and placed his other hand in the crack between the cheeks of her ass; then he closed his eyes and very quickly felt himself slipping into sleep. . . .

# 7

The sun was shining and the air was filled with the soft warmth of spring. Boxer walked briskly to the corner of 16th and M, waited for the light to turn green; then crossed and turned in 16th street and headed straight for the Russian Embassy. Just before he entered the building, he looked back over his shoulder. A man he had seen outside his hotel was behind him.

Boxer waited until the man was very close; then he quickly turned around and purposely bumped into him. He moved so swiftly that the man was too surprised to react. Boxer grabbed hold of his tie and give it a hard jerk downward.

The man tried to pull away.

Boxer jerked down again.

The man's right hand slashed at Boxer.

Boxer kneed him in the groin.

The man dropped to his knees.

"Don't ever follow me again," Boxer said. "Next time I see you, I'll put you in the hospital. Tell Kinkade not to send anyone else either."

A crowd was quickly gathering around them. Then a police car pulled up and two huge cops shouldered their way into the crowd.

"What's the problem?" one of the cops asked.

The man on his knees looked up. "No problem officer. Captain Boxer was just showing me a new pitch."

"Pitch?" the cop asked. "What kind of a new pitch?"

"Officer Wiggins," Boxer said, using the name he saw on the cop's name tag, "I don't know who the hell he is, or how he knows my name. He was following me."

The man struggled to his feet.

"What's your name?" Wiggins asked the man.

"Lacy . . . James Lacy," the man answered. "I'm a private detective." And he handed Wiggins his ID.

"Private detective!" Boxer exclaimed.

"Check this out," Wiggins said, handing Lacy's ID to his partner, who went back to the patrol car and began to use the computer terminal in it.

"Listen, Officer Wiggins," Boxer said, "I'm not going to press charges."

"Seems to me," Wiggins said, "Mister Lacy might want to do that." Then he said, "Let me see your ID mister. It's Captain Boxer, isn't it?"

Boxer handed him his wallet.

Wiggins looked at the ID card; then at Boxer. "This for real?"

Boxer nodded.

"It's for real," Lacy said.

Wiggins looked at the building behind them; then at Boxer. "There are several people watching us from the windows."

"I was going in there," Boxer said.

"Why?" Wiggins asked.

"I don't have to answer that," Boxer said.

Wiggins' partner came back. "Lacy checks out."

"You want to file charges for assault?" Wiggins asked, looking at Lacy.

"No."

Wiggins turned to the crowd of people around them. "The show is over. Just move along now. Come on, move along."

Boxer started for the building.

"I didn't say you could go," Wiggins said.

Boxer stopped, looked at him and answered, "Either you charge me, or you stop playing bad cop."

Wiggins turned very red. "How about disturbing the peace?"

"Fine, if you want to make a fool of yourself. Let's go down to the station house now."

"You're a wise ass, aren't you?"

"No," Boxer said, "and neither are you a fool. Don't try to show me how much authority you have, because I have enough to have you taken right off the force. Enough to bury you."

"He has," Lacy added.

Wiggins squinted at him.

"You don't want to test me," Boxer said.

"All right," Wiggins responded, "you can walk."

Boxer nodded; then looking at Lacy, he said, "Remember what I told you before."

Lacy nodded.

Boxer turned and walked nonchalantly into the Russian Embassy. "I want to see the Comrade Ambassador," Boxer told the guard at the door.

The guard raised his eyebrows. "I'm afraid you will have to fill out a special form and—"

"Call your naval attache," Boxer said, "and tell him that Captain Jack Boxer of the submarine *Shark* is here and would—" Before he finished the guard was on the phone.

The conversation was brief.

"Comrade Commander Bolshoi will escort you to the Comrade Ambassador's office," the guard said.

Boxer nodded.

"Sit over there, please," the guard said, pointing to a row of empty wooden chairs against the wall.

Boxer chose the end chair, fished out his pipe and was about to fill it when he saw a short, heavy-set man with iron gray hair go to the guard and speak to him.

The guard looked toward Boxer.

A moment later the man came toward Boxer and Boxer stood up. "I'm Comrade Commander Bolshoi," the man said, in perfect English.

"Captain Jack Boxer," Boxer answered.

The two men shook hands.

"The Comrade Ambassador has agreed to meet with you," Bolshoi said.

"That was kind of him," Boxer responded.

"Please follow me," Bolshoi said.

The ambassador's office was on the second floor of the building. Boxer looked straight ahead. He tried very hard not to be aware of his surroundings. But it was impossible for him not to notice that several of the doors were guarded and that the entire building was under TV surveillance.

"The ambassador's office," Bolshoi said, opening a door, in front of which stood two security agents.

Boxer stepped into the room, expecting to see the ambassador, but it was only the anteroom.

The secretary stopped working at the word processor and looked at them.

Bolshoi said something to her in Russian.

She answered, "Da." Then she picked up the phone and ran her fingers over several of the buttons. She spoke. Paused. Spoke again and putting the phone down, she nodded.

Bolshoi moved forward and opened the door immediately in front of them.

As Boxer passed the secretary, he winked.

She frowned.

He gave her a quick smile.

"Comrade Ambassador," Bolshoi said, "allow me to introduce Captain Jack Boxer of the Central Intelligence Agency."

The ambassador, a tall, broad-boned man in his early sixties, stood up, and extended his hand across the desk.

Boxer shook it.

"Please," the ambassador said, "sit down." As he spoke, he resumed his seat. "I will send for you, Comrade Bolshoi, when I need you."

"Yes, Comrade Ambassador," Bolshoi answered.

Neither Boxer or the ambassador spoke until Bolshoi was out of the room; then the ambassador asked what had taken place outside the embassy.

Knowing that their conversation was being taped, he decided to give them something to listen to. "The man made a pass at me," he said.

The ambassador raised his eyebrows. "I do not understand?"

"The man is a homosexual," Boxer said.

The ambassador frowned.

"Not my type," Boxer said. "I like women."

The ambassador smiled. "So do I."

"Like your secretary outside," Boxer said. "She's got good breasts and probably knows exactly what to do with them."

The ambassador flushed.

"But I didn't come here to discuss women," Boxer said. "I came here because I need help."

"Oh."

Boxer leaned slightly forward. "I want to send a letter to Comrade Captain Borodine, the captain of the *Q-Twenty One*.

The ambassador said nothing.

"I want to ask him to intercede on my behalf and ask your government to return the body of one of my men," Boxer explained.

"I wasn't aware that you and Comrade Captain Borodine have a social relationship," the ambassador said in an icy voice.

"It is not the usual kind of social relationship," Boxer said. "But we have on certain occasions met."

"The request is unusual," the ambassador responded. "Such requests usually come directly from your government."

"The nature of my friend's death precludes that," Boxer said. "That's something you know and so do I."

"You know it more than anyone else," the ambassador answered.

Boxer shrugged. "I didn't come here, Comrade Ambassador, to discuss —"

"And if we agree, what are you prepared to give?"

"Only my thanks," Boxer answered, "and the thanks of the dead man's widow."

"What about Senator Ross's thanks?"

"His too," Boxer said.

"He too has asked for the body of Major Thomas Redfern," the ambassador said.

"And he has not gotten an answer."

"Your raid was —"

Boxer stood up. "I came here only to ask for Comrade Captain Borodine's address."

The ambassador looked up.

"The body is of no use to your government," Boxer said.

"Major Redfern was your friend, as well as a comrade in arms?"

Boxer nodded.

The ambassador picked up a pen and on a piece of note paper with his name on it in Russian, he wrote out an address in Moscow. "Your letter will reach him at that address."

Boxer picked up the piece of note paper. "Thank you, Comrade Ambassador."

"Tell Senator Ross that I sent his request to Moscow, but as yet I have not received a reply."

"I'll tell him."

"Perhaps you will have better luck," the ambassador said, as he stood up.

"Thank you," Boxer said, reaching across the desk and shaking the ambassador's hand.

"Perhaps, Comrade Captain Boxer, you would do me a slight kindness?" the ambassador asked.

"If I can, I most certainly will."

"I have not been permitted to visit with Comrade General Yedotev and Comrade Colonel Stepanovich."

Boxer realized the ambassador didn't know that the general's knees had been shot away.

"Would you try to arrange such a visit?" the ambassador asked.

Boxer nodded. "I will try, but I am not on the best of terms with Mister Kinkade."

The ambassador smiled. "I would have been surprised if you were," he said. "But perhaps he will see the advantage of granting favor for favor."

"I can't guarantee anything," Boxer said.

"Nor could I when I gave you Comrade Captain Borodine's address," the ambassador said. "But I did what I thought should be done."

They shook hands again.

Then the ambassador picked up the phone, punched out three numbers and spoke in Russian. "Comrade Commander Bolshoi will escort you to the door," he said, as he put the phone down.

A few minutes later, Boxer was in the street again and on his way back to the hotel to write to Borodine. . . .


Kinkade entered the Army Navy Country Club and gave his coat and hat to the hat check girl. He walked into the bar.

McElroy and Trish were already sitting in a booth and with them was a man he never before had seen.

Kinkade went straight to the table.

"Thanks for coming on such short notice," McElroy said, shaking Kinkade's hand.

Kinkade bent over Trish and kissed her on the forehead.

"Mister Kinkade, Mister Lacy," McElroy said.

The two men shook hands.

"Well, now that I'm here," Kinkade said, sitting down next to Lacy, "I might as well have something to drink; then maybe you'll tell me what was so important that I had to meet you this afternoon . . . And of all places, this one."

McElroy caught a waiter's eye. "Scotch isn't it?" he asked, looking at Kinkade.

"No, I think I'll have Old Grand Dad and branch water."

"And will you bring some hors d'oeuvres," Trish said.

"Yes ma'm," the waiter answered and left the table.

"This place depresses me," Kinkade said, looking around.

"Grandfather—" Trish started.

"Excuse me," McElroy said, "but I think I should tell him . . . That's if you don't mind, Trish?"

She nodded.

"Two nights ago we dined at the Redfern's house," McElroy said, "and Captain Jack Boxer was also there as a dinner guest, though I have reason to believe that he spent the night there."

He and the Redferns are—"

"I'm aware of the relationship between the captain and the late Major Redfern."

76

Trish rolled her eyes.

"What's that supposed to mean?" Kinkade asked.

"He also appears to have a relationship with the late major's wife," Trish said.

"We don't know that for sure," McElroy said.

"What is this all about?" Kinkade asked.

At that moment the waiter came to the table with Kinkade's drink and a large platter of hot hors d'oeuvres.

"To good health and good luck," Kinkade toasted before he drank.

The other three at the table lifted their glass to him.

"I think Boxer is a rotten apple," McElroy said.

Kinkade immediately began to choke.

Trish related what happened at the dinner table and ended by saying, "I wouldn't call the captain's response exactly American, would you, Grandpa?"

"Boxer doesn't look at things the way you or I do," Kinkade said. "He doesn't consider himself a hero and he most certainly doesn't consider himself in the front lines, the way the two of you do."

"Maybe because he really isn't," McElroy said. "I want you to listen to hear what happened to Mister Lacy."

Lacy related his encounter with Boxer. "The last I saw of him, he was going into the Russian Embassy," Lacy said.

"Now why would Captain Boxer want to go into the Russian Embassy?" Trish asked.

"Well now, I'm as surprised as you about that," Kinkade said. "Maybe more. But if you have any idea that Boxer is working for them, forget it."

"Suppose though he is," McElroy said.

"But that's ridiculous," Kinkade maintained stubbornly. "Absolutely ridiculous."

"I am going to subpoena him," McElroy said.

"You're going to do *what*?"

"Grandpa, it must be done," Trish said.

"I won't permit him to answer any questions," Kinkade responded.

"That won't do you, or the Company, any good," McElroy said. "But if he is what I think he is, then I have a good shot at the White House next year. Captain Boxer just might be—"

Kinkade shook his head. "He's not like the people you're used to dealing with. Boxer won't think twice about destroying you."

"He's the one who's going to be destroyed," McElroy answered. "But to do it, I must know everything about him. I must have inside information."

"Grandpa, this will give us the kind of headlines we need," Trish said.

Kinkade ordered another drink and after the waiter was out of earshot, he said, "I don't like Boxer and I'd very much like to see him taken down a few pegs. But—"

"There are no 'buts'." McElroy said. "Trust me. I know what I'm doing."

"Please, Grandpa!" Trish said.

For several moments, Kinkade remained silent; then nodding, he said, "I'll give you what you want."

McElroy grinned. "Dinner is my treat tonight," he said expansively.

Boxer and De Vargas were standing in the foyer of the Sanchez residence. Boxer leaned against this wall. He had left the main swirl of the party to get some fresh air. The other rooms were smoky and noisy. De Vargas had joined him.

"When Sanchez gives a party," De Vargas said, looking into the dining room, "he really gives a party. This must have cost him fifteen thou."

"How did you come by that figure?" Boxer asked.

"I worked for a caterer when I was in high school," De Vargas answered.

Boxer puffed on his pipe. He was feeling mellow. He wasn't really interested in De Vargas's past, but he dutifully asked, "Where?"

"The Bronx," De Vargas answered.

Boxer cocked his head to one side and squinted at him. "I don't remember that being in your file."

"It's not. I lived there for two years; then I went back to PR. I lived in Ponce before I joined up."

"Live and learn," Boxer said, thinking about going into the living room and dancing.

De Vargas smiled.

"Well, enough of the wallflower stuff," Boxer said, starting to walk. "I'm going back in."

"Skipper?"

Boxer stopped. He knew De Vargas well enough to know that something was about to go down.

"Is it true you're taking flack because I shot up the Ruskie general?"

Boxer shook his head.

"You're not bulling me?"

"Just a rumor," Boxer said.

"If it becomes more," De Vargas told him, "you tell me and I'll take it off your back."

Boxer put his hand on De Vargas's shoulder. "You fight better than you think. Go in there and grab one of those women and—"

"Skipper," De Vargas said, "you're the fucking best we've got."

"Sure I am," Boxer grinned. "Now you get your ass in there and enjoy. There are enough women around even for a cocksman like you."

"I got mine all staked out," De Vargas answered.

"You've got to introduce me to the lucky lady," Boxer said, as they began to walk back into the dining room.

"You already know her."

"I know her?"

"Nicole Pushkin."

Boxer had seen the two of them talking together before.

"She doesn't know it yet," De Vargas said, "but she will before this blast is over."

"Good luck," Boxer said.

"Hey Skipper, you think I have a chance with her? I mean a real chance?"

"How real?"

"Maybe a real relationship," De Vargas said. "I got to

know her aboard *The Shark*. You know when I went in the drink to fish out the flyboys, she was worried about me . . . I mean, I haven't had any woman worry about me since I was a kid. It's a good feeling to know that someone cares what happens to you."

"I think you've got more than a chance," Boxer said, surprised that he had been totally unaware of the budding romance.

"Thanks, Skipper," De Vargas said.

"There's Nicole. She's with Cowly," Boxer said.

"See you around, Skipper," De Vargas said.

"See you," Boxer answered and turned toward the bar. It took him a while to thread his way across the crowded floor. Besides the women, Sanchez had invited many of his friends and all of them seemed to be dancing.

Boxer finally reached his goal and ordered a Stoli on the rocks. He was not in a party mood and if it were not for the fact that his crew was there, he wouldn't be there. Sleeping with Sue-Ann was having a strange effect on him and he didn't completely understand it. For whatever reason, it made him realize he was a lonely man. He had many friends and finding a woman was never a problem. Yet he felt terribly lonely. The truth was, of course, that he missed Louise more than he thought he would and that she had hurt him more than he wanted to acknowledge. . . .

Glass in hand, Boxer turned from the bar and saw Sanchez coming toward him.

"Skipper, how do you like this party?" Sanchez asked.

"Great," Boxer asked, amused that Sanchez used Skipper, rather than his name.

"You're full of shit," Sanchez said with a smile. "You're not even here. What the hell is wrong?"

Boxer shook his head.

"None of my business, right?"

"Right."

"You sure there's nothing I can do?" Sanchez asked.

"Nothing, Julio," Boxer answered. "I'll just have to grin and bear it, as the expression goes."

A man called to Sanchez.

"A minute," he answered in Spanish; then to Boxer he said, "If there's anything . . . I mean anything I can do to help, all you have to do is ask."

"Thanks."

"I mean it," Sanchez said, turned and walked toward the man who had called to him.

Boxer danced with various women. But the night dragged on. For the most part, Boxer preferred to stay on the sidelines. He didn't even drink much and when the buffet supper was served, he found that he didn't have much of an appetite. What he wanted most was to be alone somewhere else.

Suddenly he realized there was no real reason why he should stay. He could have one of Sanchez's chauffeurs drive him back to Washington and drop him off at the hotel.

Boxer had just about made up his mind to leave when he saw Meagan Thomas coming toward him. This was the first time he had seen her all night.

During the last cruise, Meagan had been aboard *The Shark* to do a story on its crew and had wound up remaining on *The Shark* until it had come safely back to Norfolk. This was the first time Boxer had seen her dressed in anything but a pants suit or a coverall.

"Julio," she told him, "said that you're not in a party mood."

"That wasn't for publication," Boxer answered.

"Off the record then, are you or aren't you?"

"I'm afraid not," Boxer answered. "Has something to do with my bio-rhythm, or the particular phase of the moon. Take your choice."

"Will you buy me a drink, Captain?"

With a nod, Boxer said, "But I'm not very good at small talk."

"Neither am I," Meagan answered. "When I speak, I prefer to concentrate on universals."

Boxer smiled. She had gently deflated him. "Did I sound as pompous as all that?"

"No . . . Just self-indulgent. But I know the feeling. Thank God, it's a very human one."

"Well, at least I'm human."

"I can use that drink, Captain," Meagan said.

Boxer took hold of her right arm and guided her across the space that separated them from the bar.

"A very dry martini," Meagan said.

"Stoli on the rocks," Boxer told the barman.

Stem glass in hand, Meagan turned to Boxer. "The experience of my life, the story of my life and I can't write a word of it. But here's to better luck next time for me and for you."

"That's not a bad toast," Boxer said, clinking his glass against hers.

When they finished their drinks, they danced; then they went over to the buffet.

Boxer still wasn't hungry, but Meagan announced she was "famished" and proceeded to fill her plate with lobster salad, clams and coleslaw.

"There's an empty table," Boxer said, gesturing toward the other side of the room.

"Too far," Meagan said. "I don't mind standing here and eating."

"If you don't, I don't," Boxer answered.

"This is a marvelous party. But then Julio has a talent for such things."

"And a great many other things," Boxer couldn't help saying.

"I can believe that," she said, between mouthfuls of food.

Boxer was just about to say, believe it, when his thoughts suddenly switched to Berness — the officer, who had tried to hang himself aboard *The Shark*. Then he saw him.

"Is anything wrong?" Meagan asked.

Boxer shook his head. "I just saw someone I didn't expect to see here. That man coming toward us."

"Hello, Skipper," Berness said, giving his hand to Boxer.

"I couldn't believe it was you," Boxer said, shaking his hand and then introducing him to Meagan.

"May I have a few words with you?"

"Sure."

"Now, please?"

Boxer looked at Meagan. She nodded. "Go ahead . . . I'll see you later."

"I won't be long," Boxer said, walking away with Berness at his side.

As they crossed the room, several of the men recognized Berness and greeted him warmly.

Boxer resisted asking him how he was feeling. But when they entered the foyer, Berness said. "The docs say I'm well. I've been out of the hospital about three months."

"That's great!" Boxer answered, knowing that Sanchez was responsible for having Berness at the party.

They stopped when they reached the staircase.

"It's too noisy in there to talk," Berness said.

Boxer agreed.

"Skipper, I want to return to *The Shark*," Berness said.

Boxer had had the feeling that Berness was going to ask to return to *The Shark*.

"My doc says I'm fit for duty again," Berness told him.

"Each mission has become harder than the preceding one," Boxer said quietly. "The last one was the worst . . . We almost didn't make it."

"Skipper, I almost didn't make it. I need *The Shark* to make me feel whole again."

Boxer pursed his lips.

"My fiancee didn't see much future being married to me," Berness said.

"I'm sorry," Boxer responded.

"Better now than later," Berness answered.

"I just can't give you an answer now," Boxer said.

"I can handle it, Skipper."

"You know every man in the crew will be watching you . . . waiting for you to crack."

"I can handle it," Berness repeated, paused then added, "If I don't have the opportunity to do it, I'll never know if I could."

"I understand that," Boxer said. "But I can't give you an answer now."

"I didn't expect one. But will you think about it?"

"Yes."

"Okay if I call you at your hotel?" Berness asked.

"Give me a couple of days to make up my mind."

"Thanks, Skipper," Berness responded.

"Let's go back to the party," Boxer suggested.

Berness smiled. "Why the hell not?"

# 8

Borodine entered General Kaminsky's office.

The general had been second in command of the KGB until the Americans had kidnapped General Yedotev. Now Kaminsky headed the entire organization.

"Ah, Comrade Captain Borodine, it's so good of you to come," the general said, getting to his feet. He was a stocky man, with a round, happy looking face and wise gray eyes that were out of place in it.

"It's good of you to see me, Comrade General," Borodine answered.

The two men shook hands and Kaminsky gestured to the chair at the left side of his desk.

Borodine nodded and sat down. "As you already know from Comrade Admiral Goshkov and your own people, the letter from Comrade Captain Boxer requests the body of the late Comrade Major Thomas Redfern."

Kaminsky nodded. "Have you the letter?"

Borodine fished the letter out of his breast pocket and handed it to him.

Kaminsky put his steel rimmed glasses on and for some time studied the letter. "My English isn't as good as it once was," he said.

Borodine said nothing.

"And what is your feeling about this request?" Kaminsky asked.

"I am not sure," Borodine answered. "I understand why

the body is wanted, but I am not in a position to know the political consequences that might result from returning it."

Kaminsky said, "What if I told you there would be none?"

"Then I would return it," Borodine said.

"The letter speaks of your mutual friendship and regard for one another . . . Is that so?"

"Yes," Borodine answered.

Kaminsky nodded. "I can understand such a relationship. Years ago I had one just like it with my counterpart in the west. An American too. But in the end I had to kill him. Would you do the same?"

"Yes," Borodine answered without hesitation.

"I don't mean at sea. But somewhere else. Say, for instance, Paris?"

"If I were on a mission and he tried to stop me, I'd—"

"No mission, Comrade Captain," Kaminsky said, his voice becoming hard. "I mean in cold blood?"

"No," Borodine answered quietly. He looked straight at Kaminsky. "I could not do that."

"And do you think Comrade Boxer would be capable of killing you in cold blood?"

"I cannot answer for him," Borodine said.

"A guess then?"

"No. He would not."

Kaminsky leaned back into his chair. "You may answer Comrade Captain Borodine that you will deliver the body to him in Paris."

Borodine immediately thought of Galena. "Comrade General I'd rather not go."

"You will go," Kaminsky said. "Comrade Captain Boxer would expect you to be there."

Borodine nodded.


"I didn't know you were back," Boxer said, standing in front of Lieut. Cynthia Lowe's desk.

"The admiral is expecting you," she answered formally.

Boxer looked askance at her, but said nothing.

"You may go straight in, Captain," she told him.

"We'll talk when I'm finished with the admiral," he said, as he passed her.

"There's nothing to talk about," she bristled.

Boxer didn't answer. He opened the door to Admiral Stark's office and walked in.

Stark stood up and came around to the front of the desk to shake his hand. "I was just about to phone you when you phoned me. I wanted to let you know what modifications are being made to *The Shark*."

The two men walked back to the desk. Stark resumed his seat behind it and Boxer sat down alongside of it.

"Have you seen your mother?" Stark asked.

"Planning to in a few days," Boxer answered.

Stark nodded approvingly. "Send her my best," he said.

"Thank you. I'm sure she'll appreciate it."

Stark opened a humidor and offered Boxer a cigar.

"I'll stay with my pipe," Boxer said.

"Each man to his own poison," Stark answered, taking a cigar for himself, which he cut and lit before he said, "You want to tell me why you wanted to see me, or shall I tell you about *The Shark*?"

Boxer fished out his pipe. "Doesn't matter," he said.

Stark sat back and picking up the phone, he stabbed at two buttons. "Lieutenant, will you please come into my office," he said. When he put the phone down, he explained, "She's still our resident expert on *The Shark*."

Boxer accepted the statement with a nod. He filled and lit his pipe.

After a few moments, Cynthia came into the office.

"Lieutenant, are you ready to brief Captain Boxer?"

"Yes, sir," Cynthia answered.

Stark pressed several control buttons that converted his office into a small theater.

A drawing of *The Shark* appeared on the opposite wall.

"This is *The Shark* as she was," Cynthia said. "You had one space for Ball 'copter forward." She used an electronic pointer to highlight the area. "Now there will be one aft as well. The space has been created by cutting the hull at this point and adding another twenty feet between bulkhead M and the stern. To compensate for the additional weight and size, your power plant has been upgraded. You should be able to maintain a cruise speed of five zero knots and flank speed of six zero to six five zero knots, depending upon currents."

"I'm impressed," Boxer commented.

"There's more," Stark said.

"Before the modifications," Cynthia explained, "you could access the sea only at this point." An area in the forward section of the hull was circled. "Now there's another access way here." And another section was circled on the port side of the hull, immediately forward of the aft torpedo room. "This access way will also be used in the event that *The Shark* is called upon to rescue men from another submarine. A metal shield is provided that will enable your men to work in a water-free environment to either open the hatch of a downed boat or cut their way through its hull."

"At what depth?" Boxer asked.

"The operating depth of *The Shark*," Cynthia answered.

Boxer gave a long low whistle.

"You still have two mini-subs aboard," Cynthia said. "But each can now operate away from *The Shark* for an indefinite period of time."

"Meaning," Stark added, "that the limiting factors are food, water and facilities for sleeping. The air supply is not being extracted directly from the ocean. And at depths where the oxygen content is extremely low, or nonexistent, the air will be recycled just as it is aboard *The Shark*."

Boxer nodded approvingly.

"As for the electronics," Cynthia said, "all of it has been upgraded. It will now function at temperatures between five one degrees and minus four zero degrees Centigrade and all equipment has been triple shielded against electromagnetic interference."

"That electromagnetic interference was a real problem," Boxer commented.

"All outside armaments will now be electrically heated, allowing their full utilization in extreme cold. The thermal controls switch on automatically, but have an override switch

88

on the COMCOMP."

"What do you think of the changes?" Stark asked, changing the theater back into his office.

"Excellent," Boxer answered. "If everything works the way it should, *The Shark* will be more powerful that she's ever been."

Stark nodded. "That's why we're making those changes. She's being worked on around the clock and should be ready to go to sea in about three months. Then you'll have to give her a month or so of sea trials before we know whether the modifications really fit the bill."

Boxer nodded.

"Thank you, Lieutenant," Stark said. "You may go now." Boxer added his thanks.

Cynthia glared at him and quickly left the office.

"Whatever the two of you had going doesn't seem to have ended well," Stark said.

"It never does," Boxer responded philosophically.

"Do you like the modifications you saw?" Stark asked.

"If they all function, yes."

Stark blew several smoke rings. "Is something bothering you?" he asked.

"I guess the last mission was rougher—"

"Stop the bullshit," Stark said.

"Don't worry, I'll work my way out of it," Boxer said.

"Woman trouble?" Stark asked.

"I don't know what happened to Louise," Boxer said, looking down at the highly polished wood floor. "She wrote me a 'Dear John' and—I said, I'll work my way out of it." He looked at Stark. "I have two situations. With one I need your help and with the other I need your help."

Stark smiled. "I have one for you too," he said. "But you tell me how I can help you."

"A few days ago I went to the Russian Embassy and spoke to the ambassador. He gave me Captain Borodine's address and I wrote to him on behalf of Sue-Ann and asked for Tom's body. The ambassador asked that I intercede on his behalf and arrange for him to meet with the two Ruskie agents we have. He hasn't been allowed to see either of them."

"Kinkade isn't going to like being asked," Stark answered.

"You could go to the president," Boxer suggested.

Stark blew a column of white smoke toward the ceiling. "Have you heard from Borodine?"

"I expect to in a few days," Boxer said.

"If the response is positive, I'll go to Kinkade first. He might see the wisdom of returning a kindness with a kindness."

Boxer nodded.

"What's the second situation?" Stark asked.

"Lieutenant Berness wants to come aboard again," Boxer said.

"Do you want him?"

"He was an excellent officer," Boxer said.

"You didn't answer my question."

"I don't want him to go to pieces again," Boxer said. "The next time he might not try to kill himself; he might try to kill someone else."

"Do the docs say he's fit?" Stark asked.

Boxer nodded.

"I'm afraid the decision has to be yours," Stark said. "You'll have the final responsibility if anything does happen."

Boxer cupped the hot pipe bowl in his right hand. "Would you believe there are times that I don't like making decisions?"

"I'd believe it," Stark answered. "But someone has to make them."

"I know," Boxer answered. "I sure as hell know that."

"Now I have one for you," Stark said. "It's another decision you'll have to make."

"Let's have it!"

"Lieutenant Simmons wants to sign on *The Shark*," Stark said. "I have his request in writing. The question is, do you want him?"

Boxer replaced the pipe in his mouth. "You listened to the tapes," he said. "You know what the situation was."

Stark nodded. "You could have brought him up on charges."

"I would have if he didn't finally fly," Boxer said.

"But he did have a hand in saving *The Shark*."

"No doubt about that," Boxer said. "And he's not a coward."

"Again this decision has to be yours," Stark said. "You'll have two 'copter pilots aboard. Kinkade has found a replacement for Tom. The man is a marine, Major John Furguson."

"Approve Simmons request," Boxer said. "He knows the drill and if he's willing to live with it, then I'm willing to have him aboard."

Stark nodded and jotted down a few notes. "I'll have the paper on him sent directly to *The Shark*."

"You could send it to my hotel," Boxer said.

"Done."

"And as far as Furguson goes, I'd like to meet him before he comes aboard. How about bringing him to Washington?"

Stark wrote another note. "He'll be here any time you want him."

"Set it up for next Tuesday night. Have him come by the hotel. I'll meet him in the bar."

"What are you going to do with yourself for the next few months?" Stark asked.

Boxer shrugged. "I don't really know. I'd really like to do nothing. Find someplace down on the Carolina shore and do some fishing and some reading."

"A friend of mine has a small house on Emerald Island that he rents part of the summer. If you're interested I'll find out if it's available and what the tab would be?"

Boxer nodded. "I'm interested."

"I guess that about wraps it up, Jack," Stark said, using Boxer's given name.

The two of them stood up and shook hands.

"I'll call you in a few days about Kinkade and the house," Stark said; then he added, "I'm glad you made it. I was worried for a while that you wouldn't."

"For a while," Boxer answered, "*I* was worried that I wouldn't make it. It's not the kind of thing I want to do again."

"I've had a few of those experiences myself," Stark said. "One that still gives me nightmares. Some day I'll tell you about it."

"I'll buy the dinner," Boxer said.

Stark smiled. "We'll set something up when I call you about Kinkade," he said.

"Admiral, would you mind if Lieutenant Lowe went to the Officer's Club with me for a while?" Boxer asked. "I want to straighten out a few things with her."

"I understand," Stark said. "It's fourteen hundred now. Tell her she has the rest of the afternoon off."

Boxer thanked him and left the office. "We have to talk," he said, standing in front of Cynthia's desk.

She continued to work.

"The admiral says you can have the rest of the afternoon off," Boxer said.

"I don't want the rest of the afternoon off," she said.

Boxer heaved a deep sigh and reaching down, he grabbed hold of her hands. "Either you come quietly or I make a scene."

She looked around. "You wouldn't dare."

"Watch me," he answered; then in a loud voice, he said, "Lieutenant Lowe, I asked you—"

"Are you crazy? Everyone including the admiral will hear you."

"They'll hear a lot more, if you don't come with me."

"You're a bastard!"

"I never told you I was Mister Nice Guy."

She nodded.

"What does that mean?"

"I'll go with you," she said. "I don't want to, but I don't want a scene either."

"I'll wait for you outside the main entrance," Boxer said.

"I need a few minutes to put things in order."

"Ten minutes."

"What?"

"Ten minutes," Boxer said. "If you're not there, I'll come back for you and—"

"I'll be there," Cynthia answered.

Boxer smiled and said, "I never realized how red you turn when you're angry, I only thought that happens when you

92

become excited."

"Bastard!" she exclaimed under her breath.

"See you in ten minutes," Boxer responded. He turned and walked quickly out of the admiral's anteroom.


It was hot and humid as only Washington can be in early June. As soon as Boxer was outside, he began to sweat. He looked for a shady spot. Unless he crossed the street, there wasn't any.

He took a pair of sun glasses out of his jacket pocket and put them on; then he slipped out of the jacket and folded it over his arm.

Cynthia came out of the building in less than ten minutes.

"Let's walk," he said.

"It's too hot to walk."

"Until I find a cab," he said.

"Then where?"

"Your apartment or my hotel," he answered.

"No. I don't want to fuck."

"Then you suggest a place where we can be alone and talk?" he said.

They had already begun to walk.

"I don't want to talk to you," she said.

"But I want to talk to you," Boxer countered.

Cynthia remained silent.

They came to a cross street and waited for the light to go green.

"I don't know what kind of a man you are," Cynthia said. "I don't really know if you have any feelings."

"I have never purposefully hurt you," Boxer answered.

She uttered a sound of disdain.

"Think whatever you like," he said, "but what I just told you is the truth."

They came to another cross street.

Boxer saw a cab and whistled it to a halt. "Get in," he said, opening the door.

Cynthia hesitated.

"C'mon," Boxer urged. "At least it's air conditioned."

She rolled her eyes and settled onto the rear seat.

Boxer sat next to her and pulled the door shut. He leaned forward and gave the driver the name of his hotel; then he settled back.

Cynthia turned away and looked out of the window.

"I never made you any promises," Boxer said.

"I don't want to talk about it now," she answered in a choked voice.

Boxer took hold of her hand, but she pulled it away, "Suit yourself," he said.

"If I did that, I wouldn't be here," she told him.

Boxer didn't answer. He could tell the driver was using the rear view mirror to look at them. He couldn't really blame the man for being interested. It was something to break the monotony of driving all day.

The traffic was light and they reached the hotel in fifteen minutes.

"I don't want to go to your room," Cynthia said.

"The bar okay?"

She nodded.

They sat down in the last booth.

"What do you want to drink?" Boxer asked.

"Anything that's cold and wet. What are you having?"

"A vodka on the rocks with a side of ginger ale."

"I'll have the same."

Boxer caught the barmaid's attention and ordered the drinks. Then he said to Cynthia, "This is a hell of a lot better than walking or sitting in a cab and growling at one another."

"I don't growl," she said petulantly.

"Then tell me what you've been doing?"

"I didn't want to be with you," she said.

"Good," Boxer answered. "You can go as soon as we get one or two things straightened out."

"Nothing has to be straightened out."

"Did I ever promise to be faithful to you?" Boxer asked.

"I thought we had a relationship," she countered.

"We did. We do. I enjoy being with you. I like you. And I even love you."

"You don't know what love is all about," she countered

sharply. "You've got fucking and loving all mixed up."

Boxer didn't answer.

"I didn't mind your coming to me to screw," she said. "I knew there were other women in your life. What hurts is that —"

The barmaid came with their drinks.

When they were alone again, Cynthia said, "I haven't seen you for the better part of a year."

"Part of that time you were in California," Boxer answered.

"You could have come out there any time you wanted to. You just didn't want to. Then I find out that you've fallen for a black woman."

"She's out of my life," Boxer answered.

"She's smart," Cynthia said.

Boxer picked up his drink. He didn't want to talk about Louise.

"You said we're good friends," Cynthia continued, "but I don't know how that could be. Friends are interested in one another. You're only interested in yourself."

"You're more than a good friend," he said, putting the drink down.

"In your head, maybe," she answered. "But in the real world — well, let's just say that now and then I'm a good fuck."

"What do you want me to say?"

"Anything you want to. Anything that might make me feel good about myself."

Boxer reached across the table and took hold of her hands. "You're right. I've been less than —"

She pulled her hands away. "The *mea culpa* routine doesn't suit you."

"I want us to be friends," he said.

"Friends?"

"Okay, more than friends. Sometimes, lovers."

"When? When you want to get laid? What about the times when I want to get laid? Do I call you up and say, Jack come over and fuck me, or do I just present myself to you in your hotel room?"

95

Though Boxer said nothing, he knew she was right. He had used her when he needed her and had neglected her other times.

She opened her bag, took out a tissue and blew her nose. Tears began to slide down her cheeks. "I didn't want to become weepy," she said haltingly. "But it's damn hard not to, when you love someone and that someone doesn't love you."

Boxer took hold of her hands again. "If I didn't care for you, or care about you, I wouldn't be sitting across the table from you now. You know that, don't you."

She nodded and wiped the tears from her eyes.

"Another drink?" Boxer asked.

"Are you having one?"

Boxer looked at his watch. "It's sixteen thirty. How about having dinner with me? We'll go to one of the restaurants on the riverfront."

"Later," she said. "Now I want to fuck."

He smiled.

"Get that self-satisfied grin off your face, or I'll change my mind."

"Me, self-satisfied? Never," Boxer answered.

"Always," she said.

Boxer put a five dollar bill and two singles on the table. "That should be more than enough for the drinks and a tip," he said and looked around for the barmaid. Instead, the barkeep caught his eye and bobbed his head toward the end of the bar near the door.

Boxer understood. "There might be some trouble," he told Cynthia. "Whatever happens, you leave the bar. Understand?"

"What kind of trouble?"

"Just leave the bar."

"And do what?"

"Wait for me in the lobby," Boxer said, sliding out of the booth. "We'll try to walk out together. But if I'm stopped, you continue to walk."

Cynthia stood up. "I suddenly feel very queasy." She took hold of his arm.

Boxer nodded and started to walk. His heart raced. They

were a few feet from the door when a heavy-set man with a florid face spotted him. He turned on the bar stool and said, "This is the nigger lover I told you guys about."

"Go," Boxer said to Cynthia. He let go of her arm.

One of the men stepped in front of her. "Not so fast sailor lady. We want you to see what happens to your nigger lover."

"I don't want any trouble," Boxer said. "Let the lieutenant go and I'll go outside with you."

"Keep the bitch here," the man with the florid face said.

"If you guys don't cut it out, I'm going to call the police," the barkeep said.

The man in front of Cynthia grabbed her, twisted her around and put a knife to her throat. "Stay calm and she won't get hurt."

"Okay, tough guy," the florid-face man said, "now it's your turn."

Boxer felt the rabbit punch and dropped to his knees.

The heavy set man kicked him in the chest.

Boxer heard Cynthia scream. Another kick rolled him on his side. He struggled to his knees.

A fist smashed into his face. His head snapped back and blood poured from his nose.

"Nigger lover," the florid-faced man said, "you're goin' to the hospital and you ain't never goin' to walk again. Roll him over so I can stomp on him."

"Better ta cut him," one of the other men said.

"Roll the fucker over!" the florid-faced man shouted.

Boxer felt his body being moved. He groaned in agony.

"Now mister tough guy, I'm goin' ta settle my score wid you," he said and he kicked Boxer in the ribs.

Boxer began to cough.

"That's jest fer openers," the florid-faced man said, standing over Boxer. "Now—"

Boxer rolled away.

"That's good," the man said. "I like that. You just keep rollin' like that and I'll—"

Boxer slipped the snub-nosed .38 free and pointed it at the man. "Move," he said, coughing, "and you're dead. Tell your friend to let the lieutenant go."

"You not going to use—"

Boxer squeezed the trigger and the explosion tore through the bar.

The florid-faced man dropped to the floor and clutched his right knee.

"Let the lieutenant go," Boxer said, pulling himself up to his feet.

The man was writhing on the floor. "Cut her!" he exclaimed.

Boxer squeezed the trigger again.

The slug tore into the man's shoulder. He screamed.

"The next time I'll kill you."

"For God sakes, let her go!" he cried.

"Get out of here," Boxer said. "Get out of here and call the admiral." Then to the two other men he said, "Move over to the bar, where I can see you. Barkeep, call—"

The door burst open and two cops with drawn guns rushed in.

Boxer heard the explosion and an instant later he felt as if his right arm had been hit with a red hot sledgehammer. He dropped the .38. His knees buckled. The room began to spin. He was whirling around and around inside a giant black vortex.

# 9

Boxer saw the bottom of the iceberg. It was coming straight for *The Shark*. "Dive," he shouted. "Dive . . . Dive . . ." The lights on the COMCOMP began to flash . . . reds . . . greens and yellows. He was on the bridge. The snowy sky was filled with the roar of planes; then suddenly a huge orange red ball exploded over *The Shark* and hurtled down on the ice floe. "All hands topside . . . All hands topside . . . Get those men out of there . . . Get those men . . . Get those men. For the love of God, they're burning . . . They're burning . . . They're burning!"

He opened his eyes and tried to bolt up. The effort wracked his body with pain. Breaking into a cold sweat, he went limp.

"Jack?"

Boxer recognized Kinkade's voice. Slowly he moved his eyes toward him.

"You were badly hurt," Kinkade said.

Boxer nodded. His lips were too swollen for him to speak.

"The bullet nicked your bone."

Just beyond Stark, Boxer saw Cynthia and then his mother.

"I had your mother flown down," Stark said.

His mother came close to the bed and stouched his forehead. "The doctors said you'll be fine in a couple of weeks," she said.

He nodded. Suddenly, tears streamed from his eyes. It

had been years since his mother had touched his forehead. Years since she had looked at him the way she was looking at him now. Now he was once again her little boy. . . .

He turned his head away.

"I'm staying with Cynthia," his mother said.

Boxer looked at the three of them again. Forcing himself to speak, he said, "Admiral, they would have killed me."

Stark nodded. "Lieutenant Lowe and several of the other people in the bar, including the barkeep, told us what happened."

"I want those men," Boxer said.

"Lieutenant Lowe pressed charges."

Boxer uttered a deep sigh.

"Better rest now," Stark said, "we'll be back in a few hours."

"I want to speak to Cynthia," Boxer said.

Cynthia came to the side of the bed.

"Thanks for putting up my mother," he said.

"You get some rest now," she said and kissed him on the forehead.

Boxer nodded and closed his eyes. It was painful for him to breathe and every movement made him wince.

"He'll be fine in a couple of weeks," he heard Stark say.

"He looks so helpless," his mother answered, as she left the room.

Boxer couldn't help thinking about what had happened. He went over every detail and found himself wondering why he hadn't killed the man with the florid face.

"I should have," he silently said. "I should have shot him." He sighed and drifted into an uneasy sleep.

Kinkade was in Stark's office. "Will you look at these damn headlines," he said, waving the newspapers in front of him. "Super Sub Hero Shoots Man in Barroom Brawl. Hero Fights Three. Sub Ace Shot By Police. Should I go on?"

"No," Stark said.

"What the hell are we going to do?" Kinkade asked.

"Nothing," Stark answered. "The law will take care of the three men and that will be that."

"Not so easy," Kinkade answered. "I already have several members of the House and Senate who want to know why Boxer was armed, who want to know more about him."

"Blanket it," Stark said. "You've done it before."

"What happens when the three come up for trial?" Kinkade asked. "Boxer and Lieutenant Lowe will have to testify."

"So they'll testify. There were a dozen people. More who saw what happened. They'll testify too. But none of this has anything to do with my reason for me calling you here."

"If you hadn't called me, I would have called you," Kinkade said testily.

"Boxer has been in touch with the Ruskies. He has written to Borodine to ask his people to return Redfern's body."

"What?" Kinkade shouted.

"Boxer asked that the Russian ambassador be allowed to visit the general and the colonel we have."

"This is too much," Kinkade exploded. "Too fucking much. Boxer is now conducting his own foreign policy."

"His only purpose was to obtain Tom's body," Stark said. "Nothing more."

"Then why this request—"

"Because the ambassador was kind enough—"

"Bullshit. I can't let him or any other Ruskie see those two birds until the time is right."

"They know we have them," Stark said.

"I want something more than a body from them," Kinkade answered. "I want to exchange—"

"You're not exchanging anything," Stark answered, opening the humidor and removing a cigar.

"That's not the point. Boxer should have known better than to become involved in matters that don't concern him."

Stark cut and lit the cigar. "Will you let the ambassador meet with the general and the colonel?"

"Absolutely not."

"In that case," Stark said nonchalantly, "I will go directly to the president and abide by his decision."

"I can't stop you from doing that," Kinkade answered. "But I too will speak to him."

"That's your right," Stark said. "But I'll tell you this, if it comes down to a fight between us, I'll blow you out of the fucking water. I'm getting a bit tired of your attitude. After all, Kinkade, it was and will be Boxer and his crew, who risk their lives to carry out your missions. You don't risk a fucking thing. Each man aboard *The Shark* would feel a lot better knowing their body would be returned to the States if they bought it. Think about that one before you decide to go to the president."

Kinkade stood up and glared down at Stark.

"You say what you have to say," Stark said.

"I too will abide by what the president says."

Stark nodded and said, "I'll let you know what the word is."

Kinkade was furious when he left Stark's office. He phoned McElroy from his limo. "I'll pick you up outside the Capitol," he said.

"Have you seen the headlines?" McElroy asked.

"That's what I want to talk to you about," Kinkade said.

Twenty minutes later McElroy was seated next to Kinkade. "I called Trish," he said, "and told her something important is about to happen. She'll be waiting for us outside the club."

Kinkade switched on the intercom. "Stop at the Northside Country Club."

"Yes, Mister Kinkade," the driver answered.

"We'll wait for Trish," Kinkade said petulantly. Sometimes he wondered if McElroy took a crap without Trish knowing about it. He couldn't imagine the man next to him fucking his granddaughter.

"Mind if I have a drink?" McElroy said, opening the bar.

"Pour me a scotch on the rocks," Kinkade said.

"One gin and tonic for me and a scotch on the rocks for you," McElroy said, handing Kinkade the drink. "Luck to all our enterprises," he toasted.

Kinkade hardly raised his glass.

"Trish and I are going to Paris during the NATO conferences," he said. "She wants to do some shopping and I want to see what's going on. Unofficially of course."

Kinkade glanced at him. The man had a knack for being at the right place at the right time. Politics is a combination of that and the ability to tell people what they want to hear, or to make them believe that what you're telling them is what they want to hear. McElroy possessed a large measure of that talent too. He was a natural born actor, able to assume whatever role he needed for the circumstances of the moment. The real James McElroy was an elusive creature seldom seen by anyone, much less known. Probably Trish doesn't know the real McElroy. Probably McElroy doesn't know the real McElroy.

The limo swung into the long driveway of the North Side Country Club. Trish was waiting for them. She was tanned and startlingly beautiful in a white linen suit, complete with a matching broad-brimmed, white straw hat.

She kissed Kinkade on the cheek and settled between him and McElroy. The rear of the limo was filled with the floral scent of her perfume.

"I was having a good swim, when James phoned and said you had something very important to tell us," she said.

"I'm going to help James become president," Kinkade said.

"You mean you're going to give us information on Captain Boxer?" McElroy said with a smile.

Kinkade nodded. "This time he has gone too far. I can't have a rogue elephant in the Company. No matter how effective he is, he is always a danger."

"I absolutely agree," Trish said; then she added, "See, James, I told you Grandpa wouldn't back away. James was afraid that you'd back down, that you weren't fully committed."

"I wasn't," Kinkade said. "But now I am."

"Those headlines are disgusting," Trish said. "That man must think he's some sort of throw-back to a . . . a . . . a time of pirates."

"He doesn't think that at all," Kinkade said. "He has his own set of rules and lives by them. He's fearless, but not foolish. He could be absolutely charming and if the number of women he has bedded is any indication, the opposite sex finds him very attractive. But his rules are not the Company's and that's where the problem comes into play. I have tried to replace him several times but each time I was thwarted by Admiral Stark and Williams, a man who works with the Company, but is not under its immediate jurisdiction."

"I didn't know that such arrangements existed," McElroy said.

"Lots of things exist that you don't know about," Trish commented. "Go on, Grandpa."

"Now his latest escapade—"

"He struck me as a brawler," McElroy said.

"That's a minor part of the problem," Kinkade said. "Now I know why he went to the Russian embassy."

"Why?" Trish asked.

"To arrange for the return of Major Redfern's body," Kinkade answered.

"On his own?" McElroy asked.

Kinkade nodded and explained the situation.

"But why would he even dream that you would agree to let the Russian ambassador meet with general and colonel?" Trish asked. "Any right-thinking American would know that can't be done, at least, not now."

"He is a thorn in your side," McElroy said.

"I want him removed," Kinkade answered. "I don't want him in command of a row boat, much less *The Shark*."

"You just give James the material he needs," Trish said, "and he'll make it impossible for Boxer to command anything."

"James, you'll have everything you need," Kinkade said. "But there must be absolutely no questions put forth by you, or any member of your committee about the actual missions of *The Shark*. Every one of them still carries top security classification."

"I understand," McElroy answered.

"When would you begin the investigation?" Kinkade asked.

"Two weeks after I return from Paris," McElroy said. "I will announce it in Paris and I will have Boxer trailed and photographed while he's there. Photographs of him and his Russian counterpart together will go a long way toward discrediting him."

"Remember," Kinkade warned, "absolutely no questions about the missions,"

McElroy nodded.

Trish kissed Kinkade on the cheek. "Thanks, Grandpa. This is what James and I prayed you'd do. It will put James right in the center of the political stage."

"It will give me the chance to make a grab for the brass ring," McElroy said.

"If you make it to the White House," Kinkade said, "I want it understood now that I will continue to operate the Company."

"No question about that, Grandpa," Trish responded.

"And I want it understood that I will do it without interference from any branch of the military, or from anyone on your staff, with the exception of yourself."

"Absolutely," McElroy answered. "I wouldn't want it any other way."

"Then we have a deal," Kinkade said, shaking McElroy's hand.

"Tell him, James," Trish urged.

"We have a deal," McElroy echoed.


"Comrade Captain Borodine," Admiral Goshkov said, "I'm pleased to see you again. Please sit down. I have taken the liberty of ordering vodka for the two of us."

Borodine nodded and said, "It is my pleasure to be here." Then he sat down in a booth opposite his commander.

"You thought I had forgotten about my promise to have dinner with you, eh?" Goshkov asked with a twinkle in his eyes. "But you see, I didn't forget." He looked around. "What do you think of this place?"

"Never knew it existed," Borodine answered, aware of the rich decor of the room.

"Not too many people know about it," Goshkov said. "But it is pleasant and the food is very good. The three head chefs were all trained in France."

"What kind of place is it supposed to be?" Borodine asked.

"A bistro. You'll see them when you go to France. They're charming places."

A waiter brought them two large glasses of very cold vodka.

"To the captain and the crew of the *Sea Savage*," Goshkov toasted.

Borodine clinked his glass against the admiral's and thanked him on behalf of the crew.

"I wanted to have dinner with you," Goshkov said, "because I prefer a bit of informality now and then, even though what I have to say to you is very official."

Borodine nodded.

"A few weeks after your return from Paris," Goshkov said, "you will be going on another mission."

Borodine's heart began to race. He leaned slightly forward and placed his elbows on the table.

"You will be going back to the South Pacific with several different scientists, who are oceanographers and geologists. They have a twofold purpose: the first, and most important, is to find an underwater cave, or rather a cavern, which, according to them, would be large enough to hold a dozen submarines the size of the *Sea Savage*; and secondly, to locate a large deposit of manganese nodules, which will later be retrieved."

Borodine drank some of the vodka in his glass. So far what the admiral had told him didn't require a dinner meeting in a very posh restaurant some fifty kilometers outside of Moscow. There had to be more to it.

"That cave is over a thousand meters down," Goshkov said.

Borodine finished the vodka before he said, "That's below the operating depth for the *Sea Savage*."

Goshkov nodded.

"Anything else I should know about the mission?" Borodine asked.

"You will enter the cave with the *Sea Savage* and explore as much of it as possible. The scientists believe that part of the cave is free of water."

"I'm not even going to ask why they believe that," Borodine

said.

"Something to do with the rock formations. They think a huge bubble of carbon dioxide has kept the sea out of part of the cave and if this is so, then the carbon dioxide can be replaced with oxygen under pressure, or even air. The point to all of this is that we need a South Pacific base."

"I understand that," Borodine answered. "But what you're asking me to do is risk the *Sea Savage* and its crew to find a site for that base. Comrade admiral, are the people who asked for this mission sure that we have the technology to build and maintain such a base?"

"We can do it," Goshkov answered.

"You can of course turn the command of the *Sea Savage* over to another officer."

Borodine shook his head. "Unless you take the command from me, I will never relinquish it to another officer."

"I didn't think you would," Goshkov said; then he added, "the *Sea Savage* is presently being modified for its new mission. Additional steel plating is being added at certain points along the hull to take the additional pressure. The UWIS is being upgraded. But the boat's armament will remain the same."

"The additional plating will cost us speed," Borodine said.

"According to our engineers, less than two knots," Goshkov said.

"Those two knots could be important to us."

"The extra plating is more important than the two knots," Goshkov answered.

"When do I meet my passengers?" he asked, knowing it would not serve any purpose to argue with Goshkov.

"Not until the time you sail."

"Let's hope they're not claustrophobic," Borodine answered.

"Even if they are," Goshkov said, "It wouldn't make any difference. They'll just have to learn to live with it."

"Can you at least tell me how many I'll have aboard?" Borodine asked.

"Four . . . three men and one woman."

"Woman?"

"Two men are oceanographers. The woman is a geologist and the other man is a geophysicist."

"Should I be impressed?"

Goshkov shrugged. "This mission is not my idea," he explained. "But it must be undertaken."

"I'd rather confront *The Shark*," Borodine said.

"I understand that too," Goshkov answered; then he picked up a large, ornately decorated menu, opened it and said, "I really enjoy French cuisine."

"I'm not familiar with it," Borodine said. He was about to add he had lost his appetite, but changed his mind.

# 10

Boxer sat next to Sanchez in the rear of Sanchez's air-conditioned limo. The morning was already hot and humid.

"I'm glad you agreed to cruise with me for a few days," Sanchez said. "The sea air will do you good after the ten days in the hospital."

"I guess," Boxer answered. He wasn't convinced, but he had agreed to go because Sanchez had been exceedingly kind during his stay in the hospital. He visited him every day and put a limo at the disposal of his mother so that she could come and go to the hospital as she pleased.

"It cost me five million to have her built," Sanchez said, as the limo rolled onto the dock and pulled up to Sanchez's new yacht, the *Helena*. "She's one hundred and twenty five feet long, has a steel hull and carries two thousand yards of sail on her two masts and twin diesels that will drive it at twenty knots."

"I'm impressed," Boxer said.

Sanchez smiled. "I hoped you would be."

The chauffeur came around and opened the door for them.

Sanchez got out first. "We'll sail down the coast," he said, "and head for St. John."

"That's fine with me," Boxer said, leaving the car. Looking up to where the gangplank rested on the ship he saw Cynthia. He stopped. She wore a pair of short shorts and a white blouse tied around her bare midriff.

"I didn't think you'd mind her being aboard," Sanchez said.

She waved.

"Is there any time," Boxer asked, waving back, "that you don't think of everything?"

"For a friend, I try," Sanchez answered, putting his hand on Boxer's shoulder. "And I consider you my amigo."

"And you've been a good friend to me," Boxer said. "I appreciate everything you've done for my mother."

"A nice lady," Sanchez responded, as they walked up the gangplank.

Cynthia greeted Boxer with a hug and a kiss. "I'm glad you're here," she said, pressing her braless breasts against his chest.

"I'm glad I'm here too," Boxer said.

Then Cynthia kissed Sanchez on the cheek.

"Your greeting was better than mine," Sanchez complained to Boxer.

"That's because Cynthia and I go back a long way," Boxer answered, putting his arm around her bare waist."

"Put the captain's luggage in Lieutenant Lowe's cabin," Sanchez told the steward. "Unless either one of you have an objection to sharing the same cabin?"

"None," Cynthia said.

"None," Boxer repeated.

Sanchez nodded to the steward; then to Boxer and Cynthia he said, "Several more guests will be coming aboard before we sail. And I have a few things to take care of."

"I think he's telling us to get lost," Boxer said.

"Believe me, the *Helena* is big enough to do that," Cynthia said.

"Okay, Julio, we'll get lost," Boxer said, easing Cynthia to the right. "Let's go up to the bow."

Cynthia nodded.

"When did you come aboard?" Boxer asked, as they walked away.

"About twenty two hundred last night," she answered. "But Julio asked me if I'd be willing to sail with him about a week ago. He said you would probably come along. I had some

110

time coming so I put in for a leave. You don't mind that I'm here, do you?"

"No," he said, squeezing her midriff, "no . . . I'm glad you're here."

Within a half hour, Sue-Ann came aboard. She had visited Boxer twice while he was in the hospital. Each time she had left after fifteen minutes. But now she greeted him warmly and to Cynthia she said, "I'm so glad to meet you. I've heard so much about you."

"And I about you," Cynthia answered.

"Well, I want to get out of what I'm wearing and into something more comfortable," Sue-Ann said. "I'll see you all later."

"Sure," Boxer responded, but as soon as she was out of earshot, he looked at Cynthia and asked, "What was that all about?"

"What was what about?" she said airily.

"C'mon," Boxer answered. "I know when something is going down. I may not know what, but I sure as hell know when."

"Did you screw her?"

Boxer felt the color come into his cheeks.

"She's jealous of me," Cynthia said.

"I don't believe that!"

"Believe it or not," she answered, "that's the way the cookie crumbles, as the kids used to say."

Boxer shook his head, but didn't say anything. He wasn't about to explain anything about the night he had spent with Sue-Ann. It wasn't Cynthia's or, for that matter, anyone else's business.

Shortly after Sue-Ann arrived, three women and two men came aboard. One of the men was Byron Hayes, the actor, TV personality and Company agent. Boxer didn't know the other man or any of the women.

By ten hundred, the lines were slipped and under power, the *Helena* backed out of her slip and eased into the channel.

Cynthia leaned against Boxer. "You know," she said, "if I were Sue-Ann, I'd be jealous too."

111

Boxer smiled at her. "You do wonders for my ego."

"That's the one thing on this earth that doesn't need wonders."

"Ah, so you think I'm egotistical?"

"Heroic types always are," she answered with a laugh. "They can't help it. It sort of comes with the man."

Boxer forced himself to frown.

"Even your mother said so," Cynthia told him.

"Said what?"

"That you were a difficult man to deal with. How did she put it? Ah yes, she said, 'He needs someone else besides himself to think about. Someone to tell him he's wrong, when he's wrong. He always thinks he's right.' Those weren't her exact words but they're close enough."

Boxer put his arm around Cynthia's shoulder. "And I suppose you volunteered for the job?"

"Naturally."

"And what did my mother say?"

"Oh, she knows you all right. She said, 'Even if I tell him you're a good cook and keep a clean house, he won't listen to me. He'll have to make the choice himself.' "

"I have a wise mother."

"Indeed you do," Cynthia answered. "Wise and caring."

Boxer nodded. "I know that," he answered softly.

"See you hurt really upset her. I don't think she believed anything could ever happen to you."

"That's probably true," Boxer said.

"How much does she know about what you do?"

"Nothing specific," Boxer said. "But after the shoot-out in front of the house a while back, she knows that what I do is very dangerous."

"I know that too," Cynthia said, "and if it's not easy for me to live with it, I can imagine how difficult it is for her."

"I can too," he responded. "But I don't allow myself to think about it."

Cynthia remained silent for a few moments; then she said, "I feel good. I mean really good." And she wrapped Boxer's arms around her bare waist.

"It will be even better, once we're under sail," he told her, adding, "I used to sail with my father when I was a boy."

"You two were very close, weren't you?"

"Yes. I miss him a great deal."

"I know how that feels," she said.

"In a few minutes we'll be entering Chesapeake Bay," he said, "and Julio will probably have the sails set."

"Do you want to stay on deck or go down to our cabin and fuck?"

"I owe you one," Boxer said.

"More than one," she answered. "But I'll settle for one now."

Boxer cupped her breasts. Under the thin material of her blouse her nipples were already hard.

"Let's not waste time," she said in a throaty voice.

He let go of her breasts, turned her toward him and took hold of her hand. "I like an anxious woman," he said.

"Excited would be a more accurate word."

"I like that even more," Boxer said.


As soon as they were in the cabin, Boxer locked the door.

Cynthia stripped off her blouse and dropped it on a chair. She pulled off her short shorts and the briefs beneath them.

"You're beautiful," Boxer said, slipping his polo shirt over his head.

"How can you tell?" she chided.

"Memory," he answered. It took him a few moments to strip off the rest of his clothes.

"I was beginning to think it never happened between us," she answered climbing into bed and lifting her arms toward him. "God, how I missed you!" she exclaimed.

Boxer settled down on her. Kissing her, he eased his tongue into her mouth and caressed hers.

She circled his neck with her arms and gently held him against her.

"You taste good," he said, looking down at her.

"There are parts of me that taste even better," she answered.

"How do you know that?"

"You once told me," she answered.

113

"Are you sure?" he asked, moving to her side.

She nodded. "The other part of the conversation had to do with toasts."

"Ah, I remember," he said, caressing her breasts. "You toasted my body and I toasted yours."

"Yes," she answered.

He touched his lips to each of her nipples and moved a hand down between her thighs. Even though the shades were drawn, there was enough light in the room for him to see the splattering of freckles on her otherwise alabaster breasts.

"I like holding you," she said, taking hold of his erect manhood.

He eased his hand higher on her naked thighs.

"I like that even more," she sighed, opening her legs for him.

He kissed the hollow of her stomach.

She ran a hand through his hair and then brought it down languidly onto his broad back.

Boxer kissed her suddenly with a reckless passion.

She uttered a ragged sigh; then she said, "I can feel that deep inside me."

Boxer began to gently stroke her.

"You're driving my crazy," she gasped.

"Want me to stop?"

"Only long enough so I can swing around and do something special for you," she said.

"I can manage that," Boxer answered.

"For openers," she said and began licking his manhood.

"Love it," he said as he helped himself to her own sweet sex.

"Here, let me make it easier for you," she whispered.

Boxer smiled.

"Do I still taste good?"

"Very good," he answered, feeling her tongue glide over his hard flesh. He closed his eyes and gave himself over to the enormous tide of pleasure coursing through him.

"I'm ready if you are," Cynthia said.

He drew away from her.

"You want to ride or should I?" she asked.

"Neither," he answered. "Roll onto your side?"

"Left or right?"

"I'm not choosy," he answered.

"Left then."

"Like this?"

Boxer settled behind her and entered her.

She wiggled back against him. "Not bad for a beginning," she said.

He eased one hand under her and cupped her breast and with the other hand, reached down between her thighs.

"Ah," she exclaimed, "triple action!"

"I thought you'd never guess," he said.

"That feels good," she said moving to his rhythm.

"Good for me too," Boxer answered, enjoying the feel of her against him.

She took hold of his hand and guided it to where it gave her the most pleasure, and then she reached around and caressed him.

Boxer quickened his movements.

"That's good . . . Oh, so good!"

He could feel his own passion mounting.

"I'm almost there," she said in a tight voice. "Almost there . . . Grab me . . . Grab me hard!"

He squeezed himself against her in a hard rocking motion.

"Yes . . . Harder . . . Harder!"

He felt her body tense.

She seemed to quiver and shake and cried out; "Good . . . Oh, so good . . . So good!"

Boxer's fluid gushed out of him. All of eternity seemed to exist in those few moments. Then he seemed to float back into the present.

Boxed lounged on the aft deck with the other guests. Bryon Hayes and Sue-Ann were seated across from him. The other guests were there too. It was obvious to Boxer from the way Hayes was hovering over Sue-Ann that they were sleeping together.

Cynthia sat close to Boxer and now and then, he touched

her hand or her arm. During the three days they had been together, he felt a new closeness developing between them. Boxer couldn't really define it. But he knew it was there. . . .

"In a little while," Sanchez said, "we'll be treated to a beautiful sunset."

"I'd guess we're a bit south of Cape Fear," Boxer said.

"Not bad. Not bad at all," Sanchez responded with a smile. "About an hour ago we were one hundred miles due east of the cape."

"But how could you know that?" Hayes asked.

Boxer reached for his drink, which was on a small table in front of him. "I don't know. As I said, it was just a guess."

"Don't let him kid you, Byron," Sue-Ann said, "he's more computer than man. Nothing escapes him. Everything he sees or hears goes into the computer and he comes up with the right answers."

Boxer nodded and said, "She's probably right."

"Don't knock it," Sanchez said.

Sue-Ann finished her drink and turning to Hayes, she purred, "Do be a darling and get me another one."

Boxer finished his drink, stood up and went over to the bar and asked the barkeep to "do it again." Then with a refill of vodka on the rocks, he returned to his chair.

The sun had slid considerably lower in the western sky, but still not low enough to touch off an explosion of color.

Cynthia leaned close to him. "I'm starved," she said. "Julio said, we're having prime ribs for dinner."

Boxer nodded. "It's all this fresh air that makes you hungry."

"That and plenty of activity in bed," Sue-Ann added with a smile.

Boxer darted a quick look at Cynthia. If she was aware of the malice in Sue-Ann's remark, she didn't show it.

Harry Faber — Sanchez's friend, smiled broadly, reached over to where Paige, one of the women guests, was standing and patting her rump, he said, "Certainly sex makes me hungry. But not always for food."

Boxer took another swallow of his drink.

"Captain Boxer, what are your feelings on the subject?"

Sue-Ann asked.

"I don't have any," Boxer answered. "The sea air has always made me hungry."

"In that case, you should be a very fat man," she said. "But you're not. You're lean and muscular, isn't he, Cynthia?"

"He is," Cynthia answered.

"Since you spend so much time at sea, how could that be, Captain Boxer?" Sue-Ann pressed.

"Most of the time I'm under the sea," Boxer answered.

"Under the sea?" Faber asked.

"He's a submariner," Sue-Ann said.

"Now isn't that something!" Faber exclaimed. "I never knew anyone who did that."

"Well, Captain Boxer is—"

"Forget it, Sue-Ann," Boxer said, becoming annoyed. "I'm here to relax."

She took several swallows of her drink and lifting her glass to him, she said, "Just like I am. Here to relax and fuck."

No one moved or spoke. Only the sound of the wind working on the ship and the ship moving through the water could be heard.

"We're all here to do the same thing," Sue-Ann said, breaking the silence. "And I'm not ashamed to admit it."

"Good for you, Sue-Ann," Boxer said, putting his drink down. "But none of us need your honesty. All of us are adults."

Sue-Ann nodded. "Were you an adult when you abandoned Tom?" she asked, looking straight at him. "I know you were one when you fucked me. But what about when you left him to die."

Boxer's heart skipped a beat and raced.

"What, no answer?" she mocked.

"You're drunk," Boxer said; then looking at Hayes," he added, "Take her to her cabin and let her sleep it off."

"You can't give orders aboard the *Helena*. You don't command here."

"You know how Tom was killed," Boxer said.

"I know what you wanted me to know."

"I wasn't with him. I—"

"You should have been. You should have been the one killed. You, not Tom. Not Tom." Her voice broke. "He had a wife and a child. But you let him get killed."

Boxer turned away from her. He gripped the glass so tightly it shattered, cutting his hand in several places.

Cynthia stood up alongside of him. "Let's go to the cabin," she said, looking at his bloody hand.

He shook his head.

"I'll never forgive you for leaving him," Sue-Ann hissed.

Boxer turned slowly toward her. "Tom was my friend," he said in a tight voice. "I loved him as much as any man could love a man."

"Is that why you fucked his wife?" she snarled.

Boxer ignored her. "Maybe you're right, maybe I should have been killed. But it didn't happen that way." He looked at his bloody hand, moved it out over the side and opening it, let the bloodstained pieces of glass drop into the water. Then he took his handkerchief and wrapped it around his bleeding hand. "If you'll excuse me," he said, "I'm going to my cabin."

"I'll go with you," Cynthia said.

"Not now. Now I want to be alone. Come in a little while."

"I—"

"Please," Boxer said, "give me some time alone."

She nodded.

Boxer turned and started to walk toward the bow.

"Jack," Sue-Ann shrieked, "Jack, I'm sorry." She ran to him.

He stopped and turned.

"Jack, I didn't mean it," Sue-Ann cried, sinking to her knees and embracing him. "I didn't mean it. I don't know what's happening, or why. Please Jack, please don't be angry with me . . . Please!"

Boxer reached down and pulled her up.

"I'm sorry," she sobbed. "I'm sorry. I'm having trouble handling it. Trouble with everything." She began to shake uncontrollably. "I feel as if I'm falling apart . . . falling apart."

Boxer held her close to him and looking at Cynthia, he said, "Help me get her to bed."

118

"Where are you taking her?" Hayes asked.

"To her cabin," Boxer said.

"I'll help."

"Stay where you are," Boxer said. "She needs sleep now, nothing else. And I mean nothing else. If I find you near her, I'll throw you over the side."

"You don't have the right to tell me what to do," Hayes protested.

Boxer looked at Sanchez. "Keep him away from her."

Sanchez nodded.

"Now let's get her to bed," Boxer said to Cynthia. He swept Sue-Ann into his arms and carried her.

The guests at dinner that night were subdued. And no one had much of an appetite. Boxer hardly touched his food. But he did have two cups of coffee.

"Do you think Sue-Ann needs medical attention?" Paige asked, looking at Cynthia.

"Maybe some counseling," Cynthia answered softly. "It's not easy for her."

"God no," Paige agreed.

"She'll be all right," Boxer said, noticing that Paige was a striking brunette. "Sue-Ann is made of strong stuff."

"Whatever the hell that means," Hayes commented.

"It means," Boxer said, "she's not going to fold. She'll fight it through."

"Not if she drinks the way she does," Hayes responded. "She's almost an alky now. Another—"

"I can do without your medical opinion," Boxer said, abruptly standing and going out on deck.

The *Helena* was still moving under sail. A bright half moon silvered the sea. Boxer moved forward, almost to the bow and leaned against the railing. Though he knew that Hayes was right, he found it difficult to accept, especially from him. Sue-Ann was on the skids and if someone didn't grab hold of her, she'd go down. Suddenly Boxer heard someone come toward him; he turned and saw Sanchez.

"No one there," Sanchez said, "could imagine what it was like on the mission. Without you, *The Shark* wouldn't have survived. You saved all our lives." He handed Boxer a cigar. "Major Redfern's death—well, it couldn't be helped."

"I don't blame myself for it," Boxer said, cutting and lighting the cigar. "We deal in death . . . me . . . Borodine . . . all of us. But no matter how you look at it, Julio, we're in a lousy business."

"Yes. But show me a more exciting one," Sanchez responded. "You and your men do what other men dream of doing and you do it routinely."

Boxer didn't answer.

"Come, have a drink with me?" Sanchez asked.

Boxer nodded. "If anyone had told me at the time we met that one day we'd be friends, I would have laughed in their face or decked them."

"My feelings were about the same," Sanchez said, as they started back toward the cabin. "But the cause of our first meeting was an unfortunate accident, truly unfortunate."

Neither of them spoke again until they entered the saloon and Sanchez asked, "What will you have?"

"Vodka on the rocks," he said, moving toward Cynthia, who was talking to the woman who, at dinner, had asked about Sue-Ann.

The women stopped talking and looked up at him.

"I didn't mean to interrupt," Boxer said, stubbing out his cigar in a nearby tray.

"Paige was telling me about her work," Cynthia explained. "She's a model."

"I do TV commercials mainly," Paige said.

Sanchez arrived with Boxer's drink and giving it to him, he said, "I brought one for myself too."

Boxer raised his glass. "To good times," he said.

"And good friends," Sanchez answered, clinking his glass against Boxer's.

They drank.

"Paige does the Allure commercials," Cynthia said. "The ones where the woman is nude and you see either a rear shot, or three quarters."

"Just enough to show the nipples on my breasts," Paige added with a smile.

Looking down at her, Boxer could see them. Her breasts were round and firm. Each nipple was a hard dark pink stalk jutting out from a large areola. "I see why," he said.

"I use what nature gave me," she responded.

"To nature," Boxer toasted.

"Nature thanks you," Paige said.

Boxer finished his drink and asked Cynthia if she would like to go out on deck.

"Very much," Cynthia said. "But I want to stop in the cabin for a sweater. It gets chilly once the sun goes down."

"Good idea. I'll be more comfortable with a light jacket," Boxer responded.

Boxer took hold of Cynthia's hand and gently pulled her to her feet. "See all of you later, or in the morning," he said.

"That was a nice thing you just did," Cynthia said, as soon as they were out of the saloon.

"I didn't do anything."

"Paige would have spread her legs for you right there, if you had asked her to," Cynthia said.

"I wasn't aware of it."

"Not aware of it! I thought your eyes would pop out of your head when you looked down the front of her dress."

"But they didn't and I'm here with you," he said, as they reached the door of their cabin.

"Come to think of it," Cynthia said, "I changed my mind. I'd rather stay here and let you play with my tits than go out on deck and look at the stars."

Boxer opened the cabin door. "Are you sure?"

"Absolutely certain."

"Then stop talking and get undressed," he said.

Cynthia unzipped the back of her gown and let it fall to the floor. "Naked like this, you mean?"

"Yes, like that," Boxer answered.

"Now you," Cynthia said.

Boxer stripped. "Satisfied?" he asked.

"Not yet."

He came close to her and embracing her, pressed his lips down on hers.

"There's something I've wanted to do for such a long time,"

she told him in a whisper.

"What?"

"This," she said, moving slightly away from him and easing herself down on her knees, she put her lips around the head of his penis.

Boxer ran his hands over her soft blond hair, down the sides of her neck and over the tops of her warm breasts. The movement of her tongue against his scrotum filled him with pleasure so exquisite, he closed his eyes and completely gave himself to it.

She stopped.

"Why did you wait so long?" he asked, opening his eyes and looking down at her.

"There had to be a special time. Tonight you made it special."

He helped her to stand.

"I love you Jack," she said. "I know it's dumb, but I do."

Boxer pressed her to him. "And I love you," he said.

"Now you do. And I'm willing to settle for it," she answered, caressing his penis. "Having you this way is better than not having you at all. You and I don't have to pretend toward one another."

He kissed her hard on the lips, opened his mouth and found her tongue.

"Make love to me," Cynthia said.

Boxer put his arm around her waist and guided her toward the bed.

Suddenly the phone rang.

Boxer glared at it. "Let it ring."

"Better answer it," Cynthia said.

Boxer was about to say no, when she picked it up and handed it to him. "Boxer here," he said.

"You have a radio message coming in from Admiral Stark," Sanchez said.

"What's the mode?"

"Normal signal scrambling. I'll have it patched into the telephone."

Boxer hesitated.

"They're secure. No one can tap in on the line."

122

"Patch it in," Boxer said; then covering the mouthpiece, he told Cynthia who was calling.

"Go ahead," Sanchez said, "The admiral is on."

"I'm standing by, Admiral," Boxer said.

"Good news," Stark said. "The Ruskies will release Tom's body. Captain Borodine will personally hand it over to you while you're in Paris."

"That's fine," Boxer said. "I know the senator and Sue-Ann will be pleased."

"I already called the senator," Stark said. "I understand Sue-Ann is out there sailing with you."

"Yes," Boxer answered and before Stark could tell him to, he said, "I'll tell her."

"Good," Stark answered; then he added, "Major John Furguson will be here when you return."

"I should be back a week from today," Boxer said. "If I'm not, I'll let you know."

"Enjoy yourself," Stark told him.

"I'm trying to have a good time," Boxer said, running his free hand over Cynthia's breasts.

"Do that," Stark answered; then he hung up.

Boxer put the phone down. "The Ruskies are turning Tom's body over to us in Paris. Borodine will be there to do it."

"Why so glum? I thought that's what you wanted?"

"It's what Sue-Ann and the senator want," Boxer answered. "I guess when it gets down to it, I was hoping the Russians would refuse. Bringing Tom's body back will open wounds that haven't even begun to close yet."

"Let's not think about it now," Cynthia said.

"Let's not," Boxer answered. "Wasn't I about to make love to you?"

"Then do it. Please do it!" Cynthia exclaimed.

# 11

Boxer had arranged to meet Major John Furguson at the bar in the hotel. The meeting was set for 1830. Boxer was at the bar fifteen minutes early. As soon as he settled on a stool, the barkeep rushed over to him.

"I'm sure glad to see you up and around, Captain," the man said.

Boxer nodded. "Thanks," he said.

"Vodka isn't it?" the barkeep asked.

"Vodka on the rocks."

"No twist, right?"

"Right," Boxer answered, amazed at the attention a little notoriety will bring. He almost smiled.

"You look like you've been on vacation," the barkeep said, putting the glass down in front of Boxer.

"A few days," he answered, picking up his drink.

Two more customers sat down at the bar and the barkeep busied himself with them.

The next day Boxer was scheduled to leave for Paris and he had a mixed feelings about his reason for going. When the senator first had asked him, the idea appealed to him because he had enjoyed himself on previous visits to Paris. But the trip had turned into something more. He still wasn't at all sure that bringing Tom's body home was the right thing to do. And he and Cynthia were really making it together.

Boxer set his drink down, took out his pipe, filled and lit it. He had already told Vargas that a new top man was coming aboard and Vargas, to his surprise, answered, "Skipper, it don't bother me none as long as he understands where me and the rest of the men are comin' from. There's never goin' to be another Major Redfern. . . ."

Boxer puffed on his pipe and sent a column of smoke up toward the ceiling; then he took another swallow of his drink.

The barkeep came back. "You know, Captain, I'm a navy man myself," he said.

"Oh!"

"Put two years in on the aircraft carrier *Kinkade*."

Boxer nodded appreciatively.

"You know some guys came around asking a lot of questions about you," the barkeep said.

"Probably detectives," Boxer responded.

"More like PIs, if I'm any judge," the barkeep said.

"What made you think that?"

"Cops have their ways and PIs have their ways and the two ways are different. Know what I mean?"

Boxer really didn't know what he meant but, pretending he did, he said, "Sure, I know what you mean."

"Yeah," the barkeep said, "I learned the difference when I was divorcing my wife. She put PIs on my tail."

Several more people came to the bar and the barkeep drifted away to serve them.

Boxer was certain the detectives were from the police and were just finishing their investigation of him, or they could have been from Company. But if they were anything to worry about. He drank again and looked at his watch. It was just 1800.

"Captain Boxer?" a man said from behind him.

Before he turned, Boxer saw him in the mirror. Major Furguson was in his full dress uniform. Slowly, Boxer eased himself around.

Furguson was a tall, handsome man with a fair skin and few scattered freckles on the bridge of his nose. His blond hair was close-cropped and his eyes were blue.

"Sit down," Boxer said, gesturing to the empty stool next to him.

"Thank you Captain," Furguson said.

125

"What are you drinking?" Boxer asked.

"Perrier water with a twist," Furguson answered.

Boxer ordered another round for himself and the Perrier water for Furguson; then he said, "I'm sorry I had to cancel our previous appointment."

"Just a mild inconvenience," Furguson answered. "But nothing that couldn't be adjusted."

Boxer nodded. "I'm glad," he said.

The barkeep put the two glasses down on the bar, looked at Furguson; then at Boxer and shaking his head, he mumbled, "I hate the fuckin' marines."

"What was that?" Furguson asked.

"I started to ask if you knew Major Redfern?" Boxer said.

"The Corps is small enough for the officers to know one another. But I must admit, I knew more about him than I personally knew him. He was fast becoming a legend."

Boxer raised his glass and toasted, "To the legend of Major Thomas Redfern."

"I'm sorry sir, but I can't drink to that."

Boxer frowned. He couldn't remember the time when anyone refused to drink a toast. "Then I will," he said and he drank.

"I don't believe in legends," Furguson explained. "Admiral Stark was kind enough to let me read the action of *The Shark*'s last mission. With all due respect to Major Redfern, I think the reason he was killed was that he was beginning to believe the legend."

Boxer put his glass down. "I don't understand what you mean, Major."

"He should have never entered the hut the way he had. He should have put a few rounds through the door before going in, or sent another member of the team in first. His mission was to bring those people out. He failed to accomplish that. Actually, by getting himself killed, he put the entire operation in jeopardy."

Boxer picked up his glass again. There was some logic to what Furguson said.

"I hope you understand that my comments are purely professional," Furguson said.

"Understood," Boxer responded, when he finished drinking. "Have you any more comments about the operation?"

"Lieutenant Vargas's actions were completely out of line."

"How so?" Boxer asked.

"The general had already thrown down his weapon," Furguson said. "Shooting him was an emotional reaction, not a professional one. And if I may continue, Vargas completely disobeyed your orders when he took part in the rescue of the men aboard the downed aircraft."

"That's so," Boxer said.

"And you took no disciplinary action against him?"

"None."

"May I ask why not?"

"Because Lieutenant Vargas and the other men in the strike force aboard *The Shark* are best we have. They are innovative and never yet failed to accomplish a mission."

"I took the liberty of meeting Lieutenant Vargas this afternoon," Furguson said. "He is not what you would call a model officer. I understand he is living with one of the Russian defectors."

"They have a strong attachment to each other," Boxer said.

"I'm afraid I'm not in favor of trial marriages, as such arrangements are usually called. A man or a woman who want one another should be able to make a marital commitment. I'm afraid my religious views would preclude sanctioning such an arrangement."

"I don't sanction it, Major; I accept it," Boxer said.

"Your acceptance, if you don't mind my saying so, is sanction."

"Are you married?" Boxer asked.

"Was. I have been divorced for two years. But in that time I have found Christ. I am a born again Christian and now I am capable of seeing and understanding things which I didn't know existed before I was reborn in Christ."

"Really!" Boxer exclaimed.

Furguson nodded vigorously.

"What was your over-all impression of Lieutenant Vargas?" Boxer asked.

"I will not hedge," Furguson said. "When I come aboard, I

intend to make him shape up to my standards."

"I take it, then, your impression of him was less than satisfactory?"

"Yes."

Boxer ran his hand over his beard. "You shave every day?" Boxer asked.

"Twice a day," Furguson answered.

"Many men on the strike force have beards," Boxer said.

"I will set the example for them," Furguson responded.

Boxer nodded. "Suppose they don't choose to follow it?"

"They will have no choice. They will either follow my orders, or they will not serve under me. I cannot trust men who will not shave when that is what I want them to do."

"I understand that," Boxer said. "And I cannot have you aboard *The Shark*".

"What?"

"If you come aboard *The Shark*, Major Furguson," Boxer said calmly, "I will put you under arrest. Now if you don't mind I have a date to do some fancy fucking. I am not a born again anything and absolutely delight in fucking. Barkeep, put my drinks and the major's soda pop on my tab."

"But my orders have been cut!" Furguson exclaimed.

"Screw your orders, Major," Boxer exclaimed. Without waiting for Furguson to say anything more, he stood up and walked quickly out of the bar.

"Are you going to look for her?" Irena asked.

Borodine's eyes widened. "Who?" he questioned, shifting his position in the chair to face Irena, who was preparing dinner for them.

"Galena?"

Borodine repeated his ex-wife's name.

Irena stepped away from the stove, where she had been stirring a savory beef and vegetable soup, made according to her mother's recipe.

"It hadn't even occurred to me," Borodine said.

"Then why are you going to Paris a week earlier than you

128

originally planned?"

"I don't really know. My orders—"

"What do you mean?"

Borodine stood up. This was the first time Irena showed any feelings of jealousy toward Galena. "The change in my orders came this morning. I have no idea why they were changed."

"You didn't request it?"

Borodine shook his head. "I had no reason to. There's nothing in my orders that indicates why I'm being sent to Paris earlier."

Irena pursed her lips. "Then I don't understand it."

Borodine shrugged. "Neither do I."

"But something is bothering you," Irena said. "For the past couple of weeks—ever since you found out you were going to Paris—you've been acting strangely."

"Strangely?"

"Are you afraid you might meet her accidentally?"

"The thought had occurred to me," Borodine answered. "But the odds are against it happening."

"But what if it should?" Irena pressed. "What if you should and you still found you loved her?"

"But I don't love her," Borodine said emphatically. "I don't love her. I love you."

"Then why have you been so strange? It's almost as if you're not here. I feel it even when we make love."

Borodine was about to answer: I can't help what you feel. But instead he raised his hands and dropped them.

"Tell me what's bothering you?"

"I don't know," he admitted. "I don't know what's bothering me."

"But something is, isn't it?"

"Whatever it is, it will pass," Borodine said.

"You're even restless at night. I know you get up and look out of the window."

"It's too easy," Borodine said.

"What's too easy?"

"Everything having to do with Paris," Borodine answered. "My American counter-part makes a request and it's hon-

129

ored. Not only is it honored but I was chosen to—" Suddenly he stopped and put his right hand over his mouth. There was always the possibility that the apartment had been bugged.

Irena nodded, stepped over to where the radio was and turned it on.

"Louder," Borodine whispered.

The volume went up.

"It's just too easy and when anything is too easy, I become suspicious," Borodine said.

"Maybe the change was a mistake?" Irena suggested.

"I checked. It wasn't."

Irena pointed to the radio. "Do you really think we've been bugged?"

Borodine shrugged and said, "My orders say I am to receive further instructions in Paris."

"You didn't tell me that before," Irena responded.

"It's a stock phrase. It doesn't mean anything."

"You're not going to try to find Galena?" Irena asked.

Borodine shook his head. "Let's not go back to that," he said. "I live with you. I love you. Galena is no longer part of my life."

"Even if she wanted to be part of it again?" Irena asked.

"Look, Irena, I don't want to talk about Galena. She's out of my life. I don't want to argue with you about her."

Irena turned back to the stove and began to stir the soup again.

Borodine picked up a pack of cigarettes, took one out and lit it.

"It will be ready soon," Irena sobbed.

"What the hell is going on?" Borodine growled. "What is happening here?" He had never seen Irena act like this.

"Nothing is going on," she sniffled, taking time out from stirring the soup to wipe her eyes and blow her nose.

"If nothing is going on, why are you crying?"

"Because—"

"Because you're still in love with her," Irena sobbed.

"Don't be absurd, Irena. I love you."

"I don't want to talk about it now. You tell me when you come back from Paris."

Borodine put his cigarette down and went to her. "I love you," he said. And putting his hands on her arms, he tried to turn her around.

"Don't," she said, resisting him.

"Irena, this isn't like you," Borodine said. "Not like you at all."

She whirled around. "What is like me? I'll tell you what is like me. What is like me is to want you for myself. I don't want you to share me with the memory of your ex-wife. I don't want to share you with another woman."

"But you're not!" he exclaimed.

"She's not carrying your child," Irena shouted. "I am! I'm carrying your child, Igor."

Borodine's jaw went slack.

"I know you don't want it. I'll—"

He took hold of her by her shoulders. "Will you stop shouting," he said, gently shaking her.

"I'm crying. I'm not shouting."

"Why didn't you tell me before?"

"Before what? I only knew a few days myself."

"How far gone are you?"

"The doctor thinks about three months," Irena answered.

"That's marvelous!"

She raised her tear-stained face.

"It really is marvelous," Borodine said.

"You don't have to say that just to make me feel good."

"I mean it, Irena. I really do. I want to get married as soon as possible."

"But that's not necessary."

"It is," Borodine answered. "It is. I'm not going to let the state have any child of mine. Boy or girl, I want us to raise it together."

"Are you absolutely certain?" Irena asked.

"Yes. I want you to resign your commission and devote all of your time to being a mother and a wife."

She put her arms around his neck. "I love you so much," she said, "so very much!"

He kissed her on the lips. "You can show me how much later in bed. Now you can show me by putting some of that delicious smelling soup and meat on the table. I'm starved."

She put her arms around his waist. "You're not upset about it?"

He shook his head.

"I was so afraid you would be," Irena said. "I was so afraid you'd feel trapped."

"I feel wonderful that you're carrying my child," Borodine told her.

She rested her head on his chest. "And I can't tell you how wonderful I feel that it is your child."

He kissed her gently on the top of her head. "Now that we both feel wonderful, do you think we could eat?"

"Certainly," she said, stepping away from him and turning back to the stove.

Borodine smiled. At that moment, even with the large spoon in her hand, she was more beautiful than she ever had been. There was no doubt in his mind that he was a very lucky man.


McElroy leaned against the inward curve of the concert grand piano and looked at Captain Bush and Major Furguson. Both were seated on a couch less than a dozen paces from where he was standing.

"You understand," he said, "that everything that is said here tonight must be held in absolute secrecy."

"Understood," Bush said.

"Major?" McElroy asked.

"Understood," Furguson said.

"I listened to everything you had to say about Captain Boxer and now it's my turn to tell you why I was willing to listen," McElroy said. "I am going to investigate Captain Boxer, or more precisely, my committee will."

"For what?"

"For being less than loyal to the United States," McElroy answered. "For not doing things by the book. For threatening officers who opposed him."

Trish entered the living room.

Bush and Furguson stood up.

"Gentlemen, my wife Patricia. But everyone calls her Trish."

"Please sit down," Trish said. "I just dropped in to tell you that dinner will be ready in about ten minutes. Captain, Major, I hope the two of you have planned on taking dinner with us."

"I won't hear of them doing anything else," McElroy said.

"It would be a pleasure," Furguson answered.

"I'd be delighted to stay," Bush said.

Trish smiled at them and said, "I'll see all of you at dinner."

McElroy moved away from the piano. "I have good reason to doubt Captain Boxer's loyalty to the United States. All that I heard here tonight only strengthens my feeling that he should be investigated."

"Congressman—" Bush began.

"Bill, please," McElroy said.

"Bill, do I understand that you would want me to testify before your committee?"

"Yes. I will be asking the questions and you and Major Furguson will answer them."

"Will there be any cross examination by Captain Boxer's attorney?" Furguson asked.

"There might be some," McElroy said. "But I can hold it to an absolute minimum. This investigation, gentlemen, means a great deal to me and if you help me, I will not forget it, when I reach the White House. Yes, gentlemen, that's where I'm going to go."

"I would like some time to think about this," Bush said.

"Why? Captain Boxer has dealt you several blows and yet you want to think about treating him to—"

"I do not have to think about it," Furguson said. "I know the Lord has brought me to you for this purpose."

"Good!" McElroy exclaimed.

"Boxer is many things," Bush said, "but he is not disloyal."

"He will have to prove that," McElroy answered.

Bush shook his head. "You are taking on someone who chews men like you up and spits them out," Bush said.

McElroy flushed. "Am I to understand that you admire him?"

"Yes. I do not agree with him, but I certainly have good reason to admire him. I have seen him in action. I know what he can do."

"But what about the things he didn't do? He didn't destroy the *Q-Twenty One* when he had the chance, did he?"

"No. But—"

"But that was because he had formed some sort of relationship with Captain Borodine, his Russian counterpart. Don't you find that just a bit strange?"

"Boxer is not an ordinary man," Bush explained. "His values are different."

"His values certainly are different. He doesn't seem to care whom he beds. Did you know he had a black mistress for a while?"

"I never discussed his personal life with him, or with any other member of *The Shark*'s crew."

"I have enough on him to not only question his loyalty, but question his right to command *The Shark*."

Bush stood up. "I don't like Captain Boxer, but I respect him as a man and as a superb officer and seaman."

"And what about his patriotism?" McElroy asked.

"Only a fool would question that, Congressman," Bush said; then he added, "You apologize to your gracious wife for me because I can't stay for dinner. I just remembered a previous appointment."

"I hope you will honor your word and say nothing to anyone about our conversation," McElroy said.

"I won't even bother answering that," Bush said, then added, "You needn't accompany me to the door, Congressman. I can find my own way out."

McElroy watched Bush walk out of the living room. "That man," he said, "is a fool."

# 12

Boxer flew to Paris with Senator Ross`and Sue-Ann, but for all sorts of reasons, one of which was Sue-Ann's delicate emotional state, he decided not to stay at the Ritz with them. He chose, instead, the small hotel Jean Goujon, on the street with the same name.

Boxer settled into his hotel room that had two large windows overlooking the street. Because Cynthia had asked him to, he phoned her as soon as he unpacked. After briefly chatting with her, he put through a call to Commander Wickerson, the American naval attache at the embassy.

"I was just about to phone you," Wickerson said in a nasal voice. "I have a set of orders for you from Admiral Stark. They were radioed here just ten minutes ago."

"I'll be over to pick them up in about a half hour," Boxer said.

"Very good, Captain. When you're here the ambassador would like to meet with you. My guess is that he has some instructions from the State Department for you."

"Anything else?" Boxer asked.

"Yes, the Russians are giving a small dinner tomorrow night and you were invited. I can only guess that Captain Borodine will also be there. That might be why the ambassador wants to speak with you before the formal reception for the American delegation on Saturday night."

Boxer thanked him and put the phone down. He was surprised that Borodine might be in Paris now. He hadn't expected to see him for another week. It was unlike the Russians to change their plans once they had set them in motion. But then again, there wasn't any reason why Borodine shouldn't be in Paris a week earlier, after all.

Boxer showered quickly and dressed casually in tan slacks, a yellow sport shirt opened at the neck and a brown sports jacket; he left the hotel room, rode down the slow elevator to the lobby and stopped at the desk to turn in his key.

"Ah, Monsieur Boxer, the switchboard has been ringing your room," the clerk said. "I have a message for you from Madame McElroy." And he handed him a pink message slip.

"Thank you," Boxer said and stepping away from the desk, he looked at the message, which read, "Welcome to Paris. Could you join me and my husband for dinner tonight? If you can, join us at Au Petit Coq, 10 Rue de Budapest at between 7 and 7:30." It was signed Trish and William. Boxer crumpled the paper up and stuffed it into his pocket. He had absolutely no intention of meeting them for dinner.

Boxer walked out of the lobby and onto the sun splashed street. Just outside of the hotel a woman was selling flowers and at the corner, a man was hawking fruit.

Rather than go to the embassy by cab, Boxer decided to walk. The day was warm and the streets of the city were full of people, color and a feeling of excitement.

Boxer was sorry Cynthia wasn't with him. He would have liked to sit at an outside table with her and watch the people walk by. He glanced at his watch. It was 11:45 and the cafes were already busy serving lunch. If he hadn't told Wickerson that he'd be at the embassy in a half hour, he would have stopped at a cafe for lunch and a glass of wine.

He crossed the Champs Elysée and headed to the Avenue Gabriel, where he would turn west to the embassy, which was located on the Place de la Concord. Enjoying everything he saw, he moved at a leisurely pace and arrived at the embassy later than he had said he would.

Commander Wickerson, a short, bespectacled man with wispy brown hair, seemed at a loss about how to greet Boxer. He started to offer his hand; then changed his mind and saluted.

Boxer returned the courtesy.

"Your orders," Wickerson said, "are in a priority three code."

"I'll decode them myself," Boxer said.

Wickerson nodded. "The ambassador has been waiting for you."

"Then let's not keep him waiting any longer," Boxer said.

"Right!" Wickerson exclaimed. "Will you follow me, please."

They went from Wickerson's office down a long corridor to an elevator; then up to the top floor and finally into the ambassador's outer office, where a beautiful secretary phoned the ambassador to tell him of their arrival.

"You may go in," she said, smiling at them.

Wickerson led the way, knocked softly and waited until he heard the ambassador call out, "Come," before he opened the door.

The ambassador, a man in his late sixties, with pure white hair and an engaging smile, was already standing when Boxer and Wickerson entered the room.

Wickerson made the introductions.

Boxer shook the ambassador's hand and said, "I'm sorry I'm a bit late, but the day was so beautiful I decided to walk from my hotel to the embassy."

"I understand," the ambassador said. "Please, Captain, be seated."

Boxer nodded and sat down.

"Commander," the ambassador said, "the captain will be with me for a while. Thank you for escorting him here."

"The captain will be using our decoding facilities," Wickerson said.

"I'll find you," Boxer said.

"My office is on the second floor," Wickerson told him.

As soon as the door closed, the ambassador sat down. "Cigar or cigarette?" he asked.

"Cigar," Boxer answered.

The ambassador handed the opened humidor to him. "The Secretary of State has asked me to tell you," he said, "that you must refuse the Russian dinner invitation."

Boxer cut the cigar and lit it before he answered, "You may tell the Secretary of State that I will attend the dinner and that I am not here as a representative of the United States. I am a private citizen—"

"You are far from that," the ambassador answered.

"You're right," Boxer said. "But I am here on a private matter."

"No, I'm afraid that's not so either," the ambassador said.

"I will go to the dinner," Boxer said, "regardless of what the Secretary of State wants. Captain Borodine will be there and I would be remiss if I did not meet him."

"Your chief, Mister Kinkade, is also against your going—"

"I couldn't care less about what my chief is against," Boxer answered.

The ambassador leaned forward and rested his elbows on the desk. "We don't know why the Russians are giving that small dinner party. But you can be sure it is important to them. They are not doing it just to permit you and Borodine to get together."

"Probably, you're right," Boxer admitted. "But if I did not show up, the Ruskies would know that we might be onto them. But if I do show up, they'll think we're the proverbial innocent. Besides, if I didn't show, Borodine would be insulted and I like the man too much to do that to him."

"Are you armed, Captain?"

Boxer's brow furrowed. "Why should I be?"

"I was told that you were," the ambassador said.

"I left it in the hotel," Boxer said.

"Don't be fooled by Paris. Despite its delights, it is a very dangerous city. For your own safety, carry your gun."

Boxer nodded.

"There is one more thing," the ambassador said, taking a cigar for himself. "Borodine's ex-wife works here at the embassy in our Soviet section. It might be interesting if you hinted that you know where she could be found."

"For what purpose?" Boxer asked.

"That's what we want to find out," the ambassador said, cutting the end of the cigar.

"And their agents don't know she's here?" Boxer asked.

The ambassador lit the cigar, blew smoke off to one side and said, "Not likely. Before she came here, she underwent extensive plastic surgery. She looks very different from the way she did when she was married to Borodine."

"I still don't understand the purpose—"

"Your people think it would unsettle him," the ambassador answered.

"Sounds like one of Kinkade's ideas," Boxer said contemptuously.

"It might yield very important results," the ambassador responded.

"If you or Kinkade think that it would make Borodine defect, you're both crazy. If I were in his place, I wouldn't."

"But you're not him."

"We're close enough, Mister Ambassador, close enough to know how the other would react to certain situations. Besides, I thought I wasn't supposed to be meeting Borodine until the reception here in the embassy?"

"Whether it's here or at the Russian embassy," the ambassador said, "we're asking you to hint that you know where his wife is."

"Will she be at the reception?" Boxer asked.

"It could be arranged."

"Let me think about it," Boxer said. "I'll let you know by tomorrow afternoon."

"Fair enough," the ambassador answered.

"Is there anything else I should know?" Boxer asked.

"Nothing that comes to mind now," the ambassador answered.

The two men stood up and shook hands.


Boxer found Wickerson again and together they went to the code room. Because of the priority rating of Stark's orders, Boxer was permitted to be alone when he decoded them. The entire process was computerized and in a matter of two minutes, Boxer was reading a printout.

To Cap. J. Boxer/ from Adm. Stark, CNO.

Your counterpart now in Paris. Received word from Russ. amb. changing place of turnover. Will be accomplished in Germany. East Berlin. You will be told where either by your counterpart, or notified through embassy. No explanation given for change.

Work on *Shark* ahead of schedule. Should be able to begin sea trials by end of month.

Good luck.

Adm. Stark, CNO

Boxer tore off the printout and immediately shredded it. The change in plans didn't particularly alarm him. It fitted his concept of the Russian mind. It was their Peter principle.

Boxer left the decoding station.

"Everything shipshape?" Wickerson asked.

"Everything," Boxer answered, as they stepped into the hallway.

"Is there anything I can do for you? I mean like tickets to the Folies or the opera? I can even recommend some very fine restaurants."

"No, I'm all set that way. But there is something—"

"Name it."

"Introduce me to Mrs. Borodine."

"Who?" Wickerson asked.

"The Russian woman who works in the embassy's Soviet section."

"I don't know who you mean?" Wickerson said. "I've just been aboard a month and still don't know my way around. It takes a while."

"Could you find out who she is?" Boxer asked, as they reached Wickerson's office.

"Now."

Boxer nodded. "Now."

"The ambassador could have told you who she was."

"I'd rather he didn't know I asked," Boxer said; then dropping his voice to a conspiratorial whisper, he lied, "Under orders from the CNO, a matter of naval intelligence."

"But the ambassador should know—"

Boxer shook his head. "It's navy all the way."

Wickerson hesitated for a few moments, sucked in his breath and after slowly exhaling, he said, "I'll make a few calls."

"Thanks."

The two men walked into Wickerson's office and Boxer settled in a chair alongside the commander's desk.

It took three calls before Wickerson said, "Her name is Maria Dodin. She is being sent here. Do you want to speak to her alone?"

Boxer was about to say: no, but changed his mind. "Alone if you don't mind. No more than two or three minutes."

The phone rang.

Wickerson answered it, listened a moment and said, "Send Ms. Dodin in." He put the phone down.

Boxer stood up.

"I'm going for coffee," Wickerson said.

The door opened and Ms. Dodin entered the room.

"I'll be back shortly," Wickerson said.

Boxer nodded, but his eyes were on Ms. Dodin. He couldn't imagine what she might have looked like before the plastic surgeons had worked their magic, but she was beautiful, almost too beautiful to be real. Her long, jet black hair spilled down her shoulders. Her body was small, but well proportioned. Suddenly realized he was being examined by her as intently as he was examining her.

"Is this going to be another interrogation?" she asked.

"No."

She moved to his side and looked at him. "Then why am I here?" she asked after a few moments had passed.

Boxer identified himself.

Her eyes opened wide, but she said nothing.

"You've heard my name before, haven't you?"

"You almost killed my husband . . . I mean, my ex-husband," she said in a throaty voice.

Boxer nodded. "Each of us has tried to kill the other," he said; then with a smile, he added, "But despite that we've become friends."

"I don't understand."

"It would take too long to explain," Boxer said.

"Why did you want to see me?" she asked.

"That too would be difficult to explain," Boxer answered.

"Is Igor—" She stopped and wet her lips before she continued. "Is Igor dead?"

"No, he's very much alive," Boxer said. "In fact, he's here in Paris. We're going to meet."

"You and Igor are going to meet?" she asked with disbelief.

"Again it would be difficult to explain."

"You sound like Igor. Things were always difficult for him to explain too."

"It's the nature of—"

"Your work," she said, finishing the sentence for him.

"You've heard it before, obviously."

"Too many times."

Boxer suddenly realized they were standing in the middle of the room and apologized for not having offered her a chair.

She smiled and said, "It's of no importance. But you still haven't told me why you asked to see me?"

"Curiosity," Boxer lied. Remembering his relationship with Gwen, he decided not to say anything to Borodine about Galena. Regardless of the Company's reasons, the man was entitled to live without having his face rubbed with the debris of his past.

"What?"

"Just that . . . curiosity."

She made a face but didn't say anything.

"You may go now," Boxer said.

"I hope your curiosity has been satisfied," she said icily.

"It has," he answered.

She went to the door, opened it and left the room without looking back.


Boxer felt good when he left the embassy. The sun-drenched afternoon stretched in front of him as well as the evening. He was his own man!

He crossed the Place de la Concorde and walked over the bridge to the left bank. He had no particular place or direction in mind. He made his way from one street to another on whim. Along the way, he spotted a small cafe with three tables outside and decided to have a lunch of wine and cheese at one of the tables.

Mustering what little French he remembered from his high school days, he managed, he thought with some satisfaction, to tell the troubled-looking waiter what he wanted; then he settled back in the wicker bottom chair and watched the street.

It was still lunch time and people were everywhere. Diagonally across the street, there was another cafe with five outside tables. All of them were occupied by people having lunch.

The waiter brought him a large piece of French bread, butter and knife and a glass of red wine.

Boxer asked for the cheese.

The waiter nodded and held up five fingers.

Boxer was confused. "Cheese," he repeated, using his French.

The waiter retreated inside the cafe.

Boxer was too mellow to become annoyed with anyone, or anything. He broke off a piece of bread, buttered it and began to eat it. He took a sip of the wine and wondered why wine in the cafes of Europe tasted so much better than wine anywhere else. He wasn't much of a wine drinker and could not understand those who made a fetish out of the kind of wine they chose to drink.

By the time Boxer had started to eat another piece of bread, the waiter returned with a steaming bowl of soup.

"American special," the man said brightly, as he set the bowl down in front of Boxer.

"Cheese," Boxer muttered, looking down at the soup. "I wanted *fromage*."

"*Non, vous demandez potage*," the waiter answered.

"But I wanted cheese," Boxer said in English.

The waiter's smile turned to disdainful glumness.

Boxer shook his head. Had he been in the United States or

any other English speaking country, he would have sent the dish back. But here, he didn't even know how to tell the waiter to take it back to the kitchen. He looked down at the steaming dish and though he wondered what was in it, it did smell very good.

"Okay," he said, giving up the idea of having cheese for lunch. "I'll try it." And he began to eat. It was good. There were carrots, potatoes and some sort of meat in it. He turned toward the waiter and said, "*Bon . . . Tres bon.*"

The waiter nodded. "American special," he said and walked away.

Boxer ate less than half of the soup and drank two more glasses of wine before he left the cafe and began walking again.

Years before when he had taken Gwen, his ex-wife, to Paris they ate at the best restaurants, went to the Folies, even the opera. And spent the obligatory afternoon at the Lourve. They were still in love enough to spend a fair amount of time in bed. But that was years ago and now Boxer realized he was a very different man from the one who had been here with Gwen.

By the time Boxer was tired, he found himself in front of Notre Dame, on the Rue de la Citie. Churches of any kind weren't his thing and he decided not to go inside of the cathedral. Instead, he hailed the first cab he saw and told the driver the name of his hotel.


Borodine paced back and forth in the ambassador's office. From time to time he looked at Colonel Unecha, a man dressed in a dark blue business suit, white shirt and light blue necktie.

"And you're sure that Galena is now working for the Americans?" Borodine asked, stopping at the far side of the room.

"A considerable amount of plastic surgery was done on her face and she has lost some weight," Unecha said. "But we have her fingerprints."

"How long have you known—"

144

"Comrade Captain Borodine," Colonel Unecha said, "this information has just surfaced. Had we known it before, you would have been told. Our agent in the American embassy became suspicious this morning when Galena was suddenly called to the naval attache's office. When she was gone he managed to lift a set of her fingerprints. They were brought here and we made the identification less than a half hour ago."

"Please, Comrade Captain," the ambassador said, "please sit down."

Borodine nodded and returned to the chair he had occupied before Unecha had told him about Galena.

"Comrade Captain," the ambassador said, "Comrade Colonel Unecha has some very serious doubts about your particular situation."

"My doubts," Unecha quickly explained, "are not personal. Indeed, Comrade Captain, I have nothing but the highest regard for you. But General Kaminsky apparently wants you to demonstrate your loyalty. Naturally, this would not have become an issue, if Galena had not been found working for the Americans."

Borodine began to feel the beads of sweat pop out on his back and on his forehead. "She knows nothing about—"

"She obviously knows enough for the Americans to be interested in her," Unecha said.

Borodine clamped his jaws together. There was nothing he could say to refute that.

"General Kaminsky wants positive proof your loyalty," Unecha said.

Borodine's stomach knotted. "What does he want me to do?" he asked in a dry voice.

"He wants Captain Boxer," Unecha said easily.

Borodine started out of his chair again.

"Sit down, Comrade Captain," Unecha snapped.

Borodine dropped back into the chair.

"The Americans have General Yedotev and Colonel Stepanovich. The general was shot in the knees before he was taken prisoner. We want both men back and to get them back we need someone who is valuable to the Americans."

The ambassador cleared his throat. "It reminds me of the U-Two incident. The Americans had Colonel Abel. We needed someone to exchange for him. They sent us Francis Gary Powers. Now we again need someone to exchange."

"Captain Boxer will do well," Unecha said.

Borodine shook his head.

"There is, of course, another way to prove your loyalty," Unecha said, removing a cigarette from a gold case and offering one to Borodine.

Borodine waved the offer aside. "What other way?"

"Kill Galena," Unecha said, lighting the cigarette.

"What?"

"I'm afraid you only have those two choices, Comrade Captain," Unecha said.

"I want to phone Comrade Admiral Goshkov," Borodine said.

"That's out of the question," Unecha answered. "You must give me your answer now. It must be transmitted to Moscow immediately."

Borodine looked from one expressionless face to the other. He had to make a decision, or he might find himself under arrest. He pursed his lips; then in a tight voice he said, "I can't kill Galena . . . It has to be Captain Boxer."

Unecha smiled broadly. "That, of course, was the right decision. The Americans have already been informed that Major Redfern's body will not be handed over to Boxer in Paris as planned. I am sure they accept this change as just another one of our idiosyncrasies and are in no way alarmed by it. We want you to meet several times with Captain Boxer . . . informal meetings. We want him lured to a particular place where the two of you will be attacked and he will be kidnapped."

"What about Major Redfern's body?" Borodine asked.

"It will be turned over to Senator Ross in the town of Staaken East, which is not far from Berlin."

Borodine nodded.

"You will be told where to bring Captain Boxer," the ambassador said.

"You are counting on the fact that he trusts me," Borodine

said. "But he might not trust me as much as you seem to think he does."

"That's the kind of gamble we must take," Unecha answered.

Borodine said nothing more.

Unecha stood up and, stubbing out his cigarette in the ashtray on the ambassador's desk, he said, "I am sure that General Kaminsky will be very pleased with your decision. Now I must run, I have a very important business meeting at sixteen hundred." He reached across the desk and shook the ambassador's hand; then turning to Borodine, he shook his hand. "I am, Comrade Captain, a great admirer of yours," he said smiling.

"Thank you, Comrade Colonel," Borodine answered, "I wish I could return the compliment, but unfortunately I can't."

The smile remained on Unecha's face but it left his eyes. "I was warned that you are a man who says what's on his mind. The warning was not idle."

Borodine didn't answer.

Unecha released his hand, nodded and walked quickly across the room to the door, where he stopped and faced Borodine again. "We want Captain Boxer alive. But if we can't have him that way we'll take him dead." Then he turned to the door, opened it and walked out of the office, letting it swing shut after him.

Borodine sucked in his breath and slowly exhaled.

"You made an enemy," the ambassador said.

"He was my enemy before I ever met him," Borodine answered.


With his eyes closed and his hands behind his head, Boxer lay stretched out on the bed. He had enjoyed a pleasant afternoon and felt good. He was beginning to drift off to sleep when the phone rang.

"Boxer here," he answered.

"Are you joining us for dinner, Captain?" a woman asked. Recognizing Trish's voice, he said, "I don't think any purpose would be served by it."

"I think many purposes would be served," she responded. "After all, we are on the same team, aren't we?"

"With all due respect to you and your husband, I'd rather not."

"We'll be at the restaurant at nine. If you change your mind, we'll be there for at least two hours," Trish said.

Boxer was about to answer, but Trish clicked off. He dropped the phone down into its cradle and lay back again; this time his eyes were open. The damn phone call had not only wakened him, it destroyed his good feeling.

Boxer stood up, found his pipe, filled it and began to smoke. There was no reason for McElroy to want him for a dinner guest. They were light-years apart from one another and there wasn't a snowball's chance in hell of them coming any closer. "Besides," Boxer said aloud, "I don't even like the son-of-a-bitch."

The phone rang again.

He picked it up and said, "Boxer here."

No one answered.

"Boxer here," he said again. He could hear the heavy breathing on the other end.

"Your life is in danger," a man said.

"What?"

The caller broke the connection.

For a few moments, Boxer listened to the continuing buzz; then he put the phone down and walked to the window, pushed the curtains aside and looked out. The street was bathed in twilight. He silently repeated the man's words. The accent was certainly eastern European. He turned and looking at the phone, he wondered whether he should notify Wickerson, or the resident Company man at the embassy. He certainly didn't want to have Company men following him. But neither could he dismiss the warning. Boxer went to the dresser and opened the top drawer. He took out his snub nose .38 and loaded it. He didn't like being armed, but it was the best alternative to having Company men dog his footsteps.

He undid his belt and moved the small black leather

holster along it until it rested between the broad of his back and his hip; then he relooped his belt, buckled it and secured the .38 in the holster. Unless the rear of his jacket was pushed up or the right side moved far back, no one would know he was carrying a gun.

Boxer sat down on the side of the bed, picked up the phone and dialed the Ritz.

"Senator Ross," he told the switch-board operator.

Sue-Ann answered.

"How are you enjoying Paris?" Boxer asked.

"Dad and I had a lovely walk in the Tuileries," she said, "and I bought a really wild bathing suit in a shop on the Rue de Rivoli."

"That's great!" Boxer exclaimed.

"Father said something about having dinner with the ambassador and his wife."

"Just tell him I called," Boxer said. "Nothing really important."

"I'll tell him," Sue-Ann said; then she asked, "Are you all right?"

"Fine. Why?"

"I don't know," she answered. "You sound strange."

"Maybe I'm coming down with a head cold," he answered, amazed that she was able to sense his mood.

"If you're okay tomorrow, how about doing some sightseeing with me?"

"Will do," Boxer said. "I'll call about ten hundred."

"Make it eleven."

"Eleven it will be," Boxer answered.

"See you," Sue-Ann said and hung up.

Boxer put the phone down. The entire evening was before him. "I'm going to enjoy myself," he said aloud. He slipped on his jacket and left the room softly whistling a tune whose name he couldn't remember.

# 13

Because it was a summer's night, the streets of Paris were crowded with people. Boxer enjoyed a leisurely stroll on the Champs Elysees;; then taxied to the cathedral Sacre Coeur and looked out over the city, whose lights sparkled in the darkness.

Leaning on the white stone wall across from the cathedral, Boxer found himself wondering if he should join the McElroys for dinner. After all, they had been kind enough to extend the invitation. Perhaps, they were trying to mend fences? And if that was what they were trying to do, it would be wrong for him not to help.

Boxer hailed a cab and said to the driver, *"Au Petit Coq sur la Rue de Budapest."*

The driver nodded.

A short time later, Boxer entered the restaurant. There were just a dozen tables and he immediately saw Trish at a table against the red brick wall to his left. But Bill wasn't with her.

The maitre'd approached him and in perfect English asked, "Have you a reservation, sir?"

"I'm with Congressman McElroy and his wife," Boxer answered, looking toward Trish.

The maitre'd nodded. "Please follow me," he said and escorted Boxer to the table.

"I was beginning to believe I'd have to spend the evening alone," Trish said, smiling up at him.

Boxer noticed that Trish was wearing a black cocktail dress with a plunging neckline that just managed to cover her nipples. He sat down.

"William couldn't make it," she said. "He's with the ambassador and Senator Ross."

"Sue-Ann is with them also," Boxer said.

"I just couldn't bear another one of those political dinners," she said.

The waiter came to the table and asked Boxer if he wanted something to drink.

"A vodka on the rocks for the gentleman," Trish said in flawless French; then moving her eyes to Boxer, she asked, "That is your favorite drink, isn't it?"

He nodded, not sure whether he liked the idea of the way she took command of the situation.

"William asked me to convey his apologies to you," Trish said. "He was so hoping that you would join us."

"Why?" Boxer asked.

"Because he's a great admirer of yours," she answered and after a pause, she added, "as I am."

To change the subject, Boxer asked, "What would you recommend here?"

"Everything is delicious," she said. "I ordered filet of sole almondine. If you like, I'll order for you. Since today is Friday they have a marvelous bouillabaisse."

"That's a kind of fish soup, isn't it?"

"Fish and other kinds of seafood."

"No thanks. I'll have the filet of sole."

"Shrimp before?"

"Fine."

Trish signaled the waiter and gave him the order; then to Boxer she said, "I asked him to send the sommelier to the table. I prefer a dry white wine."

"I'll stay with the vodka," Boxer said. "I don't like to mix my drinks."

"Suit yourself," Trish answered and when the sommelier came to the table and again speaking in French, she asked him to recommend a wine.

"The house white is excellent," the man said.

Trish nodded. "A small carafe would be fine," she replied.

"You handle the language like a native," Boxer said.

"I should. I lived here for three years," she told him, taking a cigarette from a gold case and leaning across the table so he could light it.

Boxer struck a match and as he touched the tip of her cigarette, he couldn't avoid looking at her breasts.

She smiled at him and moved back. "Caught you, didn't I?"

"Yes," he answered.

"But I forgive you," she said.

The waiter brought Boxer's vodka on the rocks and put it down in front of him.

"To whatever you want," Boxer said, lifting the glass to her.

Trish nodded; then she asked how he enjoyed his day.

"I had a great time," he answered. "I just walked and enjoyed myself. I even had a small mix-up in a cafe."

"Tell me about it."

When Boxer explained what had happened, Trish began to laugh. "The word for cheese is *fromage*. You used *potage*. You got the soup you ordered."

"No wonder why the waiter looked so puzzled and so glum!" Boxer laughed. "He probably thought I was nuts."

"More than likely he thought you were just another American barbarian."

"With good reason," Boxer said. "If the situation were reversed, I wouldn't have suffered in silence."

"The waiters are used to it," Trish answered. "He probably beat the hell out of his wife or kids tonight, or both."

"No!"

Trish shrugged. The movement almost freed her breasts from the narrow strips of cloth covering them. "Everyone needs an escape valve," she said, looking straight at him through a light cloud of white smoke.

"That's true," Boxer answered.

She took a deep drag on the cigarette and let the smoke rush out of her nose; then she stubbed out the cigarette in the ash tray and said, "I think I'm beginning to smoke too much."

"Then stop," Boxer said. "I'm sure you have the will power."

"I have all sorts of will power," she answered, looking at the table.

For several moments neither of them spoke; then the waiter came with the shrimp and Trish exclaimed, "Good. I didn't have any *potage* today and I'm starved."

"I'm hungrier than I thought I'd be," Boxer said.

"Do you like the shrimp?" she asked.

"Excellent."

"Done with mustard and some herbs; then broiled," Trish told him.

During dinner they didn't speak much and when they did, it was about the various exotic foods they had.

From what Trish said, Boxer learned she had been well traveled even before she had met and married McElroy. By the time they were ready for dessert, their conversation had taken a more personal turn.

"It's not easy being married to an ambitious man," Trish said.

"What about being married to an ambitious woman?" Boxer asked.

"Difficult," she admitted.

"Mind if I smoke my pipe?" Boxer asked.

She shook her head.

Boxer filled the pipe bowl and lit up.

"That smells good," Trish said. "Kind of like good leather."

"It tastes good too."

"You look good with a pipe," she commented. "It fits your style."

"I don't have a style," Boxer said.

"Everyone has a style. Some have more and some have less."

Boxer shook his head.

"What's wrong?"

"Everyone has a safety valve. Everyone has style. Why everyone?"

"Why not everyone?"

"Because it sounds as if by saying everyone you have

reduced people to . . . to being non-people."

"Now that shows a perception I frankly didn't expect," Trish admitted.

"That's because I'm not everyone," Boxer answered.

*"Touché!"* Trish said.

Boxer grinned.

"What made you finally decide to come here tonight?" she asked, helping herself to another cigarette and leaning forward for Boxer to light it.

"I thought your husband and you wanted to mend fences."

"I didn't know any needed mending."

"Our meeting at the Redfern's house wasn't exactly friendly," Boxer said.

Trish flicked some ash into the ashtray. "That night did Sue-Ann sleep with you?"

"That's not exactly any of your business," Boxer answered tersely.

"You're right. But I'm curious. My guess is that you did."

"I suddenly remembered a very important appointment," Boxer said, signaling the waiter.

"I'm sorry," Trish said.

The waiter came to the table.

"The bill please," Boxer said.

"No, it's my treat," Trish said and spoke to the waiter in French.

"Thanks for dinner," Boxer said, starting to stand. "But I have to—"

"Please wait?"

Boxer sat down.

"Thank you," Trish said.

Boxer remained silent.

The waiter returned with the bill and handed it to Trish. She paid and left a generous tip for the waiter and sommelier. "Now we can go," she said.

Boxer stood up, walked around the table and helped Trish with the light wrap she wore.

"Thank you," she said.

The two of them left the restaurant.

"I'll take you back to your hotel," Boxer said, looking for a cab.

"No," Trish answered. "That's not where I want to go."

"Okay, where do you want to go?" Boxer asked. He was angry but was trying very hard not to show it.

She didn't answer.

"I can't take you someplace when I don't know where—"

"To your hotel," Trish said.

"What? Is that supposed to be funny?"

"You asked me and I told you," she said.

Boxer suddenly realized that Trish had planned the whole thing. McElroy was never supposed to be there. This was her idea.

"I can guess what you're thinking and you're probably right," Trish said.

"Your safety valve?"

"My safety valve. I don't do drugs and I don't want to get lost in a bottle."

"Suppose I declined the invitation?"

"I'm betting you won't," she said. "Aren't you just a little bit curious whether or not I'm a good lay?"

"Are you willing to settle for my curiosity?" Boxer asked.

"I'm not settling for anything. I give as good as I get. We don't have to be lovers to enjoy a good fuck."

Boxer began to laugh.

"I'm not joking," Trish said angrily. "It's not a bad offer."

"I was just wondering what your grandfather would say if he heard this conversation," Boxer answered.

"Leave him out of this," Trish said.

Boxer saw a cab and hailed it. "Get in," he said; then sitting down beside her, he said, "You speak the language better than I do; you tell him where you want to go."

Trish gave the driver the name of Boxer's hotel.

"What were you studying during the three years you lived here?" Boxer asked.

"Art. I wanted to paint," she answered.

"And now you want to be the president's wife. Isn't that quite a switch?" Boxer asked.

"Now," she said, "I want to go to that room of yours and screw. That's what I want to do now. Nothing else."

"One question."

"I'm sure you have many questions. But ask your one question," Trish said.

"Where does Bill fit in your obviously well thought-out safety valve program?"

Trish took out a cigarette and bent close to Boxer while he lit the tip. "He can't provide what I need."

Boxer's brow wrinkled. "He's a man, isn't he?"

Trish nodded. "He's a man in every way, but he's just not interested in women."

"Does he swing the other way?"

"God forbid," Trish exclaimed. "His sex drive is almost non-existent."

"Then he knows you're with me?" Boxer asked.

"No. He just knows that I've gone out. He doesn't ask questions and I don't give any explanations."

Boxer remained silent. He couldn't be judgemental. After all, his relationship with women wasn't exactly what was preached in sunday school.

"Any more questions before we get to the hotel?" Trish asked, stubbing out the cigarette in the ash tray of the armrest.

"None."

"If you're wondering if I'm clean," she said matter of factly, "I am. I'm very careful whom I choose."

"I'm glad to know I'm in that select group," Boxer said.

"You have no cause to be sarcastic," Trish answered.

"You're right," Boxer said. "I'm sorry."

The cab stopped in front of the hotel.

Boxer paid the driver.

"What made you choose this place?" she asked, as they entered the lobby.

"It's unpretentious," Boxer answered, stopping at the desk for his key.

"Just this side of modest, I would say," Trish commented.

"If you'd prefer to go somewhere else—"

She shook her head. "No. I was only making conversation," she said.

They entered the elevator and a few minutes later, Boxer

unlocked the door to his room and switched on the light; then he stepped aside and in French asked Trish to enter.

"I hope you're not going to say *'Voulez-vous couchez avec moi'*. But then there'd be no reason for you to say that since you already know that I do."

Boxer closed the door, locked it and going up behind her, he put his arms around her.

With a sigh, she leaned back against him.

"Let me have your jacket," he said.

"Yes, take it," she barely whispered.

Boxer slipped the jacket off her and took the black velvet evening bag out of her hand. He put the bag down on the dresser and placed the jacket over the back of one of the chairs; then he removed his own jacket and put it over the back of the second chair.

"Why the gun?" she asked.

"I forgot all about it," Boxer said.

"But why are you—"

"Orders."

"Were you wearing it when I met you at the Redfern's house?"

"No."

"Then why here in Paris?"

"Someone saw fit to warn me that my life is in danger," Boxer answered. "But that's something I'm trusting you with."

"I'm not exactly in a position to reveal anything you tell me without compromising myself, am I?"

"No," Boxer answered. "I guess not." Up until that moment, he hadn't realized how much she was risking by being with him.

"Well," she said, "we didn't come here to stare at each other, did we?" And reaching up, she removed the two thin bands of material covering her breasts. "The rest of the dress comes off just as easily," she said, moving it over the flare of her hips and stepping out of it. She flung the dress onto the chair where her jacket was. "So far, do you like what you see?" she asked. Except for a pair of black lacy briefs, she was completely nude.

"You know you're beautiful," Boxer answered.

"You can take off my briefs," she said, ignoring his comment and stretching out on the bed.

Boxer stripped and lay down next to Trish. "This is one place I never thought I'd wind up with you," he said.

She turned on her side. "That's strange. Because the moment I saw you, I knew I would. Not in Paris, of course. But somewhere."

Boxer drew Trish to him and kissed her gently on the lips. Her bare breasts felt warm against his chest. He moved his hand down the broad of her back and under the lacy material of her briefs.

"Take them off," she said in a throaty voice.

Boxer rolled the briefs off.

She began to caress his scrotum.

He kissed her again. But his time his tongue found hers. Then he kissed the side of her neck and finally his lips were on the erect nipple of her right breast.

"I said I'd do whatever you wanted," Trish whispered. "and I will."

"Do what you want," Boxer answered; he was going to add that it was her safety valve, not his. But instead, he said, "I'll enjoy it no matter what you do."

"You wouldn't be annoyed if we skipped the foreplay bit and went straight to the main event?"

Boxer shook his head.

Trish straddled him and guiding his penis into her, she settled down on him. "That feels good . . . What about you?"

"Good," he said, feeling the contractions inside of her along the length of his penis. He placed his hands over her breasts and gently squeezed them.

Trish arched backwards; then with a smile, she came forward and began to move up and down.

Boxer eased one hand under her and teased her clit.

She closed her eyes.

Boxer used the forefinger of his free hand to enter her bung hole.

Trish gasped; then said, "I was going to ask you to do

158

that."

"I read your thoughts," he said.

She managed a tight smile. "What am I thinking now?" she asked.

"You're not thinking," he said, thrusting up into her, "you're experiencing."

"Faster," she said. "Move faster!" She quickened her own pace.

Boxer rammed into her.

"I'm almost there," she said, rolling her hips. "Almost there!" Her body tensed.

Boxer was almost there too.

Low in her throat, Trish began to moan.

Boxer pulled her forward and kissed her breasts; then pressed his face into the cleft between them.

Trish came down on him. She began to tremble. "Keep moving . . . Oh keep moving!"

He continued to thrust into her.

Suddenly she uttered a loud sob and her body seemed balanced on the head of his penis; then wracked by spasms, she dropped down and sunk her teeth into his left shoulder.

Boxer simultaneously felt the pain and pleasure of his own climax, which was so intense he threw his arms around Trish and held her fiercely to him.

Trish stretched out on top of him. "On the Richter scale of fucking," she said, "that was easily an eight."

"At least an eight and a half," Boxer responded.

"It was good, Jack," she said looking down at him.

"You didn't tell me you're a biter," he said.

She touched the area she had bitten. "Luckily you don't have to explain it to anyone," she said.

"What would you have done if I had marked you?" Boxer asked.

"Nothing. William would never notice. We sleep in separate rooms."

"He's a fool!" Boxer exclaimed.

Trish shook her head. "He's a very clever man."

"He's not clever when it comes to you," Boxer said.

"I don't want to talk about him."

Boxer kissed her on the lips again.

"What was that for?" Trish asked.

"For being here with me," Boxer answered.

She smiled down at him. "That was a nice thing to do and say."

"I'm just a nice guy."

"The odd thing was that I didn't realize how nice."

Boxer smiled. "Here and now it would be hard not to be nice to you."


Boxer spent most of the day with Sue-Ann, but his thoughts were about Trish. There was something about her that made him feel sorry for her and, though he couldn't define it, something about her had remained with him.

"Well thank you for being with me in body, if not in spirit," Sue-Ann said, when they got back to the hotel.

"Sorry," Boxer said. "But I have something on my mind."

"Could have fooled me," Sue-Ann responded.

"Promise I'll make it up to you."

She kissed him on the cheek. "I won't hold you to it," she said and took off across the lobby to the elevator.

Boxer returned to his own hotel room, where he showered and dressed for dinner with Borodine. He was looking forward to meeting him.

A limo from the American embassy picked Boxer up at 1800. A Company man was in the back seat.

"Slip this in your shirt pocket," the man said, handing him a small plastic disk.

"And what if they should detect it?" Boxer asked.

"They won't," the man answered. He tapped the glass partition separating the front and rear sections of the car and the driver pulled up. "There is as far as I go. Good luck, Captain."

Boxer shook his hand.

The limo started up again. At precisely 1830 Boxer entered the Soviet embassy on the Rue de Grenelle. He was immediately escorted by a man with a pock-marked face to the elevator, which was waiting for them. They went up to the second story, walked through a long hall and into an enormous dining room, where a very large mahogany table was set up with six places.

Because Borodine was the only one in uniform, it was easy for Boxer to spot him first. He was standing closer to the door than the other men. He held a drink in his hand.

Their eyes met.

Borodine smiled broadly and with his hand outstretched, he walked rapidly toward Boxer. "It is so very good to see you," he said, pumping Boxer's hand; then embracing him.

"And very good to see you, Comrade Captain," Boxer answered.

"We'll drink," Borodine said.

"Yes, we'll drink," Boxer answered smiling broadly.

They realized the other men in the room were looking at them.

"Come," Borodine said, "before we drink, I'll introduce you to the other men in the room."

Boxer dropped his voice. "Tell me which one is KGB and I'll tell him what he can do."

Borodine's eye brows went up.

"I was only joking," Boxer said.

"The KGB isn't for joking," Borodine said.

Boxer nodded.

They crossed the room. Borodine introduced Boxer to the ambassador.

"Comrade Captain," the ambassador said, "I am delighted to have been able to arrange a meeting between you and Comrade Captain Borodine."

"If it were not for the sad duty I must perform," Boxer answered, "the occasion would be a most happy one, indeed."

"Happy at least in that you are not confronting one another with anything more dangerous than a glass in your hand or a fork at the table."

"I agree with that," Boxer said.

Borodine introduced him to the other guests. All of them were members of the embassy staff. "Now we drink," Borodine said and led Boxer to the far corner of the room where there was a bar.

"That time off Africa—" Boxer began.

"I wasn't aware that a trap had been set for me," Borodine said.

"I was told about the bomb after we had separated," Boxer responded. "I tried to make radio contact. But—"

The two men stopped and smiled at one another.

"Strange," Boxer said, "but no one in this room would ever guess that we are friends."

"Better that they have no real idea," Borodine answered.

At the bar, Borodine ordered two vodkas and entwining his arm with Boxer's, he toasted, "To the men of *The Shark* and *Sea Savage.*"

"To the men of the *Sea Savage* and *The Shark,*" Boxer said. They toasted each other and drank again.

"You know," Borodine said, "my ex-wife works in the American embassy."

"Yes, I know," Boxer said. "I met her the other day."

Borodine finished the vodka in his glass and turned to the bar for another one. "I have another relationship now," he said almost sharply.

Boxer nodded understandingly.

"But if you should happen to see Galena again," Borodine said in a softer voice, "wish her well for me."

"I'll do that," Boxer answered.

"How did you manage to bring *The Shark* back to base?" Borodine asked.

"Luck," Boxer said.

"And knowing your job."

"That too," Boxer said. "Though at times it was more luck than anything else."

Borodine nodded. "I know what you mean. Sometimes there's no accounting for the way things will go."

Boxer agreed; then he said, "I want to thank you for arranging the return of Major Redfern's body. It means a great deal to his family."

"Tell them," Borodine said, "I am sorry that he was killed."

"I will tell them."

"Tell them that I am honored to have been of small service to them."

"I will."

"Was he a good friend of yours?" Borodine asked.

Boxer nodded.

"I will not try to say anything to you, because nothing I could say would make a difference."

"Your actions have been proof of your feelings," Boxer said.

"Thank you, Comrade Boxer," Borodine answered, placing his hand on Boxer's shoulder.

"Gentlemen," one of the servants called, "will you please be seated. Dinner will be served."

"We have been placed opposite one another," Borodine said. "Everyone at the table speaks English."

"I'm glad," Boxer said, "because I don't know enough Russian to ask which way to the bathroom."

Borodine laughed, and gestured to the door. "To the left once you're in the hallway," he said.

"I'll remember that," Boxer said.

At the table there were several more toasts offered to the crews of *The Shark* and *Sea Savage*. The dinner was a spectacular affair with many dishes completely unfamiliar to Boxer, but delicious beyond description.

After every mouthful of food, the Russians drank vodka from a small glass.

"As long as you eat," Borodine assured him, "you will not feel the vodka."

"Maybe that's true for a Russian, but I'm not so sure it would work for an American," Boxer answered. "But I'll try it."

Over coffee and cigars, several of the men at the table told a number of bawdy jokes.

Then Borodine, changing his voice to make it sound darker, told one, which neither Boxer or the other men thought very funny.

"Better not try to be a comic," the ambassador said.

"I told that same joke to my crew and everyone of them laughed," Borodine said in that same dark tone of voice.

"I bet you had your executive officer writing down the names of those who didn't laugh," one of the other men said.

"Listen, a captain's power has to count for something," Borodine answered, still using that dark voice.

"Not so much that we have to listen to his jokes at the ambassador's table, much less laugh at them," one of the guests said.

"Besides," said another guest, "you sound ridiculous. Where ever did you learn to use that voice?"

"Making frightening phone calls to strangers," Borodine answered.

Boxer tumbled to Borodine's act. "I understand the Comrade Captain very well," he said. "A crew must laugh at the captain's jokes, even if they're not funny."

"Only another captain could understand," Borodine commented sadly. "The rest of you could never understand."

"Take my advice," the ambassador counseled, "don't expect anyone else to understand either."

Boxer smiled.

And Borodine grinned back.

"The two of you are grinning like — like a pair of fat cats," a man at the table laughed.

"Not at all," Boxer said. "We're just two captains who understand one another."

"That's so," Borodine said still smiling. "That's so."

Boxer now knew the warning he'd received was not a prank. His life was in danger and it was possible that someone at the table might have been assigned to take him out. But who? Several of them looked as if they could do it. And where would it be done? Not there in the embassy. That would cause them too many problems.

"Not to worry," Borodine said, looking at Boxer while lighting another cigar, "All of you are safe. I will not tell another joke this evening."

Boxer raised his glass and toasted, "To all the men here: long life and happiness."

Everyone drank.

Just before Boxer was about to leave, the ambassador said, "My government has decided to turn over Major Redfern's body to you on the German border in the town of Staaken. Comrade Captain Boxer you may take possession of the body on Tuesday at nine hundred hours. Is this agreeable to you?"

Boxer glanced at Borodine. He could read nothing in his face. "Yes, it is agreeable."

"You must cross the border alone. The body will be on a handcart, which you will be able to move without any difficulty."

Boxer nodded. He wasn't at all sure how the Company or the embassy people would react to this change, but it didn't matter to him where they gave him Tom's body, as long as they gave it to him.

"Comrade Captain Borodine will be there to formally give you Major Redfern's body," the ambassador said; then he asked, "Have you any questions?"

"Will I be allowed to see the body before it is given to me?" Boxer asked.

"The casket has been sealed. You and the major's family must accept the fact that the major's body is in the casket."

"You don't give us much choice," Boxer answered.

"None," the ambassador said with a smile. Then, picking up his glass, he said, "The last toast of the evening from you, Comrade Captain Boxer."

Boxer picked up his glass, looked at Borodine; then straight at the ambassador. "To the friendship between men and peace between nations."

# 14

When Boxer entered his room, he found Trish waiting for him in bed. "I didn't think I drank that much," he said, closing the door behind him.

"I'm real," she answered.

He nodded. "I can see that. I guess I should ask how you got here. But that really doesn't matter, does it?"

"No, it doesn't."

"What does matter," he said, removing his jacket," is why you're here. I thought we both understood that last night was a one time deal."

"Tell me you're not secretly pleased to see me?" she challenged with a smile.

Boxer removed his tie and started to unbutton his shirt. "Disturbed would be a more accurate description," he said.

She drew her bare legs up. "We're not going to have too many chances to be together," Trish said in a low voice.

Boxer put his shirt over the chair, sat down on the bed and took off his shoes and socks. "You'll excuse me if I don't talk much," he said. "I've had a great deal to drink and what I really want to do most is sleep." He stood up and took of his pants.

"You went to dinner armed?" Trish asked.

"It's the only way to go," Boxer answered, going into the bathroom to shower and brush his teeth. When he came back into the bedroom, Trish was stretched out on the bed again. He lay down next to her. "Turn off the light," he said.

A few moments later the room was dark.

"Jack, I have something important to tell you," Trish said.

"You can't be pregnant so fast," he said, turning away from her.

"There's no easy way," she said.

He felt her breasts against his back. "All right, tell me what you have to tell me."

"The day after tomorrow William is going to hold a news conference."

"He's always doing that," Boxer said. "Everything he says or does is a media event."

"He is going to announce—" she faltered.

Boxer faced her. "Well, what is he going to announce?"

"That you are going to be investigated by his committee."

"What?" Boxer sat up.

"He thinks—"

"He never thinks," Boxer growled.

"Your attitude toward the Russians is suspect," she said. "There are things you've done that can be questioned."

Boxer ran his hand over his beard. "You knew this last night?" he asked.

"I've known it for a while," she admitted.

"And to soften the blow you've come to fuck?"

"Something like that," Trish answered.

"Thanks but no thanks," Boxer said.

"I came back tonight for another reason."

"I'm not interested," Boxer said.

Trish sat up. She reached over to the night table, opened her bag and took out her cigarette case. After a few moments, she handed a lit cigarette to Boxer; then she took one for herself.

"So I'm to be sacrificed for your husband's career?" Boxer asked, looking at her.

"I came here," Trish said, ignoring the question, "because I needed you."

"Need me," Boxer growled. "You don't need me. You need a husband with balls." He left the bed and began to pace in the narrow space between the bed and the dresser. "I'll tell you this: I'm not going to appear before any damn congressional committee."

Before she answered, Trish took a deep drag on her cigarette, making the tip glow in the darkness. "What you do or don't do is your decision."

"That's for sure!"

The phone rang.

"Aren't you going to answer it?" Trish asked.

Boxer walked to the night table and picked up the phone. "Boxer here," he said.

"This is Admiral Stark," the gravelly voice on the other end of the line said. "There's no easy way for me to tell you this."

"Tell me what?"

"Your mother is in the hospital, Jack."

"What happened?"

"The house was broken into and she was badly beaten by burglars."

"Beaten?"

"She's in the intensive care unit of the Norwegian American hospital."

"Have you seen her?"

"Yes . . . I was there this afternoon," Stark answered.

Boxer took the cigarette out of his mouth, stubbed it out in the ashtray on the night table next to the phone.

"Jack, are you still there?" Stark asked.

"Is she going to make it?" Boxer asked.

"She's got about a fifty-fifty chance," Stark answered.

Boxer sat down on the bed.

"Listen," Stark said, "I've arranged for you to come home. You'll fly back to Kennedy on the Concorde tomorrow morning and one of our drivers will pick you up. The senator will take delivery of Tom's body."

"Thanks," Boxer said.

"See you in a few days," Stark said and hung up.

Boxer put the phone down. "What kind of animals would beat up an old woman?" he asked. "What kind of animals?"

"I'm sorry," Trish said, moving close.

He could feel her soft breasts against his bare back. "I'd better call Air France and get the departure time for the Concorde," he said, reaching for the phone again.

168

"It leaves at nine in the morning," Trish said. "William and I will take it the day after his news conference."

Boxer shook his head. "I want to sleep, or try to. Why don't you leave."

"Because you need someone here," she answered moving away from him.

Boxer lay down and putting his hands behind his back, he stared up at the ceiling.

Trish stretched out next to him.

He could feel her naked body along the side of his own and the perfume she was wearing filled his nostrils.

She put her arm over his chest and said, "I really am sorry about your mother."

"So am I," Boxer sighed. "So am I."

"Maybe she'll come out of it and be okay," Trish offered.

Boxer didn't answer. He was thinking of all the times his mother had stepped aside to let him and his father be together. It was almost as if she considered him more his father's son than hers. Boxer pursed his lips and then he cleared his throat to ease the tightness in it.

"Sons always have a very special relationship with their mothers," Trish said.

"I don't want to talk about it," Boxer said. "I don't even want you here." And he turned away from her.

"Not too many men have done that to me," Trish said.

"Maybe more should have," Boxer answered.

"Listen," she said, "I can understand your need to feel sorry for yourself. But that's no excuse to be rude and insulting. I came here to—"

Boxer whirled around. "To fuck. Well, I don't want to fuck."

"I came here because I wanted you to fuck me."

"Am I supposed to consider that some sort of an honor?"

"Not in the least," Trish answered. "But you might realize that by my coming here tonight, I was trying to tell you something."

"Sure. Your jackass husband is going to investigate me."

"I told you that because I wanted you to understand that politics is one thing but what we have together is another."

"We don't have anything together," Boxer exclaimed, turning toward her. "Nothing." He found himself looking down at her and his anger crashed of its own weight. He shook his head. "This is crazy," he said.

"What's crazy?"

"This whole scene."

"It doesn't have to be," Trish said, stretching her hands above her head.

Boxer watched her breasts move. He saw the way her long blond hair rested against the pillow. He lowered his face to hers and kissed her on the lips. Gently at first and then with increasing ardor. His hand moved over her breasts and down the length of her body to the moist lips of her vagina.

"There's nothing crazy about this," Trish said, caressing his scrotum.

Boxer didn't answer. He pressed his face into the warm hollow of her bare stomach.

"Make love to me," Trish whispered, touching the top of his head.

Boxer entered her and began to move.

Trish put her arms around his neck. "Now is it crazy?" she asked.

"No," Boxer answered, "It makes more sense than anything else."

"I'm going to come quickly," Trish said, grabbing his shoulders.

Boxer quickened his movements.

"I'm coming," Trish moaned, thrusting her body against his.

Boxer felt the sudden surge of heat in his groin and uttered a low growl of pleasure.

After a few minutes passed, Trish said, "Now the two of us will be able to sleep.

"Are you going to spend the rest of the night here?" Boxer asked.

"Yes."

"What about William?" Boxer asked.

"He knows I'm with you," Trish answered.

Boxer uttered a deep sigh. "For now, I'm going to pretend

that I didn't hear that," he said, "or we'll never get any sleep."

Trish took hold of his hand and put it on her breast. "I want to sleep with you holding me."

"If that's the case," Boxer said, "then I might as well hold your snatch too." And he placed his other hand between her naked thighs.


As soon as Boxer saw Stark in the hospital lobby, he knew his mother had died.

"I'm sorry," Stark said. "She took a turn for the worse late last night. I was called and I flew up here."

"When did she die?"

"An hour ago," Stark said.

Boxer nodded and asked, "Is it possible for me to see her?"

"Yes. She's still in the room," Stark said.

The two of them walked into a waiting elevator and Stark pressed the button for the eighth floor.

"Have the police got any clues?" Boxer asked.

"None."

Boxer blew his nose and cleared his throat.

"How was the flight back?"

"Good," Boxer answered.

The elevator stopped and the door slid open.

"Fourth room on the left," Stark said, as they left the elevator.

The two of them walked down the hall together, but when they reached the closed door, Stark said, "I'll wait outside for you."

Boxer nodded, opened the door and walked into the room. His mother's face was covered with a sheet. He drew it back and looked down at her. The right side of her face was black and blue. Her lip was cut and there was a bruise on her neck. Boxer bit his lower lip. She was frailer than he remembered and—

A soft knock on the door made him look up.

The door opened and a young man walked in. "I'm Doctor Knight. I took care of your mother."

"Jack Boxer," Boxer said.

"I thought you'd want to know that your mother was suffering from heart disease."

Boxer raised his eyebrows.

"You didn't know?"

Boxer shook his head. "She never said a word."

"According to what I could find out from her and speaking to her own physician, she wasn't even a good candidate for a bypass."

"I never knew," Boxer said in a tight voice.

"I'm sorry to ask you this, but I'd appreciate your permission to do an autopsy."

"Yes, of course," Boxer said.

Doctor Knight produced the necessary form and Boxer signed it.

"Thank you," Knight said and left the room.

Boxer leaned over his mother's body and kissed her gently on the forehead. "The truth is," he whispered, "I never really knew you, Mom. I never did." He pulled the sheet over her face again and walked out of the room.

"I've already said my goodby," Stark said.

The two men rode down to the lobby together and walked outside.

"I could use a drink," Boxer said.

"There's a bar two blocks from here," Stark answered.

"Let's go," Boxer said.

Stark signaled the driver of the limo to follow them.

"Thanks for being here when she needed someone," Boxer said, as they stopped at the corner and waited for the light to change to green.

"She was one of my favorite people," Stark said; then in a much lower voice, he said, "But you already know I loved her."

"Yes, I know that," Boxer answered.

The two of them entered the neighborhood bar and sat down on stools with small backs on them.

Boxer looked around. The whiskey bottles stood in front of a large mirror directly behind the bar. A big screen TV was at the far end of the room.

"A Stoli on the rocks," Boxer said to the barkeep.

"And what are you drinkin'?" the barkeep asked Stark.

"The same."

The barkeep poured the drinks. "You guys with the picture people around here? They're shootin' a movie a couple blocks from here."

"Yeah," Boxer answered. "My friend here wanted to get away from the gawkers."

The barkeep nodded and walked away.

"She asked for you at the very end," Stark said.

Boxer raised his glass and drank. "You know I never really knew her. I never knew what her own dreams were. I guess I never really cared. I was always so close to my dad that she kind of faded into the background. Did you know she had heart trouble?"

"No," Stark said quietly. "I didn't know."

"I'm going to need a few days here to take care of things," Boxer said.

"Take as long as you need."

"It's not going to be that easy, Admiral," Boxer said and he told him about McElroy's upcoming investigation.

"That stupid—"

"I've already called him that a couple of dozen times," Boxer said.

"How did you find out, if he hasn't announced it yet?" Stark asked.

Boxer finished his drink and asked for another before he said, "From a very good source. Just leave it at that."

"We'll just stop it," Stark said.

"Don't try, Admiral. You'll only get full of mud. McElroy is shooting for the White House and this kind of thing will put him in the public's eyes."

"But what does he have?"

"Probably the things that Kinkade gave him. Enough to make it seem that I'm less than fit to command *The Shark*."

"And what do you intend to do about it?" Stark asked.

"Frankly, I don't know," Boxer answered, drinking again. "I don't even know if I'm angry. I guess my feelings run more toward disgust."

"I can't say that I blame you for feeling that way," Stark

said.

"There's one more thing you should know. Comrade Captain Igor Borodine risked his life to warn me that my life was in danger."

"What?"

Boxer explained about the phone call and the subsequent events at the Russian embassy. "You see, Admiral, that man, though he may be my professional enemy, is certainly my personal friend."

"That's for sure," Stark said.

"If I go before McElroy's committee I might be asked to reveal things that would put Borodine in danger and I won't do that, even if it means being relieved of my command."

"I understand that," Stark said.

"There's one more thing," Boxer said, toying with the empty glass.

"Go ahead and tell me."

"I want those men who killed my mother," Boxer said.

"The police—"

"The fucking police won't come up with anything."

"You can't go after them yourself," Stark said. "You don't know how."

"I can't. But Sanchez knows people who can. I'm telling you now, I want those men! That much I owe my mother."

Stark finished his drink. "I understand that too," he said.


To announce his committee's investigation, McElroy summoned the Paris-based contingent of the American press corps to his suite at the Ritz. For the occasion, champagne and a buffet lunch was served.

McElroy wore a blue business suit, white shirt and blue tie. His black shoes were highly polished. He looked very much like a successful business man.

Trish wore a tailored gray suit, with a light pink blouse that was open at the neck. Arm in arm she and McElroy circulated around the room, chatting with each of the reporters.

"It's about that time," McElroy said, looking at his watch.

Trish nodded.

The two of them walked to the far side of the room where a lectern had been set up. McElroy stepped behind it and Trish stood at his side.

"Ladies and gentlemen," McElroy said in a loud voice, "may I please have your attention . . . Please ladies and gentlemen, may I have your attention."

The talking diminished, then ceased altogether.

"I summoned you here this afternoon to inform you that I am returning to Washington tomorrow morning in order to convene a special session of the special investigating committee which I am honored to chair. This special session will investigate the activities of Captain Jack Boxer."

A whisper ran through the room.

"All of you are familiar with his name, as are most Americans. But certain things have been come to light regarding his attitude toward the Soviet Union, things that in my opinion need clarification—"

"Are you trying to tell us that Captain Boxer is soft on the Russians?" a redheaded reporter asked.

"I am only telling you that my committee intends to have certain of the captain's actions explained."

A dozen flash bulbs went off.

"Aren't you treading into areas that are highly classified?" another reporter asked.

"In a democracy everything must be out in the open," McElroy answered.

"Congressman, can you be more specific about the particular incidents that you want Captain Boxer to explain?"

"Not at this time," McElroy answered.

"Congressman, are you aware that Captain Boxer's mother died yesterday?"

"Yes."

"Will that delay your investigation?" the same reporter asked.

"No. Our national security must take precedence over anyone's personal difficulties. Naturally, I extend my condolences to Captain Boxer. But the nation will be better off once it knows that the captain is fit to command *The Shark*."

"Are you saying, Congressman, that he is presently not fit to command *The Shark*?" A woman reporter asked.

"That is what my investigation will determine," McElroy answered.

"Congressman," a reporter shouted, "you wouldn't be using this investigation to put yourself in the public's eye, would you?"

"Ladies and gentlemen," McElroy said, "I have nothing else to say on the matter. I, or other members of my committee or staff will release additional information to the press as the investigation proceeds. I thank all of you for coming." He stepped toward Trish and whispered, "How do you think it went?"

"Well," she answered.

He nodded.

A reporter asked McElroy and Trish to pose together.

"Just one," McElroy said and with his arm around Trish's waist, he smiled into the camera. Then to Trish, he whispered, "I want to speak to you."

"Now?"

"Now," he answered and taking hold of her arm, he steered her through the crowd of reporters into the bedroom.

"Leaving them wasn't very bright," Trish said. "Reporters have a way of sensing things."

"I had no objection to you sleeping with Boxer," McElroy said. "You can sleep with whomever you want."

"Thanks. But I thought that was settled between us about a month after we were married and that was seven years ago."

"But you spent the night with him. You didn't come back until after seven in the morning."

Trish went to the dresser and looked at herself in the mirror. "So I spent the night with him!" she exclaimed.

"It's not to happen again," he said. "It's too dangerous. Too much is at stake."

Trish didn't answer.

"Right now you have him," McElroy said. "In a few months you'll want someone else. Right now I'm the star and if we're to get to the White House that's the way it must be.

176

We must be the typical American couple. We must appear to be very much in love. We—"

"For Christ's sakes, don't tell me what we must be. I know all too fucking well what we must be. Now you go back out there and smile at the reporters. I'll be out in a few minutes."

McElroy looked as if he were about to speak, but Trish spoke first. "Don't say anything. Not another fucking word!"

McElroy turned and left the room.

Trish sat down on the bed, lit a cigarette and puffed at it greedily.


Stark, Williams and Kinkade met in Stark's office. Stark called the meeting to hear what Kinkade had to say about McElroy's investigation.

Stark remained behind his desk. Kinkade and Williams sat facing him.

"The question," Williams said, "is whether or not that damn committee is out to hang Boxer."

"That seems to be the reason for the investigation," Stark said. He looked straight at Kinkade. "How much material did you give McElroy?"

"Everything he asked for," Kinkade answered.

Stark's eyes went to Williams. "Did you know anything about this?"

"No," Williams replied.

"Listen," Kinkade said, "there is a certain area where Boxer has left himself open to questioning. He has acted many times contrary to my orders and often his judgment was opposite from—"

"Kinkade," Stark said, "you have opened up a hornet's nest. I'm not going to permit Boxer to answer one question. He'll plead the 5th, or if necessary, insanity. But I won't let him stand before McElroy and justify his decisions to that political snake."

"Then he'll be charged with contempt of Congress," Kinkade said.

"He'd be better off answering the questions," Williams said.

Stark leaned forward. "So this is your way of getting Boxer, eh?"

"This is my way of getting rid of someone who refuses to play on the team," Kinkade said.

"You made a mistake, Kinkade," Williams said.

"That remains to be seen," Kinkade answered. "But as things stand now you'd better cut orders relieving Boxer of his command."

"No," Stark answered. "I will not do that."

"McElroy intends to make the same request to you in writing and if you do not act on it, he will request the president to act."

"I'll cross that bridge when I come to it," Stark answered sharply. "But let me tell you this, Kinkade, you and I have been on different sides of the fence before, but this puts us in different camps. Understand Kinkade, that's not a threat; it's a fact. From now on you will not mount a single covert operation involving any of my people unless I have full command of the situation and I mean full. None of your people will ever again direct naval personnel. Do you understand that?"

"That too remains to be seen," Kinkade said, standing up.

"Indeed it does," Stark answered. "But I tell you this, Kinkade, I'm not going to let that fucking White House hunter ruin one of my men."

"You've made that very clear," Kinkade said. "Now if you'll excuse me, I have several important things to take care of."

Stark nodded.

"You coming?" Kinkade asked Williams.

"No," Williams answered. "I want to discuss a few things with Stark."

"Suit yourself," Kinkade said and he left the office.

Williams waited until the door was closed before he said, "It's not going to be easy for Boxer to defend himself."

Stark stood up and began to pace. "Yeah, I know it. Many of Boxer's actions could be given the wrong slant and McElroy is smart enough to give them just that."

"Make sure that Boxer has a lawyer there," Williams said.

"I know that. He won't accept one."

178

"Make him. At least make him see the wisdom of having someone who would have the expertise to challenge a question?"

"Right now Boxer is occupied with the death of his mother," Stark answered. "As soon as he returns to Washington, I'll have a long talk with him."

"The best way to stop McElroy is to find out something about him that he wants to hide," Williams said.

"What? He and his wife are the perfect Mister and Mrs. America," Stark answered, lighting a cigar and puffing on it violently.

"It's worth a try."

"Who would you use?"

"I'll give Sanchez a call and have him come up to New York. He'll be sure to know someone who could handle it."

"I'd really like to nail the bastard," Stark growled.

Williams stood up. "Truthfully I didn't think Kinkade would go this far to get rid of Boxer."

"Neither did I," Stark said, "and obviously we underestimated the situation."

Williams nodded and offered Stark his hand, "I'll do what I can to help Boxer."

"Thanks," Stark said, shaking Williams' hand.


The actual funeral took place three days after Boxer had returned. *The Shark*'s entire crew came to the chapel in Brooklyn. Gwen was there and so was Meagan. Since his mother's will stipulated that she be cremated and her ashes scattered at sea, like those of her husband, there was no cortege to the cemetery.

Just before the casket was removed, Stark stood up and clearing his throat, he asked the minister if he could say a few words.

"Of course . . . Please."

Stark moved slowly to the podium and clearing his throat, he said, "Those of you who were here for Captain Boxer's funeral are aware that my relationship with the Boxer family goes back many, many years. But only Jack knows that once long ago I asked the lady, to whom we have come to pay our last respects, to marry me. She chose then Ensign Boxer. In the years between then and now I have seen her go from a young beautiful woman, to a beautiful mother and finally to a beautiful woman of some sixty-five years. And never in all those years had I ever heard her say a harsh word about anyone. She was truly a wonderful lady."

Stark stepped away from the podium, stopped for a moment at the closed casket and kissing the palm of his right hand, he touched the top of the coffin; then he returned to where he had previously sat.

Cynthia spent the night with Boxer and the following day the two of them flew down to Washington for Redfern's funeral in a small cemetery, not far from where the Redferns lived.

Again all of *The Shark*'s crew was there and this time it was DeVargas, who came forward at the grave side and looking straight at Sue-Ann, he said, "The words don't come easy for me. But no man here owes more to the major than I do. I would have spent my years in service in prison, if it weren't for the major. He saw something in me that I didn't even know was there. He gave me a sense of respect for myself and for the Corps. For all that he gave me, I can never repay him. But with your permission Mrs. Redfern, I'd like very much to name my firstborn son after him?"

"Yes, of course," Sue-Ann said.

DeVargas saluted her and called the rifle squad from *The Shark* to attention. Moments later seven rounds were fired in quick succession; then taps were played as the sealed casket was lowered into the grave.


Boxer returned to New York to dispose of his mother's belongings and to take care of legal matters.

The day Boxer went to the family lawyer, he was informed that he was now worth in excess of three million dollars.

"You have a right to use the money any way you want," the lawyer said.

"For the moment," Boxer answered, "I can't think of

anything I'd want to use it for. But if I do, I'll notify you."

"There's no need to do that. The bank will take care of it."

Boxer thanked the bald-headed man and cabbed it back to his mother's house, where he found Sanchez waiting for him in a hired limo.

"You called this morning and said you wanted to see me," Sanchez said.

"Thanks for coming," Boxer said, opening the front door.

"I have some other business here later this evening," Sanchez said. "So I decided to fly up early."

"Drink?" Boxer asked.

"Something with ice in it," Sanchez answered. "It must be ninety-five outside."

"Something like that," Boxer said, pouring ginger ale over ice. "I'll turn on the air-conditioning. It will cool down soon." He gave Sanchez the glass and led the way into the living room. "Have a seat," he said.

Sanchez sat down on the couch. "What are you going to do with the house?"

"I haven't decided yet, but I'll probably sell it," Boxer said, in between sips from his glass.

"You should get a good price for it," Sanchez commented.

"Julio, I want your people to find the men who killed my mother," Boxer said.

"Then what?"

"I'll make that decision then," Boxer said.

"What do the cops say?" Sanchez asked.

"They're working on it."

"I'll try to find them," Sanchez said.

Boxer nodded. "Thanks Julio," he said with a nod. "Thanks."


Two days after Sanchez's visit, Boxer returned to Washington. He had dinner with Cynthia in a small, Italian restaurant and told her that he wasn't going to stay with her.

She said nothing.

"I'm not going to be very good company for a while," Boxer said.

"I didn't expect you to entertain me," she answered.

"I know that. But how do you think I'm going to be with this investigation coming up?"

Cynthia shrugged. "I can't force you to do what you've already made up your mind not to do."

Boxer reached across the table and squeezed her hand.

"I'm going to ask you a blunt question, Jack," Cynthia said.

"Ask."

"What are you going to do when you want to get laid?"

He hesitated for a moment. "Blunt answer, all right?"

"Blunt answer," she repeated.

"Probably call you," Boxer said.

"And do I have the same privilege when I want to be fucked, or am I being fucked here and now at this table, without my thighs being spread and your cock inside of me?" Her voice was tight with anger.

Boxer didn't answer.

"This time I really thought we had a relationship going."

"We did."

"Past tense."

"I don't want—"

"It can't always be what you want."

"I know that."

"Then why don't you act as if you know it," Cynthia challenged.

"Because now—"

She stood up. "I don't want any explanations," she said. "None . . . Don't call me, Jack. Once and for all, get out of my life." And sobbing she ran from the table into the street.

Boxer uttered a deep sigh, dropped two twenty dollar bills on the table and, aware that every one in the place was looking at him, he left the restaurant.


Two hours later, Boxer checked into the hotel he always stayed at when he was in Washington. The desk clerk handed him a letter and a phone message.

The letter found its way via the American embassy in

Paris to Boxer's hotel in Washington.

Boxer examined the outside of the letter. There was no return address on it and the writing didn't look familiar. He looked at the phone message. It was from Trish. All it said was: See you soon. Because it wasn't signed, he knew it was from her.

Boxer went up to his room, opened the letter and began to read it:

Dear Comrade Captain Boxer:

I was informed of your loss this morning and wish to extend my sincerest condolences to you and other members of your family. I too have elderly parents and your loss has reminded me of my obligation to them. Though I write frequently, I never seem to have the time to visit. I shall make the time.

It was a pleasure to see you in Paris and I hope that at some future date our meeting can be as peaceful.

By now you know the body of Major Redfern was turned over to Senator Ross and the major's wife in Paris as planned and not in East Germany. I had the opportunity to meet Senator Ross and Mrs. Redfern. Both were charming.

I remain your friend,

Comrade Captain Igor Borodine

Boxer knew the risk Borodine had to have taken in order to send it. He put the letter down and clearing the tightness in his throat, he said aloud, "I owe you one, friend. I owe you one." Then for the first time since his mother's death he buried his face in his hands and wept.

# 15

By the middle of September McElroy's committee, consisting of himself, four other congressmen and eight aides, began their hearings. The sessions were conducted behind closed doors, in a windowless room in the Capitol.

Boxer and Seth Talbert, his lawyer, sat at a table directly in front of the committee.

McElroy opened the hearings. "The purpose of this committee is basically a simple one," he said. "Given the tensions between the United States and the Soviet Union, we cannot afford to have less than an absolute commitment from any individual who serves the country. It is our purpose to explore the—"

"Mister Chairman," Talbert interrupted, "will you define what you mean by absolute?" Talbert was a very tall and very thin man. He spoke softly, but there was no mistaking that he came from New York.

"Total."

"Meaning?" Talbert asked.

"Absolute obedience to orders."

"Anything else?" Talbert asked, scribbling a few lines on the pad in front of him.

"The willingness to destroy the enemy whenever the opportunity presents itself."

"One more question, Mister Chairman," Talbert said.

"Yes, what is it?" McElroy asked unable to mask his annoyance.

"Are the Soviets your enemy?"

"They are the enemy of every American."

"That I take it means yes."

"It does," McElroy answered.

Talbert nodded. "A moment longer, Congressman, and I'll be finished."

"When you're finished, Mister Talbert, maybe I could begin," McElroy quipped.

The other members of the committee snickered.

"Patience Congressman, patience. So you're a good American and as such you should shoot the first Russian you see. But Mister Congressman, you have not done that. And yet you expect others to do it?"

"Those who follow the flag—"

"You mean are in the military?"

"Please, Congressman McElroy, I would and I'm sure the other people in this room would prefer less euphemistic language. We're simple folk here."

This time Talbert's comment brought forth laughter.

McElroy flushed. "The military then," he said.

Talbert nodded and let him finish his opening statement without further interruptions. But while McElroy was speaking, he leaned close to Boxer and said, "All of it won't be as easy as this was."

Boxer didn't answer.

The hearing was adjourned after McElroy had one of the other congressmen read into the minutes of the hearing a list of particular actions which the committee wanted Boxer to explain. Some of them involved the Russians and some did not. When the reading was finished, the congressman asked, "Does Captain Boxer wish to make any comment now?"

Boxer was about to say something, when Talbert stood up and said, "He does not. But he reserves the right to comment on everything that has just been made part of the record of this hearing any time during the course of these proceedings."

"Granted," McElroy said.

"Let the secretary record it as such," Talbert said.

"Secretary," McElroy said, "will you please record Captain Boxer's request as having been granted by the chair."

"Thank you Congressman McElroy."

The session came to an end.

On the way out, Talbert asked Boxer if he could logically defend his actions in all the circumstances that the committee intends to investigate.

"No," Boxer answered.

"Well then, we'll have to find the logic, won't we?"

Boxer looked at him.

"Didn't anyone tell you that you and I are going to be living together until the trial — for that's exactly what it is — is over and you're acquitted."

"Acquitted of what?"

"Treason," Talbert answered, as they stepped out into the hazy sunshine. "Now let's have some lunch."

For the next two weeks, McElroy made Boxer look more and more suspect. He never openly said that Boxer might be a Russian agent but he implied it several times a day.

Kinkade was his star witness.

"Then what you are saying, Mister Kinkade, if I heard you correctly, was that Captain Boxer on several different occasions either did not follow your orders, or acted beyond the scope of your orders."

"That is true."

"And on one particular occasion, during a mission, Captain Boxer became sexually involved with a woman —"

"Objection, Mister Chairman," Talbert said, raising his hand. "The mission had already been completed and since that is the case, then the captain's sexual conduct did not in any way endanger the mission."

"A mission is not completed until *The Shark* returns to home port," McElroy said. "Isn't that so, Mister Kinkade?"

"Yes," Kinkade answered.

"I have a question, Mister Chairman," Talbert said.

"I would like to clarify your position on the matter of Captain Boxer's sexual conduct, which by now you have explored to a considerable degree with other witnesses and are about to delve still further into it with Mister Kinkade —"

"Your question, please."

"Sorry, I was following your style, Mister Chairman, and just got carried away."

McElroy glared at him.

Talbert waited until the laughter subsided and said, "Will your investigation show that there is a direct relationship between Captain Boxer's sexual behavior and his political beliefs?"

"Why—"

"Prove that, Mister Chairman, then you certainly endanger many of your political colleagues."

Again there was laughter in the room.

"I intend to prove, Mister Talbert, that Captain Boxer abandoned his command in favor of the bed."

"The record clearly shows the number of hours that Captain Boxer was on the bridge of the *Tecumseh*," Talbert answered.

"Mr. Talbert," McElroy said, "we are dealing with a flawed man and—"

Boxer was on his feet. "McElroy, I told you once and I'll tell you again: you're a horse's ass." And he stomped out of the room.

"I apologize for the captain's outburst," Talbert said, as he ran after Boxer and grabbing him by the arm said, "Congratulations, you just became a horse's ass too."

Boxer shook his hand off. "I don't have to sit there and listen to that shit."

"Yes, you do, if you want to command *The Shark* again," Talbert said.

"I saved that woman's life," Boxer said. "She tried to kill herself because she was going back to face several years in prison. She came to me because—" Boxer threw up his hands. "What the hell is the use of trying to explain something like that?"

Talbert put his arm around Boxer's shoulder. "Don't try. That's what I'm there for. Now will you go back?"

"Not today," Boxer said. "I need some air. I need a drink. It's Friday and I've had a bellyful."

"Okay," Talbert said, removing his arm, "I'll tell the committee that you respectfully ask the session be adjourned until Monday morning. But that will give McElroy a win by default."

Boxer shrugged. "If I go back there and he says something else that rubs me the wrong way, I just might punch the son-of-a-bitch out."

Talbert sighed. "Okay," he said, "we'll let him have this one."

"Thanks."

"Go somewhere and rest for the weekend," Talbert said. "McElroy and his team are just getting warmed up."

"I just might do that," Boxer said. "See you Monday morning." And he walked slowly down the hallway to the main lobby of the Capitol building.

Outside, Boxer stopped to put on his sunglasses; then he began to walk. The day was hot and humid. He removed his jacket and carried it over his arm; then he loosened his tie and opened his collar button.

There wasn't any doubt in his mind that he was at his lowest and that he was beginning to give some thought to resigning. There wasn't any reason for him to undergo the humiliation of having to sit and listen to McElroy or any or the other congressmen question his actions.

Suddenly Boxer decided to leave Washington for the weekend and drive down to Emerald Island, on the coast of North Carolina. He hailed a cab and returned to the hotel, where he stopped at the desk to see if there were any messages for him.

There weren't any.

Boxer asked the clerk to make the necessary arrangements for a car. "Something in the way of a small wagon will do fine," he said. "I'll take it as soon as possible and return it Sunday evening."

"It might be difficult to get something for the weekend on such short notice. But I'll try."

Boxer thanked him and said, "I'll be in the bar."

"I'll phone you as soon as I have something," the clerk said.

Boxer nodded and walked away from the desk. This just wasn't one of his good times. He entered the bar and settled down on a stool.

The barkeeper recognized him and said, "Vodka on the rocks, Captain?"

Boxer nodded and took a pretzel stick from a nearby bowl. He was trying to decide what to do if he couldn't rent a car, when the barkeep said, "There's a phone call for you, Captain."

"Where—"

The barkeep brought the cordless phone to him.

"Boxer here," he said.

"You're difficult to reach," the woman on the other end answered.

Boxer didn't immediately recognize the voice.

"I'm free this weekend," the woman said. "Are you?"

"Who are you?"

The woman laughed lightly. "Forgotten so soon," she mocked. "And I thought I meant more than the sun and the stars to you."

"Trish?" he guessed.

"You win the woman if you want her," Trish said.

Except for one telephone message, he hadn't heard from her since he had been in Paris.

"Me for the weekend, are you game enough for that?" she challenged.

"Can you meet me at my hotel," Boxer said. "I'm trying to rent a car. I want to drive out to the North Carolina coast for the weekend."

"We'll use my car," Trish said. "But that's too far to go. Too much time will be wasted driving when it could be better used in bed."

"Do you have a better suggestion?"

"The eastern shore of Virginia. It's closer and there's a motel on the other side of the—"

"I know the one," Boxer said.

"Agreed we go there?"

"Agreed," Boxer answered.

"Pick you up in a half hour," Trish said and hung up.

Boxer switched the phone off and set it down on the bar. He picked up another pretzel stick and munched at it. He wasn't sure that Trish was what he needed. But he recognized the fact that he needed someone.

"Ready for your drink?" the barkeep asked.

"Ready," Boxer answered.

Trish arrived fifteen minutes late. "Traffic," she complained, as Boxer put his carryall in the car and settled down next to her.

"You want to drive?" she asked.

"No, I want to sleep," he said, aware that she was well tanned, dressed in a white pants suit and was wearing a red headband to keep her long blond hair in place.

"The seat tilts back," she said, easing away from the curb and entering the stream of traffic.

Boxer adjusted the back of the seat and closed his eyes. "If you get tired," he said, "I'll drive."

"I'll let you know," she said.

Boxer didn't answer. He could smell her rose scented perfume and liked it. After a while, he sensed they were on the highway, but he had no desire to open his eyes and check whether or not they were.

"Are you sleeping?" Trish asked.

"No."

"Mind if I turn on the radio?"

"No."

The sound of a woman singing filled the car.

Boxer didn't pay too much attention to the song, but he heard Trish hum along with it.

"I'm glad we're together," Trish said.

Boxer pretended to be asleep. He felt her hand glide lightly over his head.

"I know you're not sleeping," she said.

"I'm trying to," he answered.

"You shouldn't continue to call William a horse's ass," she said.

Boxer sat up and readjusted the seat. "How did you know that?"

"I listened to the tape," she said.

Boxer fished out his pipe, filled and lit it. "That woman was on her way back to go to prison," Boxer said and he told her the whole story, including how she had been murdered.

"Was the killer ever found?" she asked.

"I don't know," Boxer lied. He wasn't about to tell her that he had one of Sanchez's men take the killer out.

Trish fell silent.

Boxer moved catty corner and looked at her. She certainly was a beautiful woman.

They were on the Chesapeake Bay Bridge when Trish said, "Even with the story that you told me, you can't justify having the woman in your bed to the committee."

"I won't try," Boxer responded. "But I really don't want to talk about the investigation. I want to relax and—"

"Fuck," she said, looking at him for a moment."

"Yes."

She smiled and said, "So do I, Jack. So do I."

They checked in the American Motel at two thirty in the afternoon. They had an upstairs room in the rear of the motel that gave them a beautiful view of the bay, which was separated from the motel by a large expanse of very green grass.

Trish drew the shade and pulled back the bedspread. "I'm not shy," she said. "I want to screw now."

"Okay, but you'll have to earn it," Boxer answered.

"And what does that mean?"

"Use your imagination," he said.

"Like this," she said, slowly unbuttoning her jacket.

"What you do is up to you," Boxer said.

Trish removed the jacket. Her breasts were bare and as tan as the rest of her. She looked down at them and then at Boxer, smiled at him and began to gently play with her already hard nipples.

"Here," she said in a low voice, "They're ready for you to suck on." Moving to where he was standing, she placed her hands on each breast. "This one first," she said, offering him the right breast.

Boxer put his mouth to the warm nipple and moved his tongue over it.

"Suck on it," Trish said. "Ah, yes . . . Hard like that. Now the other one."

With the nipple of her breast in his mouth, Boxer ran his hands over her bare back and down to her still clothed bottom.

She moved away. "Don't be greedy," she said. "Eventually you'll have all of it." She undid the top button of her slacks and unzipped them. Then she eased them down to the floor and stepped out of them. She wore thin white briefs. "Now there are several things my imagination tells me I could do," Trish said.

"I can believe that," Boxer answered.

"I'll try this," she said and moving close to him, she took hold of the zipper tab and pulled it down; then she reached into his shorts and freed his penis.

Boxer tried to embrace her.

She stepped away. "Since I have to use my imagination, you can't touch me."

"That wasn't part of the—"

"It is now," she told him.

"Your move," Boxer answered.

She moved closer to him and taking hold of his penis, she slowly rubbed its head over her briefs; then over to the warm skin above her blond love mound and finally she inserted it between her thighs and held it there.

"Now you can play with my tits," she said.

Boxer put his hands on her breasts and gently squeezed them.

Trish began to roll her hips.

Boxer felt the movement along the shaft of his penis.

"How's my imagination working?" Trish asked, playing the fingers of her right hand over his scrotum.

"Not bad for an amateur," Boxer answered.

"If there's one thing I'm a pro at without being a pro in the business sense," she said, "it's fucking."

Boxer didn't answer. He bent his head down and sucked each hard nipple again.

"Take your clothes off," she said, letting go of his penis and stepping back a few paces.

Boxer stripped.

Trish slid her briefs off and stepped out of them; then she climbed into the bed.

Boxer started to follow her.

"Not yet," she told him.

"But why—"

Trish was moving her body slowly and sinuously, as if she were dancing. Then she began to slide her hands over herself, touching her breast, moving between her thighs and over the cheeks of her buttocks; then between her thighs.

Boxer wanted to join her and started toward the bed.

"No," she said. "Not yet. Just watch." She splayed her naked thighs and caressed their insides.

His own excitement mounting, Boxer watched her spread the lips of her vagina with one hand and played with her clit with the other.

"I thought you'd like to watch me do this," she said in a tight gaspy voice.

Boxer nodded.

She smiled and closed her eyes. "Should I tell you what's the most erotic thing I can think now?" she asked.

"Tell me!"

"Your tongue moving on my clit," she answered.

"Is that what you want?" he teased.

"For openers," she said. "Here, I'll make it easy for you." And she moved sideways so that the lower part of her torso was off the bed. "All you have to do is kneel down between my open thighs."

"Since you started the operation," Boxer said, "you finish it."

"Bastard, I always knew you were a bastard."

"Hey, I'm going along with your imagination — the no touching rule. Remember that rule was your idea, not mine."

"I withdraw it."

"Now when it suits you," Boxer said.

Undulating, she diddled herself more vigorously.

"I can see you need help," Boxer said.

She answered with a low moaning sound.

Boxer knelt between her naked thighs and kissed the warm inside of one and then the other.

Trish began to tremble. "Do it," she pleaded. "Eat me!"

Boxer placed his mouth against the wet lips of her vagina. "That's it!" Trish gasped, pushing herself against his mouth.

"How's that for openers?" he asked.

She grabbed hold of his head and pulled it against her.

Boxer tongued her clit. She tasted slightly sour and smelled of roses.

"I can hold back long enough for you to come inside of me," Trish said.

Boxer stood up.

Trish reached back and grabbing hold of a pillow, she put it under her buttocks. "Now come into me," she said, rolling up on her back.

Boxer entered her.

She uttered a loud sigh of pleasure and wrapped her bare thighs around his back.

He put his lips to hers. They were soft, warm and yielding. Their tongues met. Boxer put his hands over her breasts. He began to move inside of her.

"Go deep," she whispered. "Go deep." She stroked his scrotum; then teased his bung hole.

Boxer kissed her nipples and gently scored them with his tongue.

Trish thrust her pelvis up. "Faster . . . Go faster . . . Oh my God!" She raked his back with her nails. Her thighs tightly grabbed Boxer's back. Suddenly she uttered a wordless cry. Her body tensed; then went limp; tensed again and shuddered.

Boxer climaxed with enormous intensity. Everything seemed to dissolve. The only thing that seemed to matter was the woman beneath him. He buried his face in the hollow between her heaving breasts.

Trish sighed. "Next time," she whispered, caressing his face, "I'll give you head that will blow your mind."

"Promise?" he asked, beginning to lift himself off her.

"Don't go . . . Stay on me."

Boxer eased himself down on her again.

"I promise," Trish said, answering her question.

She ran her finger through his hair. "I am happy to be with you," she said.

"So am I," Boxer answered.

Trish was silent for several moments; then in a whisper, she asked, "Do you think we could be lovers?"

He put his hands over her breasts. "I thought we were."

"I mean, not for just a fuck," Trish said. "Something more."

"Could you handle something more?" Boxer asked.

She nodded; then asked, "Could you?"

"I'd be willing to find out," Boxer answered.

Trish wrapped her arms around his neck. "You'd be easy to love," she said.

"You'd have to try it, before you could say that," Boxer said, bending over and kissing her lips.

"Then I'll try it," she whispered.


On Monday morning at nine o'clock, Boxer and Talbert were back in the committee room, waiting for McElroy to begin the session.

"You look as if you got some sun," Talbert commented to

Boxer.

"I spent the weekend on Virginia's eastern shore," Boxer answered.

Talbert nodded. "You look better than you did Friday. Ah, here's McElroy. He doesn't look too good."

Boxer made no comment.

McElroy began the session by letting the committee hear several sections of tape which were recorded when Bush revealed that he had planted a bomb on the hull of the *Q-21*.

As soon as the tape was finished, McElroy asked, "Captain Boxer, was that your voice on the tape?"

"Yes."

"And the other voice was Captain Bush?"

"Yes."

"Will you tell the committee, what transpired immediately prior to the conversation they just heard?"

"Captain Borodine and I congratulated each other on having survived an undersea storm."

"And what did you do during that conversation?" McElroy answered.

"I had gold transferred to the *Q-Twenty One*."

"Why?"

"Borodine had helped *The Shark* to survive and in my opinion deserved something for—"

"But you had fought him for the gold and had won."

"Yes."

"Did you have the authority to give that gold to Captain Borodine?"

"No."

"Did you contact anyone at your headquarters and ask for permission—"

"I used my own authority," Boxer said. "Captain Borodine—"

"That gold belonged to the United States, Captain. It was not within your authority to do anything with it, except to return to your home port with it."

"That is your opinion," Boxer answered.

"Now to the real heart of this investigation," McElroy said, "will you please tell this committee why you attempted to contact Captain Borodine to warn him—"

"That's right," Boxer said, leaping to his feet. "That's right. To warn him that a bomb was planted on the hull of his boat. That is not the way I repay a kindness."

"But Captain Bush had received his orders from the highest authority in the organization."

"Kinkade was a fool to issue that order," Boxer said.

"So you took it upon yourself to warn Captain Borodine."

"Yes."

"And that led you directly into a Russian trap, didn't it?"

"No."

"A trap no doubt set by Captain Borodine."

"He had nothing to do with it."

"And how do you know that?" McElroy asked.

"He told me," Boxer answered.

"Where?"

"In Paris."

"And you believe him?"

"More than I would you," Boxer shot back.

"Had you been in communication with Captain Borodine before your meeting with him in Paris?"

"You know I have and you also know the reason why," Boxer answered.

"Wouldn't you be more comfortable if you were seated?" McElroy asked smoothly.

Boxer sat down.

"He has you on the ropes," Talbert whispered. "Answer his questions with a simple yes or no. Don't give your opinions."

"Captain Boxer, isn't it your sworn duty to destroy the Q-Twenty One?" McElroy asked.

Boxer looked at Talbert and whispered. "I can't answere that with a simple yes or no."

"Captain," McElroy pressed, "I asked you a question and—" An aide came up behind McElroy and tapped him on the shoulder. "Excuse me," he said and gave his attention to the aide, who bent over him and whispered something to him. McElroy nodded and turning to Boxer and Talbert, he said, "I have been summoned to my office for a few minutes. The committee is in recess for next half hour." And he stood up and left the table.

"What the hell do you think that's all about?" Boxer asked.

"I wouldn't even want to guess," Talbert said. "Let's get out of here and get cup of coffee."

"I didn't do myself any good, did I?" Boxer asked, as they left the room.

"No good at all," Talbert answered.

Boxer shook his head. He was beginning to think about asking Stark to let him resign.

McElroy went straight to his office. Kinkade and a man he didn't know were waiting for him.

"This is Mister Slattery," Kinkade said to William.

"Congressman," Slattery said, shaking his hand.

McElroy sat down behind his desk. "Whatever it is," he said, "it must be important, or you wouldn't be here."

"It concerns Trish," Kindade said.

McElroy raised his eyebrows.

"Slattery came to me and said he had something that concerns Trish but he wouldn't tell me what it is unless you were present."

"Who are you, Mister Slattery?" McElroy asked.

"Philip Slattery," the man answered.

"What do you do, Mister Slattery?" Kinkade questioned.

"Things . . . like take pictures and make tape recordings," Slattery answered.

McElroy began to sweat. Kinkade knew nothing about his marriage to Trish. There was no reason for him to know.

"Let me show you some pictures," Slattery said, reaching into the pocket inside his jacket and taking out a small envelope. "These are three by fives, but of course they could be blown up." He tossed the envelope on the desk. "Your wife and Captain Boxer," he said.

Kinkade reached for the packet before McElroy could move.

"Those pictures were taken with a camera hidden in the motel room," Slattery said.

Kinkade gasped.

"The tapes are as explicit," Slattery said.

Kinkade tossed the pictures on the desk. "Did you know she was fucking him?"

McElroy glanced at the pictures.

"Well, did you?"

197

"Your granddaughter," McElroy said tightly, "has fucked a great many men. I don't keep track of who she fucks."

"Do you fuck her?" Kinkade shouted, jumping out of his chair. "Do you even sleep in the same bed with her?"

McElroy turned very white. "What I do or do not do, is none of your business."

Kinkade turned on Slattery. "Blackmail, eh? How much—"

Slattery held up his hand. "End this investigation," he said, "or these pictures and the tapes will find their way to the press."

McElroy's jaw went slack.

"Who sent you?" Kinkade yelled. "Who?"

Slattery smiled. "End the investigation today, Congressman."

"He can't," Kinkade said.

"If he doesn't, he's finished," Slattery said flatly. "I want a yes or no now, Congressman. What will it be?"

McElroy dropped his head. "Yes," he mumbled.

Boxer and Talbert walked down the steps of the Capitol together.

"I don't understand why McElroy should recess the committee indefinitely," Boxer said.

"Neither do I," Talbert said. "But I can guess it had something to do with him going back to his office. But it's over and that's all that should concern you."

"Thanks for all you did," Boxer said, offering his hand.

"I didn't really do anything, Captain," Talbert said. "You just got lucky."

"Have a drink with me to celebrate?"

"Sure, why not."

"There's a place a few streets from here," Boxer said.

Talbert nodded. "I sure would like to know what made McElroy back away. He had you just where he wanted you."

Boxer nodded.

"Would you do those things over again?" Talbert asked.

"Yes," Boxer answered. "I couldn't do anything else."

Talbert smiled. "I would have been disappointed if you had said anything else, or had hesitated before you answered. The drinks are on me, Captain."

"We'll alternate," Boxer said. "I'll buy the first round and you

198

the second; then I'll take the third."

"By then I'll be under the proverbial table," Talbert laughed.

"Then I'll have the opportunity to help you," Boxer said, "and that would be a real pleasure."

It was ten o'clock at night. Boxer entered the White Deer, a cocktail lounge two miles west of Leesburg, Virginia. He scanned the room and spotted Trish in a booth. He walked quickly to where she was.

She lifted her face.

He bent over her and kissed her on the lips.

"Thanks for coming," she said, taking a cigarette from her golden case.

Boxer sat down, picked up a book of matches, struck one and held it out to Trish. "You said it was important," he said.

"It is," she answered, blowing smoke toward the ceiling.

"I have something important to tell you too," Boxer said.

"I know," Trish answered.

Boxer raised his eyebrows.

"The investigation is over," she said.

Boxer smiled. "I guess he tells you everything."

"Let's have something to drink," Trish said.

"That's okay with me."

"I'd like something to eat," Trish said. "I haven't had dinner yet."

Boxer signaled one of the cocktail waitresses.

"I'll have a very dry Martini and cornbeef sandwich on rye," Trish said.

"Vodka on the rocks and that cornbeef sandwich sounds like a good idea," Boxer said.

Trish waited until the waitress was gone before she said, "William was forced to call off the investigation." She stubbed out the cigarette. "You didn't know that, did you?"

Boxer shook his head. "He left the committee room for a while and when he returned he said that because new information had come to light the investigation was suspended until further notice. That was it; then he left the committee room again."

Trish leaned back and closed her eyes.

At that instant Boxer wanted her more than he ever had before. He reached across the table and taking hold of her hands, he said, "After we eat let's go to a motel."

"We were followed," Trish said, opening her eyes.

"Followed here?"

She shook her head. "On the weekend."

Boxer let go of her hands. "You mean—"

"This is what I mean," she said, opening her bag and removing an envelope from it. "Photographs," she said.

Boxer took the envelope from her, opened it and looked at the pictures. "There must have been at least three different cameras involved," he said.

"There are tapes too," Trish said.

"Do you have them?"

"William does."

Boxer put the pictures back in the envelope and returned it to Trish.

"A man by the name of Slattery threatened to give the pictures and the tapes to the press if the investigation wasn't terminated," Trish explained, taking another cigarette. "My grandfather saw those pictures too," she said.

"You smoke too much," Boxer said.

"I know. Now will you please light my cigarette," Trish answered. "Thanks . . . Do you know a Mister Slattery?"

Boxer shook his head.

"I didn't think so," Trish said.

"I had no idea—"

The cocktail waitress returned with the drinks. "Your sandwiches will be right out," she said.

Boxer nodded, picked up his vodka and drank.

"William and Grandpa think that Slattery is working for the Russians," Trish said.

Boxer gagged on his drink and started to cough.

"William at least is sure of it," she said.

When he could speak, Boxer said, "He's way off base . . . way off."

"I told them that," Trish said. "But it won't do any good with William. But I think my grandfather will eventually realize that the Russians had nothing to do with it."

"Kinkade—sorry, but that's the way I refer to him—hates my guts. Now, that he has seen those pictures and heard the tapes, he must want me dead."

Trish nodded. "He does."

Boxer drank more of the vodka; then he asked, "Where does all of this leave us?"

"William wants a divorce," Trish said matter of factly.

"And what do you want?"

Without hesitation, she answered, "You."

Boxer nodded.

"But not in marriage, at least not right away," Trish said. "We can live together. But I don't want to be married."

"If that's what you want, that's the way it will be."

The cocktail waitress brought their sandwiches. "Will there be anything else?" she asked.

"Another one of these," Boxer said, holding up his empty glass.

"I'll have another martini too," Trish said.

"What's your grandfather going to say when he finds out we're living together?"

"He'll be furious," Trish answered, picking up a half of the sandwich and biting into it. "But," she added, after she had swallowed, "he'd finally say, 'As long as you know what you're doing and you're happy doing it, I don't care.' You know, he really is a dear man."

"He's not a dear man to me," Boxer growled, "and never will be one. That's something you have to realize from the very beginning."

"He couldn't understand how I 'could do those things'—as he called what he saw in the photographs—with you."

"And what did you answer him?"

"The truth," Trish said. "I told you that I was physically attracted to you from the moment I first met you and that you're a skilled and gentle lover."

"He must have loved that."

"He didn't answer," Trish said.

For a while both of them concentrated on eating their sandwiches.

Trish finished hers first and said, "That was really good and I was very hungry."

"You can have the other half of mine," Boxer said.

"I'll split it with you," Trish said.

Boxer cut the remainder of his sandwich and put half of it in Trish's plate. "I'm sorry you were embarrassed by the photographs, but I'm damn glad the investigations are over. Your husband, as Mister Talbert put it, had me on the ropes."

"I wasn't at all embarrassed by the pictures themselves. What bothered me was that a stranger saw me naked and doing things with someone I care about and heard me say things that I haven't said to any other man, even if—Well, you know what I mean, don't you?"

"Yes, I know what you mean," Boxer answered.

"Do you still want to go to a motel when we finish eating?" Trish asked.

"Yes," Boxer answered, reaching across the table to caress her face.

She took hold of his hand and put the palm against her lips. Then she whispered, "I'm glad the investigation is over too."

Boxer nodded. "I know that," he said.

# 16

"Depth two thousand one seven five feet," Borodine read the numbers as they came up on the Digital Depth Indicator. "Bottom coming up fast," he said, looking at the Underwater Imaging Screen.

Immediately to his right was Doctor Louisa Suslov, one of the four geologists aboard the *Sea Savage*. Borodine could smell her lavender perfume. Clustered on his left were the three other geologists: Dr. Alexander Kassov, a short man, heavy-set, jovial, with a pock-marked face; Dr. Gregory Chekurov, a tall, bald headed man, who could almost always be found in his cabin reading; and Dr. Vladimir Travkin, a man about the same age as Borodine, who spent most of his time mooning after Dr. Suslov.

From previous experience, Borodine knew that one of the four was, in addition to being a geologist, a KGB officer. But he had no idea which one it might be, though now and then, for no particular reason, he suspected it was Dr. Chekurov.

"Level indicator, going to null," Borodine said. "Will you look at those rock formations!" he exclaimed, turning his attention to the UWIS.

"Just as we predicted," Chekurov said. "Comrade Captain, you are looking at formations made as recently as a thousand years ago, or less."

"I'm impressed," Borodine said. "Now which one of you has the grid chart?"

Kassov produced it.

Borodine laid it out on the console and studied it for a moment or two.

"The cave has to be in the immediate area," Kassov said. "If we search—"

Suddenly a red light on the console began to flash.

Borodine lifted the phone, pressed a button and listened.

"Comrade Captain," the communications officer said, "a priority ten message is coming in from Moscow."

"Roger that," Borodine said. "I'll be there in three minutes. Viktor take the CON. Continue on present course."

"Aye, aye Comrade Captain," Viktor answered.

Borodine hurried from the bridge to the Communications Room.

"The decoding station is ready," the communications officer said, handing the message sheet to Borodine.

"Nothing else coming in?"

"Nothing, Comrade Captain," the officer answered.

Borodine nodded and went into a closed off section of the area. He switched on the light, sat down at the decoding computer and turned it on and began to type in Priority Ten.

The computer asked him to identify himself.

He typed in his name, rank and serial number.

The computer asked for his code number.

He typed in 2-22-29.

The computer responded with: INSERT MESSAGE.

Borodine typed several lines of numbers and letters. Even as he worked the first words came up on the screen.

Date. Oct. 1, 1995. Moscow. Priority 10 Message For Comrade Captain Borodine's eyes only. Terminate present mission. Make for Lat 5° N, Long 170° East search for the GM Frigate *Storozhevoy*. Contact Moscow when said vessel is found. Proceed at flank speed. This is a condition red situation. End of message.

Borodine pressed the STORE key. The message left the screen and went into a special file that only he, or someone else with the proper ID could access. In the event that he was killed or badly disabled, Viktor would be that person.

Borodine turned off the computer, stood up and switching off the light he left the decoding area. "If you hear any unusual transmissions," Borodine said to the communications officer, "let me know immediately."

"Aye, aye, Comrade Captain," the officer answered.

Before returning to the bridge, Borodine went to his quarters and sat down. He needed to think for a few minutes. The *Storozhevoy* was one of the newest ships in the fleet. She and several other vessels were on a routine mission in the south Pacific. She was equipped with latest surface to air missile systems and the most sophisticated anti-submarine devices available. Her weapons systems were capable of destroying several submarines at the same time.

Borodine took a cigarette from a pack on his desk, lit it and blew smoke from his nose. He hoped that the condition red did not mean war.

He stubbed out the cigarette in the ash tray and returned to the bridge. The four scientists were still there.

"I have the CON," he said to Viktor.

"Aye, aye, Comrade Captain," Viktor answered.

Borodine sat down at the console. He decided to break the news to the four doctors by announcing to the entire crew that the mission had been scratched. He switched on the MC. "All hands . . . All hands," he said. "now hear this . . . This is the captain . . . We are terminating this mission . . . We are terminating this mission."

"I don't believe it!" Louisa exclaimed.

The three men were speechless.

"Orders from Moscow," Borodine said.

"A message must be sent —" Dr. Kassov began.

Borodine shook his head. "Our status has been changed. No message can be sent unless it is of military nature. And until further notice, all of you are banned from the bridge."

"But what has happened?" Dr. Chekurov asked.

"Nothing that either of you have to concern yourselves about. I would appreciate it very much if all of you would leave the bridge now. Thank you."

Borodine waited until the bridge was cleared; then he dialed the latitude and the longitude into the NAVCOMP. He switched on the MC again. "Stand by all hands, we're going to five zero

zero feet." He changed the setting on the COMCOMP. Then he keyed the EO. "Give me flank speed," he said.

"Going to flank speed," the EO answered.

Borodine watched the DDRO. They were passing through the two thousand foot level. He checked all systems. There were no malfunction indications.

He motioned Viktor to come closer. "We have a condition red," he said in a low voice.

Viktor's eyes opened wide. "War?"

Borodine shrugged. "I don't know. The message ordered us to a new position." He said nothing about the *Storozhevoy*.

"Are we going to alert status?" Viktor asked.

"Not yet," Borodine answered. "I want to get closer to our destination." He scribbled the latitude and longitude on a piece of paper and handed it to Viktor.

"That's two thousand miles from here!"

Borodine nodded.

"We should be there in fifty hours," Viktor said.

Again Borodine nodded and said, "Destroy that piece of paper."

Viktor turned and fed the scrap of paper into the shredder. "Do you think we are going to war?" he asked.

Borodine made an open gesture with his hands. "Your guess is as good as mine," he answered.

"That's what the men will think once we put them on alert status."

"I can't help that," Borodine said. "But I will delay going to a full alert as long as possible."

"What about our guests?" Viktor asked.

Borodine looked at the DDRO. He switched on the MC. "Coming to five zero zero feet . . . All systems normal," he announced. "Coming to level." He watched the ENI. "Null on ENI. Level at five zero zero feet." He switched off the MC, looked at Viktor and asked, "What about our guests?"

"For one thing, what do we do with them if there is any kind of a situation?"

"They remain with us until we receive instructions from Moscow," Borodine answered.

Viktor smiled. "Which one do you think is KGB?" he asked.

Borodine shrugged. "Chekurov . . . but that's because he looks the part."

"Do you think he'll reveal himself?"

"Probably, when we go to alert status."

The conversation between the two men lapsed and Viktor moved back to his station, while Borodine made another systems check; then he leaned back into the command chair and thought about the message, the more it seemed as if the red condition had something to do with the *Storozhevoy* and not the fact that war was imminent. Perhaps some disaster has occurred aboard the ship, or perhaps some disease had broken out amongst the crew and—

"Comrade Captain," Viktor said, "Doctor Suslov asks permission to speak with you."

"Have her come to the bridge," Borodine said.

"She asked that the conversation take place in your quarters."

Borodine agreed and gave the CON to a junior officer. "Keep an eye on him, Viktor. Make sure he doesn't sink us."

Viktor smiled. "He's too afraid to do anything but breathe and that he's doing sparingly."

Borodine left the bridge and went to his quarters. Dr. Suslov would be the first woman to enter the small room.

A knock at the door brought his attention to it. "Yes?"

"Doctor Suslov to see the Comrade Captain," an escorting seaman said.

"Have her come in," Borodine answered.

The seaman opened the door, stepped back, waited until the doctor was in the room and then he closed the door.

"Please," Boxer said, gesturing to one of the two empty chairs.

"Thank you, Comrade Captain," Suslov said, as she sat down.

Borodine offered her a cigarette, which she accepted. "If you would like coffee, I could have it brought here."

"No thank you," she said with a smile. "The cigarette will do fine. Besides, I drink too much coffee as it is."

"There are very few amenities aboard a boat, even a boat as large as this one," Borodine answered.

She nodded sympathetically.

"Is there anything I can do for you?" Borodine asked.

"To put it bluntly, Comrade Captain, I'm disappointed in you."

Borodine suppressed a smile and managed an, "Oh!"

"Don't you think I and my colleagues should have been informed about the mission's termination before the crew?"

Borodine raised his eyebrows. He would have never guessed she was KGB.

"We are after all the reason why the *Sea Savage* is here," Dr. Suslov said.

"You and your associates may be the reason why we are here," Borodine said, "but the decision to inform everyone aboard the *Sea Savage* at the same time was mine."

"It was a regrettable one," she said, stubbing out her cigarette in the ashtray. "From now on, you will consult with me before you make such decisions." And opening her bag, she withdrew a wallet, showing him her identification.

"Major, eh!" Borodine exclaimed.

"Now if you will be so good as to tell me the contents of the message that canceled the mission," she said.

"That message, Major, was for my eyes only," Borodine said.

"I have the authority—"

Borodine stood up. He was tired of having to deal with KGB agents in any form, whether they were suave men like Colonel Unecha in Paris, or a lovely looking woman like Dr. Suslov. "Before you make a mistake about your authority aboard the *Sea Savage*," Borodine said, "there is only one captain, one authority. I will not consult with you about anything that does not require that consultation."

"And who will determine what requires it and what does not?"

"I will," Borodine said.

"I'm afraid I cannot accept that," she answered.

"You have no other choice."

"Indeed I do, Comrade Captain. You will send a message to Moscow asking for—"

"I will not send a message to Moscow," Borodine said, cutting her short, "and I will not continue this conversation. As long as you are aboard the *Sea Savage* you and all your colleagues are under my command. You do understand what that means?"

"Yes. But I intend to lodge a complaint with your political officer and take the matter to my command when we return."

"I would not expect you to do anything else," Borodine said. "Now, I must return to the bridge."

"Are you dismissing me?" Dr. Suslov asked.

"Yes."

She stood up, looked straight at him and shaking her head, she said, "You have just made a very serious mistake, Comrade Captain Borodine. I will not let this matter pass."

Borodine went to the door, opened it and said to the waiting seaman, "Please escort Doctor Suslov back to her area."

"Aye, aye Comrade Captain Borodine," the seaman said, saluting him.

Borodine returned the salute, and stepped aside to allow Dr. Suslov to leave the cabin. Then he closed the door and returned to the bridge.

"I have the CON," he told the young officer.

"Aye, aye, Comrade Captain," the man answered.

Borodine summoned Viktor and said, "It's Doctor Suslov."

"KGB?"

"Yes."

Viktor gave a low whistle; then he said, "At least she's better looking than most of the others."

"But no less ruthless, I'd be willing to bet."

"You're probably right," Viktor answered.

"Under no circumstance is she to be allowed to send a message to Moscow without my prior approval in writing," Borodine said.

"I'll inform the COMO section."

"Do it immediately," Borodine said, checking the various readings on the COMCOMP. The more he thought about his conversation with Dr. Suslov, the angrier he became with her, with the KGB and with a government that has to maintain a special organization to keep its people under constant surveillance.

Admiral Stark and Williams were in Kinkade's office. He had summoned them an hour earlier and now the three of them were seated at a conference table.

"We have something very strange happening," Kinkade said. "Reports have reached us from Russia that there has been a mutiny aboard the *Storozhevoy*."

"My God!" Stark exclaimed.

"If it's true, it's been the first time since the *Kronstadt* mutiny in nineteen twenty one," Williams said.

Kinkade nodded. "We have reason to believe that it is true because of the sudden increase in communications between Moscow and her ships in the Pacific. And we also intercepted a message sent from Moscow to the *Q-Twenty One*. The *Q-Twenty One* has been ordered to abandon its present mission and go to a red alert. It is now moving at flank speed to the last known position of the *Storzhevoy*, which was here." Kinkade pressed several buttons on a hand control and a large map of the southwestern Pacific Ocean appeared on the far wall. A moment later a brightly illuminated spot indicated the *Storzhevoy's* last position. Another spot indicated the *Q-21's* position. "At flank speed that puts the *Q-Twenty One* about fifty hours away from the *Storzhevoy*. But she won't be there. The *Q-Twenty One* will have to search for her. In fact the whole damn Russian Pacific fleet seems to be doing just that. But there's a lot of ocean out there and a ship can be damn difficult to find."

"There are thousands of atolls and islands, where she can hide," Stark said.

Kinkade nodded. "Our best guess is that she's doing just that. She's not moving during the day. We know that because we've made daylight overflights over a few thousand square miles of ocean where she should be. She's sailing at night and she's sailing blacked out."

"Sailing to where?" Williams asked.

"Possibly Australia," Kinkade answered.

"She has a long way to go before she gets there," Stark said.

Kinkade nodded. "We're going to try to see that she does get there. I want *The Shark* at sea as soon as possible. If *The Shark* can reach her, then—"

"It will have to find her first," Stark said, aware that Kinkade had avoided using Boxer's name. "And there's another problem: *The Shark* has been made larger and must undergo sea trials before she's ready for an actual mission."

"No time for that," Kinkade said.

Williams agreed. "Too much is at stake. If there's a chance to get hold of the *Storzhevoy*, then we should take it. How long would it take for *The Shark* to put to sea?"

"Twenty hours," Stark answered.

"How long would it take her to reach the last known position of the *Storozhevoy*?" Kinkade asked.

"Nine days."

"By then it might be too late," Williams said. "But it's certainly worth a try. During that time we might get a more precise idea where the *Storozhevoy* is and be able to vector *The Shark* to her."

"Whatever tests have to be made, can be made while she's underway," Kinkade said.

"Can you reach Boxer?" Williams asked.

Stark nodded.

"Where is he?"

Stark looked at Kinkade. "He's vacationing with the former Mrs. McElroy."

"Oh . . . Yes. I had forgotten about that."

Stark enjoyed watching Kinkade squirm. "I'll contact him as soon as I return to my office," he said.

"Would you ask Captain Boxer to see me before he leaves?" Kinkade said.

Stark nodded.

"Is there anything else that we should discuss now?" Williams asked.

"Nothing that I can think of," Stark answered.

"There is one more thing," Kinkade said. "I know, though I have no proof, that the two of you were behind what happened to my granddaughter and for what it is worth, I will some day repay that kindness with a kindness of my own. I am a patient man. I will wait."

Stark had a belly full of Kinkade and he wanted him to know it. "I'll put it to you this way," he answered, "whether or not we were responsible for it doesn't mean anything. Your granddaughter just likes the way Boxer fucks. Maybe if McElroy gave her good bang once in a while they'd still be married."

Kinkade flushed.

"I don't have anything else to say," Stark said, as he stood up. "I'll let you know, Kinkade, as soon as *The Shark* puts to sea."

"I'll go with you," Williams said, standing. Then looking at Kinkade, he said, "Don't ever threaten me again." And he followed Stark out of Kinkade's office.

Boxer had arranged to meet Kinkade in the lobby of the Watergate Hotel. Kinkade was already there when he arrived.

"Thank you for coming," Kinkade said politely.

Boxer nodded.

"The bar here, or the roof top garden?" Kinkade asked.

"You choose. You're the one who asked for this meeting."

"So I did," Kinkade answered. "I like the view from the roof top."

They rode the elevator without speaking.

Boxer had agreed to meet Kinkade only because Trish had asked him to. His own inclination was to avoid the man.

When they stepped out of the elevator, Kinkade gestured to the right. "I like to sit at a special table when I come here," Kinkade said. "It's in the corner and it practically gives a two hundred and seventy five degree view."

Boxer didn't answer.

"Ah, the table is unoccupied!" Kinkade exclaimed, heading for a table for two placed between huge panes of glass. "We can watch the sun go down," he said settling in a chair.

A barmaid came to the table.

"Old Grand Dad and branch water," Kinkade said.

"A Stoli on the rocks," Boxer ordered.

"What do you think of this view?" Kinkade asked, turning toward the pane. "Just look at that crimson sky!"

"Kinkade, you didn't bring me here to admire the view," Boxer said.

"No," Kinkade answered, "But I thought a certain amount of casual conversation might make it easier for the both of us. But I see that I was wrong."

"Wrong as you'll ever be," Boxer answered. "For one thing, I sail tomorrow morning at zero seven hundred. This will be my last night with Trish."

Kinkade stiffened. "You never make something easier," he said harshly.

Boxer shrugged.

The barmaid brought their drinks.

"To *The Shark*'s success," Kinkade toasted.

Boxer echoed Kinkade's words, raised his glass and drank.

"I don't think we ever liked each other," Kinkade said, putting down his glass. "If we did, it lasted so briefly that I have forgotten about it."

"Nowhere in the regs does it say that I have to like you," Boxer answered.

"And even if did, you wouldn't obey them," Kinkade said.

Boxer smiled. "At least you've got that part right."

"I want to talk about you and Trish," Kinkade said.

Boxer shook his head. "You've picked the wrong topic."

"She means a lot to me," Kinkade said.

"She means a lot to me too."

"Are you going to marry her?" Kinkade asked.

"That's none of your business, Kinkade."

"Suppose I tell you that I'm the executor of a five million —"

"I'm worth half that now. What do I care how much she's worth?"

Kinkade took another swallow of his drink. "I don't want her to make another mistake. I was against her marriage to McElroy."

"Are you telling me that you're against my marrying Trish?"

"No."

"Then what are you saying, or trying to say?" Boxer asked, trying to control his anger.

"I want you to marry Trish," Kinkade said. "I want her to have a stable life. I don't want her to go from man to man . . . I don't want her to become a whore."

Boxer finished his drink. "Trish needs time," he said, in a less belligerent voice. "We'll see how things go when I return."

"Do you want to marry her?" Kinkade asked.

"I've thought about it," Boxer answered. "But, to tell the truth, my past record with long term relationships hasn't been that good."

"I know that," Kinkade said.

"I suppose you do," Boxer responded.

"I don't want Trish misused," Kinkade said.

"That's not my style," Boxer said. "But right now she's not ready for marriage."

"Are you in love with her? I mean —"

"Kinkade, you're way out of line," Boxer said. "You want me to tell you that I'll marry Trish. Well, I can't. She's not sure and neither am I. We do some spectacular fucking. But you already

213

know that from the photographs and the tapes. I can't tell you anything else now."

"But that's lust!"

Boxer shook his head. "I enjoy it," he said. "I don't name it."

"What about love as God meant it to be?" Kinkade asked.

"God and I have never been on speaking terms," Boxer answered. "I don't know what you think He meant love to be and I frankly don't give a damn."

"Then how will you answer for your lust when your day of reckoning comes?"

"If there is a day of reckoning," Boxer said, "tell me how will I answer for the many men I killed?"

Kinkade shook his head. "You did that for your country."

"If you think God will accept that, than he surely must accept the fact that I fuck for my pleasure and the pleasure of the woman I'm with. Kinkade, stop worrying about my day of reckoning and whether or not Trish and I will marry. The first isn't worth your time and the second, as I said before, is none of your business. Now, I think I'll have another drink; then I'll give Trish a call and meet her for dinner. Do you want a refill?"

Kinkade shook his head and putting his hand over the empty glass, he said in a quiet voice, "I've had enough. More than enough!"

Boxer raised his eyebrows questioningly. "Are you all right?" he asked.

"Tired," Kinkade answered, "just very tired."

Boxer was about to say something sympathetic, but changed his mind. As far as he was concerned, Kinkade was his enemy and would always be his enemy.

Suddenly Kinkade started to stand, clutched at his chest and dropping back to the chair, toppled it backwards and fell to the floor.

# 17

Borodine sat at the COMCOMP. He was very tense. The SO had just ID'd the *Storozhevoy*.

For the past three days the *Sea Savage* hunted for the *Storozhevoy*. Moscow's second message had been even terser than the first. It had said find and destroy the *Storozhevoy*. No further explanation. Hoping to get some insight into what was happening, Borodine had asked for clarification. But the message had been repeated.

Borodine switched on the MC. He dreaded this moment and hoped it never would have come. But it had and he had to act. He had to treat the situation as if it was just another mission.

"Now hear this . . . All hands, now hear this . . . This is the captain." He covered the mike with one hand and took a deep breath and slowly exhaled before he spoke again. "We have found what we were sent here to find: the *Storozhevoy*, and we have been ordered to attack and destroy it."

Viktor came to the COMCOMP.

Borodine nodded and said, "All hands to battle stations . . . All hands to battle stations." And switching off the MC, he sounded the alarm.

The SO immediately reported, "Target bearing two five six degrees . . . Range fifteen thousand yards . . . Speed three zero knots."

"Roger that," Borodine said. He keyed the EO and said, "Flank speed."

"Going to flank speed," the EO responded.

Suddenly the telltale pinging sounded through the *Sea Savage*.

"It didn't take them long to find us," Viktor commented.

Borodine didn't answer. He knew that the *Storozhevoy* had thrown out her sonar net — small buoys that were instrumented to pick up targets and radio the information back to the ship's sonar system.

"Helmsman, come to course, two five five degrees," Borodine ordered.

"Coming to course two five five degrees," the helmsman answered.

"Activate ECM," Borodine ordered.

"ECM activated."

"Forward and aft TO, arm and load your torpedos."

Both officers acknowledged the order.

Borodine looked at the DDRO. The *Sea Savage* was a thousand feet down. "DO stand by, going manual diving control . . . Going to manual diving control." He reset several switches and checked the depth gauge immediately above the COMCOMP. "Manual control achieved," he said.

"Roger that," the DO answered.

"Make three zero zero feet," Boxer said.

"Making three zero zero feet," the DO answered.

"Target turning . . . Range twelve thousand yards . . . Speed four zero knots."

"Roger that," Borodine answered.

The pinging passed through the *Sea Savage* again.

Borodine switched on the MC. "Rig for attack," he said.

"Target bearing eight two degrees . . . Range twelve thousand yards . . . Speed four zero knots."

The first salvo of missiles exploded below and to the starboard side. The *Sea Savage* rolled violently.

Borodine keyed the DCO. "Any damage?"

"Negative," the DCO answered.

"Coming to three zero zero feet," the DO reported.

"Roger that," Borodine answered.

Two more missiles exploded aft and below the *Sea Savage*.

"No damage," the DCO reported.

"Stand by to fire torpedos one and two," Borodine ordered.

"Torpedos one and two ready," The TO answered.

"Fire one and two," Boxer ordered.

"Torpedoes one and two fired," the TO answered.

The bow of the *Sea Savage* lifted slightly; then settled back.

Borodine switched on the UMIS and watched the torpoedos streak toward their target. One suddenly exploded and the other did the same thing.

"Fire torpedos three and four," Borodine ordered.

"Several small targets bearing eight two degrees, range ten thousands yards . . . Speed fifty knots."

"Helsman, come to course nine zero degrees," Borodine ordered.

"Coming to course nine zero degrees," the helmsman responded.

Borodine couldn't see the Killer Darts on the UMIS. He switched on his own Sonar Scope and saw them plainly enough. The KDs were underwater missiles that were fired in clusters.

"Dive," Borodine said, keying the DO.

The *Sea Savage* began to drop off at the bow and slide deeper into the depths.

"Fire torpedos three and four," Borodine ordered.

"Torpedos three and four fired," the TO answered.

The boy eased upwards, then went down sharply.

Borodine looked at the UMIS. The torpedos were streaking toward the *Storozhevoy.* "Rearm torpedo tubes one, two, three and four."

"Roger that," the forward TO answered.

"Helmsman," Borodine said, "come to course one nine zero."

"Coming to course one nine zero," the helmsman responded.

"Seven zero zero feet," the DO said.

"Bring her level at seven five zero feet," Borodine said.

The KDs passed about the *Sea Savage.*

"Helmsman, change course to two two degrees," Borodine said.

The pinging grew louder.

Borodine looked at Viktor. "We're inside their net," he said.

"Changing course to—"

Three explosions violently shook the *Sea Savage*. The lights went out; then back on.

"Comrade Captain," the DCO said, "first generator damaged . . . Number five ballast tank ruptured."

217

Borodine switched on the MC. "All section officers report casualties."

"Comrade Captain," the EO reported, "switching all electrical power needs to standby generators."

"Roger that," Borodine answered.

"Reducing speed," the EO said, "to two five knots."

"Can't you give me at least three zero knots?"

"Negative," the EO answered.

"Ten four," Borodine said.

"Seven five feet," the DO announced.

"Roger that," Borodine said, looking at the level indicator; then moving his eyes to the clock, he realized that more than enough time had elapsed for the torpedos to have reached their target. The *Storozhevoy* had evaded them.

"Torpedo tubes one, two, three and four rearmed," the forward TO said.

"Roger that," Boxer answered.

The pinging from the *Storozhevoy's* sonar buoys grew louder.

"She must have put out more than the usual four," Viktor said.

Borodine nodded. "Wouldn't you, if you were her captain?"

Before Viktor could answer, three explosions hammered down on the *Sea Savage*.

Several automatic alarms sounded simultaneously. Red lights came up on the COMCOMP. The *Sea Savage* had been breached.

"Forward torpedo room flooded and sealed," the DCO said. "Three electrical fires in section four."

"Unable to hold seven five zero feet," the DO said.

"Blow ballast tanks one, two, nine and ten," Borodine ordered.

The sound of high pressure air being forced into the ballast tanks filled the *Sea Savage*.

"Tanks blown," the DO reported. "Still losing depth."

"Fires under control," the DCO announced.

"Blow all ballast," Borodine said.

The *Sea Savage* was struck by two more explosions. She rolled to her port side. The lights went out again and remained out for several seconds.

Another series of red lights began to flash.

"We're losing depth," the DO reported.

"Fire in the aft torpedo room," the DCO reported. "Section isolated. Automatic flooding taking place."

Borodine frowned. The men inside the aft torpedo room were already dead from the fire or would drown from the water.

"Main drive shaft damaged," the DCO said.

"Roger that," Borodine answered and keyed COMMO. "Send a message to headquarters . . . Give them our position; tell them we're going down in two thousand feet of water, that we have many casualties on board . . . Tell them to initiate rescue procedures immediately."

"Aye, aye, Comrade Captain," the COMMO answered.

"Then send out a May Day and keep sending until further orders," Boxer said.

"Aye, aye, Comrade Captain," the COMMO said.

Borodine switched on the MC. "All hands hear this . . . All hands, this is the captain . . . We have been badly hit . . . We are going to find a place on the bottom where we will wait until we are rescued." He switched off the MC and asked each section officer for a casualty report.

Other than men trapped in the torpedo rooms, there weren't any casualties.

Borodine looked at the depth gauge. The *Sea Savage* was slowly diving through the thousand foot level.

"How come no more missiles?" Viktor asked.

"Their sonar buoys must have lost us," Borodine answered, studying the damage display on the COMCOMP. The *Sea Savage* was mortally wounded. Her ballast tanks were badly damaged. She even lacked the power to move foward.

"One thousand five hundred feet," the DO announced.

"We're going to land bow first," Borodine said flatly.

"Diving planes are inoperable," the DCO answered.

Borodine switched on the MC. "Hear this," he said. "Hear this . . . We're going to have a rough landing on the bottom . . . I'll give you warning when to brace yourselves for the shock." Borodine watched the depth gauge. The deeper the *Sea Savage* went the faster she headed for the bottom. Borodine took out a handkerchief and wiped his brow. Up until that moment, he had not realized that every part of his body was covered with sweat. "All hands stand by . . . All hands stand by," he said over the

MC. "We're going down fast." He switched on powerful lights on the bottom of the *Sea Savage's* hull and moved his eyes to the UWIS. The ocean floor was coming up fast. The bottom was littered with boulders. A huge worm-like creature with its own source of light swam by. He checked the depth gauge; they had passed through the two thousand foot level. "Stand by. All hands brace yourselves!" He grabbed hold of the edge of the COM-COMP.

The *Sea Savage's* bow slammed into the bottom. The under side of the bow crunched against a huge boulder.

Borodine was wrenched out of his chair and left hanging onto the COMCOMP.

The *Sea Savage* shuddered; then her stern crashed down. She rolled to one side then to the other.

Red lights on the COMCOMP began to flicker.

"Water coming into the mess area," the DCO said.

"Can it be stopped?"

"Negative."

"Move all hands into the bridge area," Borodine said. "And seal off the damaged area."

"Roger that," the DCO answered.

"COMMO, are you sending that May Day?" Borodine asked, keying his communications officer.

"On automatic," the COMMO answered.

"Comrade Captain," the DCO said, "we have lost three of our air scrubbers."

"Roger that," Borodine answered. He turned to see the men and the four geologists move into the bridge section.

"Forward section completely closed off," the DCO reported.

"Roger that," Borodine answered. He switched off the outside lights and began readjusting the controls on the COMCOMP. The *Sea Savage* now consisted of the bridge area, the sail above it, and the area immediately aft of it, as far as the torpedo room bulkhead.

"Comrade Captain," the EO reported, "the reactor cooling system is beginning to fail."

"How much emergency power do we have?"

"Batteries have been designed to last two days. More if we cut the power use to a minimum."

"Shut down the reactor and switch to batteries," Borodine said.

"Roger that," the EO answered.

Borodine didn't have to use the MC to speak to the crew. All of them, with the exception of the EO and four of his rates, were standing within a few feet of him. He stood up and stepping away from the COMCOMP, he said, "I know all of you are asking yourselves what are our chances of getting out . . . They're not good."

A low murmur came from the crew.

"The *Sea Savage* is too badly damaged to—"

"Comrade Captain, have you informed Moscow of our situation?" Dr. Suslov asked.

"Yes."

"Then we will certainly be rescued," Suslov said.

Borodine took a deep breath and slowly exhaled. "That is by no means certain, Doctor. The crew must be told the truth. Our nearest rescue craft is in Vladivostok. It would take at least a day to fly it here and the rescue operation would take even longer. We will do our best to keep everyone alive until we are rescued. But I want all of you to understand that such an operation will be very difficult and it may not succeed." Again he paused to take a deep breath and slowly exhale. "I have enough pills for everyone to make death as painless as possible. Should that time come, when we have to make that choice, it will be by vote and will have to be unanimous."

Everyone began to speak at once.

"I have never heard such a defeatist speech in my life," Dr. Suslov said, raising her voice above the others. "Comrade Captain, as of this moment I remove you from command—"

"Major Suslov," Borodine said, "you will regard yourself as a member of my crew and act accordingly, or I will have you bound and gagged."

"You wouldn't—"

"You men there," Borodine said, pointing to two of them, "seize Major Suslov and gag her."

The men moved quickly, stuffing a handkerchief into her mouth.

"Bind her hands," Borodine said.

"Comrade Captain, how long can we remain here?" one of the

young officers asked.

"We have enough power for two days, maybe three, if we're lucky. The power must be used for the air scrubbers."

"What about food?" one of the crew members asked.

"We have none. But we do have water."

"In a little while it's going to get very cold," Borodine said. "Those of you who can get to your clothing pass out your extra clothing to the men who need them. All officers are ordered to do the same. Do not move around any more than is absolutely necessary. The COMCOMP will be manned by officers on a twenty four hour basis. Every officer will spend at least one hour on duty at the COMCOMP. For obvious reason only, the COMMO officer is excused from duty at the COMCOMP. Are there any more questions?"

"Comrade Captain, is there anything we could do that might help us get out of here alive?" one of the seamen asked.

"Nothing," Borodine said. "Our lives are in the hands of others. We must wait until they come and rescue us." He stepped back, looked at Major Suslov and said, "Take her to my quarters and set her down in my bunk. Tie her feet before you leave her."

"Aye, aye, Comrade Captain," one of the two seamen said.

Borodine returned to his chair in front of the COMCOMP and sitting down, he covered his face with his hands. He was too weary to think and yet he was thinking about Irena and the baby she was carrying. There was practically no chance of ever seeing the child and that saddened him, almost as much as he was saddened by the possibility that he might never again hold Irena in his arms and make love to her.

"Igor," Viktor said, coming up to the COMCOMP, "why don't you get some rest. I'll stay at the COMCOMP."

Borodine dropped his hands from his face. "In a little while," he answered.

"It's getting cold already," Viktor said.

Borodine nodded. "Send one of the men to my cabin and have them take all my sweaters and coats and give them out to the men."

"What will you use?"

"I'm wearing enough," Borodine answered.

Viktor turned around and gave the order to one of the men;

then he said to Borodine, "I was beginning to think the *Sea Savage* couldn't be sunk."

"I know what you mean," Borodine said with a nod.

"Do you think the surface ships will get the *Storozhevoy*?"

"Maybe," Borodine answered. "But I'd have to admit that part of me says just the opposite."

"And we don't know why we were ordered to sink her," Viktor said, shaking his head.

"Mutiny probably."

"That would be my guess too," Viktor answered.

Borodine shrugged.

The conversation lapsed and Viktor drifted away from the COMCOMP.

Borodine wondered how long it would take before one of the men couldn't take the waiting and cracked? He pursed his lips. No matter how difficult it was, he was determined to do whatever was necessary to keep himself from going berserk . . . To himself he believed that he and all the others in the *Sea Savage* would be rescued before they voted to take their own lives.

Boxer sat at the COMCOMP of *The Shark*. He motioned to Cowly and said, "That May Day has to be coming from the *Sea Savage*. She's down all right. The *Storozhevoy* must have done a job on her."

"Any word on the *Storozhevoy*?" Cowly asked.

"Nothing. My guess is that she was caught by surface craft and destroyed," Boxer said.

"Now what do we do. We're still two and a half days from her last reported position."

"The Ruskies won't be able to get a rescue craft anywhere near there for a couple of days and that's if they fly it in. By the time they finally get it into operation — well, Borodine and his crew might not live that long."

"Even if we do reach it," Cowly said, "we might not be able to do anything. Our equipment is built to fit over the escape hatches of our boats."

Boxer nodded; then in a low voice, he said, "But we have to try. I owe Borodine one and this is as good a way to pay it back as any

I know."

"The whole area will be swarming with Ivan's ships."

Boxer nodded. "We have to try," he said.

"What about Langley?"

"Nothing about them," Boxer said. "The acting chief is too damn green to make any noise about anything and Kinkade is still in the hospital."

"That man was lucky you were there to keep him alive," Cowly said.

"I did it for Trish," Boxer answered.

"It doesn't really matter who you did it for," Cowly answered, "the fact is that you did do it. You could have let him die and no one would have known that you might have saved him."

"I would have known," Boxer answered and he switched on the MC. "All hands, now hear this . . . Now hear this . . . We are going after the *Q-Twenty One*. She has been sunk. She is sending a May Day signal. This time we're going to try and save as many of those Ruskies as possible. We may not be able to, but we're going to try. Once we get into the area, we're going to have Ruskie ships all over the place and that means we might have trouble. But we're going to do everything to avoid trouble. This time we want to save the men on the *Q-Twenty One*. We don't want to kill them." He switched off the MC and nodding to Cowly, he said, "The Ruskies will probably set up a screen about a hundred miles out from the *Q-Twenty One*'s position. As soon as we reach that screen, we'll stay close to the bottom. I don't think we'll have any problem getting through their screen. The problem will come when we start rescue operations. We won't be able to mask the noise and that will clue them off that someone is down there trying to get into *Q-Twenty One*."

"What if they should decide to attack?" Cowly asked.

"I don't want to think about it," Boxer answered. "But with a bit of luck, the most we would need is an hour. Just time to get inside and get the men aboard *The Shark*. I don't plan on spending a great deal of time there. If we can enter through the hatchway, fine. We don't have the time to do it any other way."

"Any way you do it, if you get those men out it will be a miracle."

COMMO keyed Boxer. "Skipper, message from Langley."

"Roger that," Boxer said, pushing a switch that put the message on the video.

From: Kinkade
To: Captain Boxer
    Abandon mission. *Storozhevoy* sunk by aircraft. Return to base.
Kinkade

"I thought you said he was in the hospital," Cowly said.

"He probably is there and is running the Company from his bed," Boxer said.

"That would be typical," Cowly answered.

Boxer keyed the COMMO. "Send the following answer to Kinkade. Use red code. Received your message. Will attempt to rescue crew of the *Q-Twenty One*. Will keep you advised. Sign my name to it."

"Aye, aye, Skipper," the COMMO answered.

"That should send him into cardiac arrest," Cowly said.

"It won't," Boxer answered. "But it surely will make him angry."

Cowly smiled.

"We'll stay on our course for the next couple of days," Boxer said. "We don't have to do anything special until we come close to that protective screen."

"Just sit back and think about how easy it will be to rescue men two thousand feet below the surface of the ocean," Cowly said with a hint of a smile on his lips.

Boxer shrugged. He'd be doing just that. But he knew that it wouldn't be in the least bit easy.

Borodine entered his quarters. Major Suslov was stretched out in his bunk. He had completely forgotten about her.

She glared up at him and made sounds behind her gag.

Borodine went to the bunk and shook his head. "I'm sorry it has to be this way," he said. "But I can't have you running around trying to take charge of things." He pushed her toward the wall and lay down next to her.

She shook her head and though her feet were bound, she tried to kick him.

"If you don't stop thrashing around," Borodine said, "I'll put you on the floor. I want to get some sleep." He closed his eyes and uttered a weary sigh. "The trouble with you and the rest of your people is that you don't know too much about reality. The reality of this situation demands that every man knows where he stands. And Major, at this moment, none of us stand too good."

Suslov stopped moving.

Borodine suddenly became aware of her perfume and he turned to her. "This is the first time I've been in a bed with a beautiful woman who was bound and gagged," he said.

Her eyes never left his.

"If I take the gag off will you promise not to try to give any orders?" Borodine asked.

She nodded.

Borodine reached around to the back of her head and undid the gag.

"May I please have some water?" she asked.

Borodine went to his desk and from the pitcher on it, he poured some water into a plastic cup and held it to Suslov's lips.

She drank greedily and then said, "That water feels wonderful."

"More?" Borodine asked.

She nodded.

Borodine held the cup to her lips again until she drank all of it. He put the empty cup back on the desk and lay down again.

"We don't have much of a chance, do we?" she asked.

"Not much," Borodine answered, closing his eyes again.

"If I promise not to make any trouble," she asked, "would you untie me. Being tied makes me feel even more helpless than I otherwise would."

Borodine hadn't thought about that when he had ordered her tied. He sat up again and untied her hands and then her feet. "You're free to go," he said.

"As long as I'm free to go, I choose to stay," she said.

Borodine shrugged and settled down next to her again. He closed his eyes.

"I'm frightened," Suslov said in a whisper. "Really frightened."

"You'd be a fool not to be," Borodine answered. "I'm

frightened. Every man aboard is frightened."

"But I've been trained not to be," she said.

"Nonsense. You were never trained for this kind of a situation and even if you were, you'd still be frightened. Now I must get some sleep," Borodine said.

"I know it's absurd," she said, "but do you know what I'm thinking about?"

"No."

"Sex."

"Better join the others," Borodine said.

"Are you surprised?" she asked.

"No."

"Will you—"

"No."

"Will you hold me?" she whispered. "Please hold me!"

Borodine put his arms around her and pressed her against him. She was completely devoid of passion and wondered whether she would be afraid to swallow the pill should she have to?

# 18

Borodine sat at the COMCOMP. His head pounded. He was finding it difficult to think, to look at the glowing red lights on the signal panel. The bridge itself was in a demilight. But even in that, he could see the forms of the men. Some leaned against the bulkheads; others were stretched out on the floor. The air was already foul.

"You're going to have take that vote soon," Viktor said, coming up to Borodine.

Borodine nodded. "We've got to give it more time."

"Not so much time that most of us are suffocated. Igor, I don't want to go that way."

Borodine put his hand on his friend's shoulder. "A little longer," he said.

"Has Moscow answered our message?"

"Yes. Help is on its way. Headquarters said help is on its way. Now sit down and rest."

"Some of the men are hallucinating."

"Now and then, so have I," Borodine answered.

Viktor eased himself down to the floor and leaned against the COMCOMP.

Borodine looked at Suslov. She was leaning against the periscope well. All of her KGB training had not prepared her for something like this. All the starch had gone out of her.

Suddenly Borodine heard a familiar sound. The sound of a propellor turning in water. "Don't let me imagine it," he whispered. Sucking in his breath, he listened intently. It was real; he wasn't imagining it.

Viktor moved.

"You hear it too?" Borodine asked.

"It's not close," Viktor answered, pulling himself to his feet.

"Not close but not that far either."

Several of the other men were beginning to stir.

To save them from any doubts, Borodine said, "Something is out there."

"Maybe it's coming from the surface?" Viktor suggested.

"It would have a different sound. This one is coming from our port side," Borodine said.

"Sound travels very far underwater. That could be hundreds of kilometers from where we are," Viktor answered. "It could even be an American submarine?"

"Or one of ours?" Borodine countered.

Viktor didn't answer.

By now everyone was listening to the sound.

Suslov scrambled to her feet and came to Borodine. "Is it a rescue craft?" she asked. "Is it?"

"It might be," Borodine answered.

"But can't we do anything? Can't we signal them?"

"We need every bit of power we have," Borodine answered. "We can't do anything but sit tight."

"And what if they can't find us? What if they come too late?"

Borodine shrugged. The same thoughts had been going through his head and probably the heads of every man there.

Suslov leaned against the COMCOMP. "If we get out of this," she whispered, "I want you to promise that you'll make love to me."

Borodine nodded.

"I can think of nothing else," she said.

"Don't let it bother you," Borodine answered. In one of his hallucinatory episodes, he had imagined it too.

"The sound," Viktor said, "is gone."

Borodine listened. "Gone," he said flatly.

"What does that mean?" Suslov asked.

"I don't know," Borodine answered. "I don't know."

"You must know," Suslov cried, flinging herself at Borodine. She pounded on his chest with her clenched fists. "You must know . . . You must!"

Borodine grabbed hold of her wrists and brought her against him.

She was sobbing.

"Save your strength," he said gently. "Save your strength. Maybe we'll get lucky."

"I don't want to die," she wept. "I don't want to die. . . ."

Borodine caressed the back of her head. He didn't know what to say to her, except the truth. "I don't want to die either," he whispered. "But soon I will have to make the choice to die."

She looked up at him.

He nodded. "I promise you it will be swift and painless."

"How long would it take?" she asked.

"Only moments," Borodine answered.

She rested her head against his chest. "I have such strange thoughts," she said. "Such strange thoughts. I am not a loose woman."

"I didn't think you were," Borodine said.

"I spent most of my life studying."

Borodine nodded sympathetically. But he really didn't want to continue the conversation. His head throbbed and speaking to Suslov was making it throb even more.

"I've had three lovers in my life," she said.

Borodine didn't know what to say.

"Such strange thoughts," Suslov said again.

"Maybe you'd feel better if you sat down," Borodine said gently; then added, "All of us have strange thoughts at a time like this."

"I want to give myself to every man here," she said.

"And I'm sure every man here wants you," Borodine answered. "But —"

Suddenly she let go of him and went limp.

Borodine eased her down to the floor and felt her pulse. It was weak.

After a few moments her eyes opened. "What happened?"

230

she asked.

"You fainted," Borodine said. "But you'll be all right."

She nodded. Suddenly she flushed and asked, "Did I say or do anything unusual?"

Borodine shook his head. "Nothing," he answered. Absolutely nothing. Then as he stood up, he heard the sounds of the engine again. It was still far away but it was there. "Do you hear it, Viktor?" he asked.

"Yes. But it won't make any difference to us," Viktor answered. "You must decide to vote soon, Igor . . . Soon. . . ."


Boxer sharpened the image of the *Sea Savage* on the UWIS. She lay ten thousand yards ahead of *The Shark* and eight zero feet below her. "Stand by all hands," he said over the MC. "We're going to hover directly over the *Sea Savage.*"

Using a newly installed Sound Deflector System, Boxer was able to slip through the cordon of surface ships guarding the *Sea Savage.* His only real concern now was the possibility that a Russian killer sub might be prowling around and although it could not go down to where *The Shark* was, it might have torpedos that could.

"Cowly, is the Emergency Air Team standing by?" Boxer asked.

"Suited up and ready," Cowly answered.

"Now hear this," Boxer said over the MC, "going from auto system control to manual." He reset several switches. "Helmsman report?"

"Course one five nine degrees," Mahony reported.

"Roger that," Boxer responded and asked for a report from the Diving Officer.

"Depth two thousand five five feet," the DO said.

"Roger that," Boxer responded and gave his attention to the UWIS again. He was sweating profusely and using a handkerchief wiped the sweat from his brow.

Except for the hum of the blowers *The Shark* was silent.

Boxer keyed the EO. "One five knots," he said.

"Going to one five knots," the EO answered.

Boxer checked the speed and direction of the current. It was moving south-southwest at less than a half a mile an hour. Once *The Shark* was in place on top of the *Sea Savage* even a much stronger current wouldn't matter.

"We'll drift the last few hundred yards," Boxer said to Commander Wales, the DCO for *The Shark*, "then it's in your hands."

Wales, a short, wiry man with red hair and pale blue eyes, nodded and said, "If we're lucky, we'll go through the hatch. But if we have to cut through that's going to take time. Probably more time than we'll have."

"How much time will you need to cut—"

"Pardon me, Skipper, but I think I have a third way," Wales said.

"Okay, tell me about it."

"Separate the part of boat where the men are from the rest of it and carry it to the surface; then take the men aboard."

"What?"

"We can explode off any part of the hull from any other part of it."

"That's right."

"Then all we have to do is sling that section we want under *The Shark*. Bring it close to the surface. Pump air into it and it will surface. The rest will be easy."

"Getting it slung under us won't be easy and if it should slip its slings—"

"Skipper, it's risky as hell. But if we have any other choice then it's worth a try."

Boxer nodded. "Let's hope we have a choice," he said.

"Skipper," COMMO said, keying Boxer, "a code ten message is coming in from HQ."

"Roger that. I'll be there in a few minutes," Boxer answered; then turning to Cowly, he said, "Take the CON. Hold her steady as she goes."

Cowly nodded.

Boxer left the bridge and hurried to the communications center.

"Everything is set up," the COMMO said.

Boxer took the message and went into the decoding

232

enclosure. He ID'd himself to the decoding computer and then typed in the string of numbers and letters. Almost as fast as he typed the message came up on the screen.

Date Oct. 11, 1995

From: Kinkade
To: Cap. J. Boxer

Our sources say there are survivors in the *Q-Twenty One*. Do not attempt rescue. Repeat do not attempt rescue. Destroy the *Q-Twenty One*. Repeat destroy the *Q-Twenty One*.
Acknowledge this message.

/ Kinkade

Boxer pressed the erase button, switched off the decoding computer and left the enclosure. "Send the following message to Kinkade," he told COMMO. "Disregarding your order of October eleven. Boxer."

"Is that it?" the COMMO asked.

"Short and sweet, as the saying goes," Boxer answered.

"Aye, aye, Skipper," the COMMO answered.

On the way back to the bridge, Boxer stopped to see Vargas and his men, many of whom would be taking part in the rescue operation.

"Everything is go," Vargas said.

"Remember, Spic, you stay inside *The Shark* this time, or I'll tell your Ruskie sweetheart," Boxer said.

Vargas flushed. "She'd sure as hell would be pissed at me," he answered.

Boxer clapped him on the shoulder. "No unnecessary chances," he said.

"None," Vargas answered.

Boxer returned to the bridge. "I have the CON," he said, taking Cowly's place in front of the COMCOMP.

"I just did a distance to target check," Cowly said. "We were five thousand yards from it. She's listing to the port side about five degrees. And there's a substantial boulder on her starboard side close to the bow."

Boxer looked at the UWIS screen. "Are we going to have problems because of that list?" he asked, glancing up at the DCO.

"It would be easier if she were even keeled," the DCO answered.

"Maybe we can nudge her over," Boxer said. "The two mini-subs might be able to do it."

"It's worth a try," the DCO responded.

Boxer switched on the MC. "Now hear this . . . This is the captain speaking . . . Now hear this . . . I need four volunteers. Two officers and two EMs. The *Q-Twenty One* is listing to her port side. By using the two mini-subs to ease her over, we're going to try to put her on an even keel. It might not work; then again it might. But there's also the danger that she'll roll further to the port side and if she moves too far over and too fast — Well, all of you know what could happen. Volunteers report to the bridge on the double." Boxer switched off the MC and put the mike back on its bracket.

"Berness is coming," Cowly said in a low voice.

Boxer glanced over his shoulder. He didn't expect Berness to volunteer. So far Berness had performed as well as any other officer. He was assigned to the CIC. Coppes was immediately behind Berness. The two enlisted men were from the engine room.

"All of you men know what the score is," Boxer said. "It could be a piece of cake, or it could cost you your lives. If any one of you have any doubts, now is the time to change your minds." He waited a few seconds; then he said, "One officer and one enlisted man in a sub. Report to the launch bay area. And good luck."

Boxer keyed the Launch Bay Officer. "Prepare to launch both subs," he said.

"Aye, aye Skipper," the LBO answered.

"Skipper," the DCO said, "we're closing fast with the target."

Boxer keyed the EO. "Three knots," Boxer said.

"Three knots," the EO answered.

Boxer turned to Wales and standing up, he said, "The

CON is yours."

*The Shark* hovered fifty feet above the *Sea Savage*.

Boxer stood directly behind the DCO and watched two divers move along the hull of the *Sea Savage*.

"Aft and forward sections," one of the divers reported, "are destroyed. Casualties in both."

"Roger that," the DCO answered.

"Will plug in an air hose just below the sail," the second diver said. "If anyone is alive, they'll be in the bridge section."

The two divers were suited in diving gear that weighed several hundred pounds and gave them a spherical shape. They moved very slowly. One carried a long metal tube and the other dragged a hose, the end of which was attached to a special device in *The Shark* that pumped out oxygen-enriched air.

"How long can they stay out there?" Boxer asked.

"Two hours at the most," the DCO answered. "I have another team ready to go."

The SO keyed Boxer. "There's activity on the surface," he said.

"Roger that," Boxer answered; then to the DCO, he said, "The Ruskies upstairs seem to be nervous."

"I can't worry about them now," the DCO replied.

Boxer smiled, but didn't comment.

"They've reached the spot where they're going to attach the hose," the DCO said.

Boxer looked at the UWIS. Both divers were on their knees.

"We're getting response to our tapping," one of the divers said.

"That's great!" Boxer exclaimed and relayed the news to Cowly, who gave a thumbs up signal.

"Now comes the tricky part of getting that hose in. It's actually blown into the sub by explosives and the immediate rush of air through the hose makes it swell into a water-tight seal. The specs say it can be used at depths up to three thousand feet."

"We'll soon find out if they're right," Boxer said, licking his dry lips.

"Once we have air into her," the DCO said, "we'll try to put her on an even keel."

Boxer concentrated on the UWIS. The divers were actually working directly below *The Shark* in a circle of intensely bright light.

A sudden burst of bubbles erupted from the hull of the *Sea Savage*.

"The hose is in!" the DCO said.

"Good work!" Boxer exclaimed.

Borodine and several of the members of the crew had answered the tapping that had come from the outside and as soon as the air hose exploded into the *Sea Savage*, they began to shout, "Air . . . Air . . . We're saved . . . We're saved . . . Air!"

One by one the other men began to stir. Each one took several deep breaths.

Viktor grabbed hold of the edge of the COMCOMP and pulled himself to his feet. "I never thought it would happen," he said.

Borodine nodded. The pounding in his head ceased. "I was just about ready to call for a vote," he said.

"I'm glad you didn't."

Borodine looked down at Dr. Suslov. He wondered how much she'd remember. Probably very little, or nothing at all.

She was starting to get to her feet.

"Feeling better?" Borodine asked.

"Much," she said with a nod.

Suddenly the tapping began again.

"It's the Morse Code," the communications officer said.

"Are you sure?" Borodine asked.

"Yes, Comrade Captain—" the man stopped.

"What is it?"

"I'm not sure but I think *The Shark* was spelled out."

"Answer. Ask if they're from *The Shark*," Borodine said.

The communications officer took off his shoe and began striking the side of the hull. When he stopped the tapping came from outside. "Stand by," he said. "*The Shark* will attempt to rescue you. Stand by, in a few minutes we will try to put you on an even keel."

"Who and what is *The Shark*?" Suslov asked.

"The American counterpart of what we are," Borodine answered.

Again the tapping began. "Captain Boxer asks if Comrade Captain Borodine is alive?" the communications officer said.

"Answer yes," Borodine said.

"Do you really intend to let the Americans take us?" Suslov asked.

"Take is the wrong word," Borodine said. "We are being rescued." He pointed to the opening where the air was coming from. "That came from the Americans. That saved our lives. Without it all of us would be dead."

"You don't know that," she answered.

"I do," Borodine said. "I was about to ask for a vote; everyone would have voted to take the pill."

"But —"

"There are no buts," Borodine answered. "The Americans are here. Our people aren't. If the Americans can get us out, then we'll go with them. There's only one alternative and anyone who wants to take it has my permission to remain on board the *Sea Savage*."

Suslov didn't answer.

"Now we wait," Borodine said. "We wait and hope that we can be rescued."

"I think the lights have become dimmer," Viktor said in a low voice.

Borodine checked the battery. "It's completely down," he said. Just as he spoke all the lights went out. "I have two torches in the drawer to my right," he said. "Viktor can you get them?"

"Yes."

"Everyone else stay where you are," Borodine said.

Viktor switched on one of the torches and handed it to Borodine.

237

"You hold one and I'll hold the other," Borodine said, switching off his torch. "We'll use them only in an emergency. Everyone keep calm and stay where you are."


Boxer watched the two mini-subs move into position. Berness had his craft forward of the sail and Coppes was aft.

"Stand by," the DCO said, speaking to them by radio.

"Standing by," Berness answered.

"Standing by," Coppes said.

"When I give the signal," the DCO told them, "gradually increase your power . . . Now!"

The mini-subs strained against the hull of the *Sea Savage*.

"Are you at full power?" the DCO asked.

"Full power," Berness said.

"Full power," Coppes replied.

Suddenly the *Sea Savage* began to move.

"She's easing over," the DCO said.

"Can feel it," Coppes said.

"Ease off then," the DCO ordered.

Both subs backed away.

The SO keyed Boxer. "Target . . . Bearing two eight one degrees . . . Range twenty thousand yards . . . Speed three five knots . . . Depth . . . One thousand feet."

"ID?" Boxer said.

"Alfa class submarine," the SO reported.

"Roger that," Boxer answered.

"She's over about three degrees," the DCO said. "One more push should put her on an even keel."

Boxer nodded.

"Move back into position," the DCO said.

The two subs eased against the hull of the *Sea Savage*.

The SO keyed Boxer. "Target bearing two eight two degrees . . . Range sixteen thousand yards . . . Speed three eight knots . . . Depth one thousand feet . . . Closing fast."

"Roger that," Boxer said.

"Move, you bastard, move," the DCO said aloud. "She's giving . . . She's on even keel!"

Boxer took the mike from the DCO. "Listen up, Berness

and Coppes . . . We've got a wolf on the prowl at two eight two degrees . . . Range sixteen thousand yards . . . Speed three eight knots . . . It's closing fast . . . I want you guys to stop it."

"Roger that," Berness answered.

"Roger that," Coppes echoed.

Boxer turned to the DCO. "Better get to it. We don't want to hang around here longer than necessary."

The DCO switched on the MC. "Now hear this," he said. "Now hear this . . . We're going in for the final stage of the rescue operation. Everyone at their stations."

Boxer nodded.

The DCO maneuvered *The Shark* into position above the *Sea Savage*'s escape hatch. "Stand by DCO," he said.

"Standing by."

"Down seven zero feet," the DCO said. He checked the picture on the UWIS and keyed the EO. "One thousand two zero zero rpms on the port engine."

"One thousand two zero zero rpms on port engine," the DCO said.

The EO repeated the order.

Boxer watched *The Shark* slide over the hull of the *Sea Savage*.

"Now!" the DCO exclaimed, hitting two switches simultaneously.

The cylindrical structure dropped out of the bottom of *The Shark*'s hull. Immediately high speed pumps cleared the water out of it.

"We're down on the deck," the DCO said, drawing his sleeve across his sweaty brow.

Boxer nodded, took a deep breath and exhaled.

"Rescue team go to it," the DCO said.

Three of Vargas's men entered the cylinder and attempted to open the hatch.

"Won't come," one of the men said.

"Burn it open," the DCO answered.

"Target in visual sight," Berness radioed.

"Destroy," Boxer ordered.

"Roger that," Berness answered.

The sound of an explosion rolled over *The Shark*.

"Coppes caught it," Berness said. "Firing two torpedos."

His brow furrowing, Boxer said, "Roger that."

Two men used an oxy-torch to cut through the hatch cover.

"Skipper," the COMMO said, keying Boxer, "the Ruskies are burning up the airways."

"Roger that," Boxer answered.

"Hull breached!" the DCO exclaimed.

"Good work," Boxer said. "Good work."

"Rescue team go get them," the DCO said.

Another explosion rolled over *The Shark*.

"Skipper," Berness said, "Target badly damaged. Going in for the kill."

"Negative. Return to base. Acknowledge."

"Returning to base," Berness answered.

"Ten four," Boxer answered.


Borodine switched on his torch and pointed it at the open hatch. Two men jumped onto the deck of the *Sea Savage*. An instant later the end of a rope ladder clattered onto the deck.

Borodine turned the torch on Dr. Suslov. "You go first."

She hesitated.

"Go," he ordered.

Moments later she disappeared into *The Shark*.

The three civilian geologists followed; then the men, leaving only Borodine and Viktor.

"I'll go last," Borodine said.

Viktor nodded and went up the rope ladder.

Borodine left the COMCOMP and walked slowly to the ladder. The two crew men from *The Shark* gestured to the ladder.

"In a moment," Borodine said in English. He looked back at the COMCOMP. It was harder for him to leave the *Sea Savage* than he had thought it would be. Much harder. Suddenly he turned to the rope ladder and quickly climbed into *The Shark*.

"Rescue operation completed," the DCO said.

Boxer switched on the MC. "All hands, stand by to get underway." He turned to Cowly. "Secure from rescue operation."

"Aye, aye Skipper," Cowly answered.

It took several minutes for the rescue cylinder to be retracted into *The Shark* and pumped free of water.

Boxer keyed the DO. "Give me eight zero feet."

"Aye, aye Skipper," the DO said.

*The Shark* slowly rose eighty feet.

Boxer keyed the LBO. "Stand by to recover mini-sub," he said.

"Standing by," the LBO answered.

Boxer was anxious to be underway. He keyed Berness. "We're coming toward you," he said, looking at Berness on the UWIS.

"Roger —"

Boxer watched Berness's mini-sub disintegrate before he heard the explosion. "Christ!" he exclaimed closing his eyes. An instant later he hit the klaxon, sounding General Quarters.

Boxer keyed the EO. "Flank speed."

The men in *The Shark* heard the pinging of the Russian sonar.

"Flank speed," the EO responded.

Two explosives went off to *The Shark*'s port side and another well aft of her stern.

Boxer keyed the DO. "Make one thousand feet," he said, "then drop back to one thousand five zero zero feet."

"Aye, aye Skipper," the DO answered.

*The Shark* rose swiftly through the water.

She was surrounded by explosions, but none of them were close enough to do any damage.

"One thousand feet," the DO reported. "Going to one thousand five zero zero feet."

*The Shark* started to sink again.

"Helmsman, come to course five two degrees," Boxer said.

"Coming to course five two degrees," the helmsman answered.

The pinging stopped. The Russians had lost them.

"Have the men secure from General Quarters," Boxer said.

"Aye, aye Skipper," Cowly answered.

Boxer took a deep breath and slowly exhaled. "Take the CON," he said. "I want to make sure our Russian guests have what they need."

"Do you want me to write the letter to the Coppes and Berness family?" Cowly asked.

"No," Boxer answered, "that comes with the job."

Cowly nodded.


As soon as Boxer entered the mess area, Borodine leaped to his feet and went to greet him.

"Welcome aboard *The Shark*, Comrade Captain," Boxer said, vigorously shaking Borodine's hand.

"This is the last place I expected to be," Borodine answered. "For myself and on behalf of my crew, I thank you. But now what will happen to us?"

"I don't know," Boxer said, scanning the faces of the *Sea Savage*'s crew. "How many did you lose?"

"More than half," Borodine answered.

Boxer shook his. "I lost two in the last attack," he said; then suddenly he realized he was looking at a woman. "You had a woman—"

Borodine smiled. "She is a member of a civilian team of geologists. We were actually on a scientific mission."

"Oh, You must tell me about it."

Borodine flushed. "Not a completely scientific mission," he said.

Boxer spotted Viktor and waved to him. "I'm glad to see your EXO is alive." Then he added. "I'll make arrangements for the woman to have her own room. But the rest of you will have to remain in this area."

"I understand," Borodine answered.

"I must return to the bridge," Boxer said. "If there is anything you want tell one of the guards."

"Comrade Captain," Borodine said, "all of us owe our lives to you."

Boxer smiled. "Maybe the rest do, but you and I are even, Comrade Captain."

"Friends are never even, as you put it," Borodine said.

"Maybe you're right," Boxer answered. "Maybe you're right." He turned, left the mess area and went to the Communications Center. "Send the following message in priority ten code. Today's date. To Kinkade from Captain Boxer. Have Captain, EXO and twenty members of the *Q-Twenty One*'s crew on board *The Shark*. In addition to the aforementioned people I have four civilian geologists, one of whom is a woman. I will try to contact a Russian ship to return them. Sign it Captain Jack Boxer."

The COMMO read it back.

"Sounds good to me," Boxer said, certain Kinkade would go up in smoke when he read the message. But he didn't give a damn.

# 19

Borodine, Viktor, and the *Sea Savage*'s political officer Comrade Lieutenant Karanski spoke in low tones at the far end of the mess area.

"Colonel Suslov had identified herself to me earlier this evening," Karanski said.

"And to me," Viktor added.

Borodine nodded and offered the two men cigarettes from the pack given to him by Boxer at dinner.

Both men took the cigarettes, lit them and greedily sucked in the smoke.

"The Americans make a better cigarette than we do," Viktor said, letting the smoke rush out of his nose.

"Major Suslov says we cannot allow the Americans to intern us. That if that happens we will be subjected to deep interrogation sessions, even drugged."

"The decision of what to do with us—" Borodine started to say, but was interrupted by Karanski, who said, "Excuse me, Comrade Captain, but we hold the decision."

"Meaning?" Borodine detected Suslov's work here and Karanski's fear of what might happen to him if he didn't agree with her.

"I have already organized the men into attack teams," Karanski said.

"Attack teams!" Borodine exclaimed, leaping to his feet.

"We must try and take control of *The Shark*," Karanski said.

"Is this Suslov's idea?" Borodine asked, still standing.

"It is something the three of us agreed on," Viktor said. "We must not be taken to the United States."

Borodine sat down. He had always thought Viktor was as much like him as another man could be. But here was a heretofore unrevealed difference. Viktor too was frightened by what the KGB might do to him.

"To be certain of success," Karanski said, "we need you to lead the men."

"*The Shark*'s crew is double our strength," Borodine said. "And they have their assault force on board. We don't have ours with us."

"The men will look to you to lead them," Viktor said.

"They will," Karanski added.

"Just think of what it will mean to every man if we could bring *The Shark* back to Russia," Karanski offered. "Instantly we would be national heroes. Our lives would be forever changed."

Borodine stubbed his cigarette out in a makeshift plastic cup ashtray.

"We must try," Viktor said.

"It won't work," Borodine answered. "We would have to capture the bridge."

"No," Karanski said. "We'll go for the Communications Center; once we have that we can signal our ships. Comrade Captain Boxer would not be able to fight a squadron of our ships. He would be forced to surrender, or risk being sunk."

"Suppose he chooses to fight?" Borodine asked.

"No sane man would," Karanski said.

"Viktor, would you fight?" Borodine asked.

"As long as there was a chance of winning, I would; but if I knew I'd lose no matter what I did, I would not fight."

Borodine pursed his lips; then in a low voice he asked, "How would you know when to stop? Maybe at the very moment you decide to throw in the towel, just a bit more effort would see you through?"

"Are you trying to tell us that Comrade Captain Boxer would risk having *The Shark* sunk?" Karanski asked.

Borodine nodded.

"Then that's a gamble we must take," Karanski said.

"It's a very big gamble," Borodine added.

"The men will fight better with you leading them," Viktor said.

"When is all of this supposed to take place?" Borodine asked.

"The watch changes at zero two hundred. The men coming off watch will come in here to eat or for coffee. Some of us will attack them, take their uniforms and leave the mess area. The guards immediately outside will be overpowered and their arms taken. Our first objective will be the Communications Center; then the whole forward section."

"What will you do for arms?"

"My guess," Viktor said, "is that there are two arms rooms. One forward and one aft. The way it was aboard the *Sea Savage.*"

"Remember there are one hundred assault troops on board. Their quarters—"

"Are aft, according to Major Suslov," Viktor said; then digging into his pocket he withdrew a sketch. "She drew this a few hours ago. Her cabin is aft of the bridge, across from Comrade Captain Boxer's. She will do everything possible to distract him."

"Will you lead the men?" Karanski asked.

Viktor uttered a deep sigh. He did not want to repay Boxer's kindness with this kind of betrayal. "You know the men of this boat risked their lives to save us."

"To capture us," Karanski said.

Again Borodine pursed his lips. He would not be able to change their minds. He did not want to be part of it, yet he owed his men the leadership they had come to expect from him. If there was the slightest chance for the plan to succeed, he had no choice other than to lead them.

"Better fill me on all the details," Borodine said.

Karanski smiled broadly.

"I told you," Viktor said, "that the Comrade Captain would be with us."

"What would have happened if I said no?" Borodine asked.

"You would have been killed," Karanski answered.

Borodine raised his eyebrows, but was too surprised to say

anything.

"It would have had to be done for security reasons," Karanski said.

"Of course. I understand. For security reasons." He finished the sentence silently . . . *a whole nation lives in fear of your shadow.*

The watch changed.

Borodine waited for the six men to come off duty. "Remember," he whispered, "overpower them. I do not want them killed. There are enough of us here to do it swiftly and without killing."

Several of the men nodded.

"Everyone stay in their cot until I leave mine," Borodine said.

"They're coming!" A lookout stationed close to the door said.

"Get in your cot . . . Everyone pretend to sleep," Borodine said.

The six men entered the mess area. They spoke in low tones and went directly to the coffee machine first; then to the food dispenser.

Borodine watched them carefully. They were similar to many of his own men. In their early twenties. Quick to laugh and — He stopped thinking about them. Several of them were smoking cigarettes. It was time to move. He left his cot.

It was over quickly. The six men were thrown to the floor, gagged and bound in less than a minute.

"All right," Borodine said, "six of you get into their uniforms."

His men changed clothing quickly.

"There are three of you for each one of the guards," Borodine said. "Remember they're armed . . . Okay, do it!"

The six men left the mess area.

The guards were standing in the passageway to the left and right of the entrance to the mess area.

Borodine watched his men. As soon as they were in the passageway, they split into two groups of three, started past

247

the guards; then whirled around. One of them punched the guard in the stomach, the second man wrenched the M22 rifle from him and the third man delivered the rabbit punch that knocked him to the deck. As soon as he was down, he was dragged into the mess hall, gagged and bound.

Borodine looked at his watch. "Four minutes," he said to Karanski.

The political officer smiled and nodded.

"Okay," Borodine said, "our first objective is the arms room. Two of you in uniform takes the rifles. The other four follow them. As soon as they secure the arms room, bring weapons back here. This shouldn't take more than six minutes. Go."

"All of us failed to mention that we hold the food and water supply," Viktor said, settling down on a chair next to Borodine.

"Food yes," Borodine answered. "But not the water. They can tap into the water line in a dozen different places."

"Do you hear anything?" Karanski asked, coming to where Borodine and Viktor were seated.

"Nothing," Borodine answered.

"Is that a good sign or a bad one?"

Borodine shrugged and checked his watch. Three of the six minutes had already passed.


Boxer answered the soft knock at his door with a terse: "Come."

"Excuse me, Comrade Captain," Dr. Suslov said. "But I am unable to sleep. I thought perhaps you might have a sleeping pill?"

"I do," Boxer said standing and opening the top drawer of his desk. "They're somewhere in here."

"So this is the way an American captain lives!" she exclaimed.

Boxer found the plastic container and handed it to her.

"Thank you," she answered.

"Your quarters aren't very spacious," she said.

"Not very," Boxer admitted, aware that she was an attractive woman.

She smiled at him. "But I guess you don't even notice that?"

He shook his head. "Even if I did, it wouldn't make any difference."

"I could never live in such a small area," she said. "I like lots of room." She looked toward the bunk. "There's hardly enough room for a man to sleep there. At home I have a very large bed. I like large beds."

"So do I," Boxer said, wondering where the conversation was going.

"Comrade Captain would you mind if I stayed with you a while?"

"Please," Boxer said. "It was stupid of me not to ask you in."

Suslov entered the cabin and sat down on a chair. "It's good to be able to speak to someone."

Boxer returned to the desk. "I know what you mean," he answered.

"These past few days have been a nightmare," she said.

Boxer filled his pipe and lit it.

"I like a man who smokes a pipe," Suslov said.

Boxer blew smoke toward the ceiling. "I'm a good listener," he said.


"They did it!" A man exclaimed from the doorway.

An instant later another man ran into the mess area with an armful of rifles, another followed with belts of ammo and a third with grenades.

"Everyone armed?" Borodine asked.

"Everyone," Viktor answered.

"Karanski," Borodine said, "take five men and secure everything forward."

"Aye, aye Comrade Captain," Karanski answered.

"Viktor, take three men and hold the mess area," Borodine said.

"Aye, aye Comrade Captain," he answered with a twinkle in his eyes.

"The rest of you follow me," Borodine said. He moved quickly into the passageway. The Communications Center was immediately forward of the bridge. The door was closed. "Three men remain here. Stop anyone coming from the bridge."

"Aye, aye Comrade Captain," a junior officer answered.

"When I open the door," Borodine said, "I will go in first. As soon as the rest of you are in fan out. Remember do not shoot unless it's absolutely necessary. Ready? We go!"

Borodine flung open the door, walked inside the room and pointed the rifle at the startled officer. "Do not move, or speak," Borodine said.

The other men entered behind him.

"All right," Borodine said to the men on duty, "move away from your equipment. That's right. Come toward the door." Then moving his eyes to one of the petty officers, he said, "Take two men and deliver them back to mess hall."

"Aye, aye Comrade Captain," the rate answered.

Borodine went to the main control console, picked up the mike and threw the main MC switch. "Comrade Captain Boxer, this is Comrade Captain Borodine speaking from the Communications Center. My men have control of the entire forward section of *The Shark*. I repeat we hold the entire forward section of *The Shark*."


The first sound of Borodine's voice brought Boxer to his feet. Reflexively his right hand hit the alarm button three times, while his right switched on the MC. "All hands. Stand by, this is the captain speaking." He glanced down at the MINICOMCOMP. His thoughts raced. He couldn't risk a fight while *The Shark* was submerged. He had to get *The Shark* to the surface as quickly as possible. "Forward section being sealed off," And he pushed a toggle from left to right. "All hands stand by . . . All systems on auto. Initiating emergency surfacing procedures." He checked the DDRO. They were 500 feet down. Boxer dialed in a ten degree elevation the bow and stern diving planes. "All ballast being blown!"

*The Shark* was filled with the sound of hissing air.

"Vargas, arm your men," Boxer said. "Report to me on the bridge in five minutes. Cowly send two armed men to my quarters immediately. All hands battle stations. Battle stations." And he hit the klaxon four times.

The door opened and two armed men entered.

"Take Doctor Suslov back to her room," Boxer ordered. "She is not to leave it. If she makes any attempt to leave, shoot her."

"Aye, aye Skipper," the men answered in unison.

Grinning, they took Suslov from the cabin.

Boxer ran to the bridge. Vargas was already there.

"I've checked our transmissions," Cowly said. "They're continuous."

"Borodine is probably calling every Ruskie ship in the Pacific," Boxer commented.

"Skipper, we're going through the five zero level," Cowly said.

Boxer switched on the MC. "Stand by to surface. We'll be coming up hard." He looked at Cowly. "What's the weather topside?"

"Last check rain with a one five knot wind from the southeast," Cowly answered.

Boxer spoke to the crew again. "Passing two five feet . . . Brace yourselves," he said. "Brace yourselves!" He put down the mike and held onto the edge of the COMCOMP console.

*The Shark* breached, bow first; then slamming back into the water, rolled violently from side to side.

"Sail up," Boxer ordered.

"Sail going up," Cowly repeated.

Again Boxer switched on the MC. "Comrade Captain Borodine," Boxer said. "I ask you and your crew to surrender before lives are lost in your attempt to capture *The Shark*."

"I must answer no, Comrade Captain Boxer," Borodine said.

Boxer switched off the MC. "Sail detail topside," he said. Cowly repeated the order.

"Here's the way I see it," Boxer said. "Borodine needs time. He has no intentions of fighting us."

251

"No comprendez," Vargas said. "If he doesn't want to fight, why did he take half the fuckin' boat?"

Boxer looked at Cowly.

"He doesn't have to fight, Spic," Cowly said. "He figures that the rest of the Ruskie navy will do it for him."

Boxer nodded.

"I get it now," Vargas said. "He knows that you wouldn't risk staying down with his jabokies armed and he's sending messages like they're going out of style."

Boxer nodded. "Sooner or later the Ruskies will get a fix on us and come to Borodine's aid. We can't fight the whole damn Ruskie fleet. He knows it and knows I know it. He just has to sit and wait."

"What the hell are we going to do?" Vargas answered.

Boxer rubbed his beard with his right hand. "First, we're going to stop his transmissions. Cowly, have the DCO cut the power lines to the Communications Center."

Cowly nodded.

"I'm going to force him to fight or surrender," Boxer said. "And I'm going to do it within the next few hours." He switched on the MC. "Comrade Captain Borodine, in the next few minutes the power to the Communications Center will be cut. You will not be able to transmit. I urge you to surrender before it is too late."

"Comrade Captain Boxer," Borodine answered, "Russian ships are already on their way here. It is I who now ask you to surrender *The Shark*, yourself and your crew to me and my men."

Boxer switched off the MC.

"He's bluffing," Vargas said.

"If he's not, we're in deep shit," Cowly commented.

"Organize two assault teams," Boxer said, looking at Vargas. "Six men in each. We'll send one from the bridge, through the forward bulkhead door and one through the forward deck hatch."

"Aye, aye Skipper," Vargas answered.

Boxer switched on the MC. "Comrade Captain Borodine, you have exactly five minutes to surrender. If you do not, you and your men will be attacked. Five minutes, Comrade